CROWNED IN BLOOD

MELISSA CUMMINS

Cover by Melissa Cummins

Editing by Waddle Editing

Proofreading by Pinpoint Editing

Formatting by Melissa Cummins

Published by Melissa Cummins on October 22nd, 2024

ASIN/ISBN: 978-1-958769-22-5

Also by Melissa Cummins

Chronicles of The Otherworld

Part 1. The Vampire War

Dark Vampire and Witch Romance (Interconnected Standalones best read in this order)

Night Shade

Night Fury

Night Fall

Part 2. Feral Wolves - Coming Soon

Dark Omegaverse/Shifter Romance (Standalones read in any order)

Carnal Claim - Coming Soon

Bitten To Obey - Coming Soon

Primal Hunger - Coming Soon

Savage Embrace - Coming Soon

Part 3. Fae - Coming Soon

Dark Fae Romance (Standalones best read in any order)

Fae Book 1 - Coming Soon

Fae Book 2 - Coming Soon

Fae Book 3 - Coming Soon

Standalones

My Brutal Beast

Crowned In Blood

My Vicious Beast - Coming Soon

DEDICATION

To those who believe they are broken. That the scars of the past define them. That no one would ever love them enough to break down the walls they hide behind and see them for who they truly are.

Every single beautiful shard of you is worthy, priceless, and deserving of love. Don't you dare settle for less.

I remember exactly where I was when this book came into my mind. It was October 10, 2021. I had just released Night Shade and was sorting through the rush of my author feelings.

I had the TV playing in the background and there was a commercial that kept coming on. It was a play on Rapunzel where she refused to let down her hair for the prince because she was busy making coffee.

I thought it was funny, but paid no mind to it. But after it played for the third time, I thought about how cool it would be to have this tough, strong woman who refused the "prince" of her story. To have a fairytale retelling of Rapunzel where she says, "No. I don't need you, your fake love, and the cage you want to lock me up in. I have better things to do and you're not worth my time."

The moment I woke up, I recorded an audio message of the plot of Crowned In Blood. You can listen to it on my Patreon here if you like.

I wanted so badly to drop everything and dive into that book, but I'd just started a series, was still working full time plus on call hours, and it was too much to write two books at the same time for me then.

Three years later, I finally wrote the book that has been on my mind every day and night since, and it's changed my life. It's changed how I write, what I want to write, and the trajectory of my author career.

I listened to the audio message a month before I finished this book and the same excitement I had then, is the same excitement I had every time I broke open this book and started writing. I've never loved a set of characters I've published more than these two and I hope you love them too.

Content & Trigger Warnings

Crowned In Blood is intended for mature audiences. This story contains references to and detailed depictions of child neglect, child abuse, physical, emotional, mental, and sexual abuse (including sexual assault), domestic violence, starvation, PTSD, panic and anxiety attacks, disassociation, extreme violence, murder, racism, kidnapping, explicit language, and sexually explicit scenes.

This book also mentions: Suicidal thoughts, suicide, death of a parent, removal of body parts, torture, pregnancy by marital rape, and pregnancy by rape (not the FMC in either case).

The following kinks have also been included in this work: Praise, Pleasure Dom behavior, degradation, punishment, spanking, DD/LQ behavior, breath play, breeding, shibari, and primal play.

Playlist

Want to listen along while you read? Search Crowned In Blood by Melissa Cummins on Youtube or scan the QR code below:

Lovely by Billie Eilish & Khalid
Here by Alessia Cara
Like that by Bea Miller
Elastic Heart by Sia
Wild Side by Cross My Heart Hope To Die
DARKSIDE by Neoni
Royalty by Egzod, Maestro Chives & Neoni
KNIVES by Neoni & Savage Ga$P
KEHLANI by Jordan Adetunji
Motive by Ariana Grande & Doja Cat
Keep Me Up by Charlotte Lawrence
Dangerous Woman by Ariana Grande
Boyfriend by Ariana Grande & Social House
I Wanna Be Yours by Arctic Monkeys
Shake It Out by Florence + The Machine
Flowers by Raye
Little Girl Gone by Chinchilla

Shameless by Camila Cabello
Shut Up And Listen by Nicholas Bonnin & Angelicca
Let Me In by Tanerélle
Heartburn by Dizzyeight
Left Me Yet by Daya
We Go Down Together by Dove Cameron & Khalid
Arres by Melanie Fontana & Serhat Durmus
Crash&Burn (Feat. O'neill Hudson) by Bea Miller
Work Song (Official Video) by Hozier
Love Me Like You Do (From "Fifty Shades Of Grey") by Ellie
Goulding
Savage (bitmastr remix) by Bahari
Die 4 U by Billie Eilish & Kami Kehoe
Infinity by Jaymes Young
Speechless by The Veronicas
A Thousand Years by Christina Perri
Dance Me To The End Of Love (Bonus) by The Civil Wars

PROLOGUE
CATALINA

Killer.

Monster.

I was called both from the moment I was born.

My father was at a rally, campaigning for a seat in the Senate, when my mother went into labor. By the time he arrived, she had already passed.

There were dozens of photos of my father's tears over the loss of his wife, Alana. And even more articles questioning how he was going to manage in a world without her, especially while trying to navigate life with a newborn.

But Simon Herrera persevered.

He took me with him wherever he could and pushed for new laws to protect children and their families, predominantly for low- and middle-income households.

The press went wild.

There were countless images of him holding a small, smiling version of me wrapped in the prettiest lace and the softest, most sparkling outfits.

Everyone believed I wanted for nothing, that everything I could have ever desired would be placed in the palm of my hand. And it was those images that helped my father succeed to the Senate.

He was a pioneer, a "real man," who put his child first. An authority women compared their men to, saying, "If he can take care of his daughter while running for the Senate, why can't my husband take care of the kids for an afternoon?"

Women supported my father. They believed in him, wanted him to win, because they secretly wanted him.

But it was all a lie.

To them, he was a good, just person. A man dedicated to his family. Someone who loved me more than anything in the world.

They were wrong.

Simon Herrera was a monster—one even worse than me.

As a child, I didn't truly understand my fear of my father. I hardly remembered anything before the age of four, only that the photos which hung in his office—his *mementos*—terrified me. But there was one summer that no matter how hard I tried, I could never forget.

I'd been dragged to a public rally. My father had chosen a thick velvet dress for me to wear, because it matched his outfit best and had small reflective stones. But he hadn't accounted for the heat.

Sweat dripped off my brow, constantly getting into my eyes. I kept swiping at them, messing up my short brown bangs. I tried to tough it out as long as I could, but my headache turned into nausea. And then I committed the worst offense of all—I stopped smiling and waving and cried.

My father took me home as soon as he could. And the moment we stepped inside, he loosened his belt, wrapped one end around his fist and said, "I'll give you something to cry about."

He beat me mercilessly, screaming, "This is all your fault," and if I "would have just kept smiling," he wouldn't have had to resort to whipping me.

I begged him to stop, promised I'd never do it again, but he told me he wouldn't. Not until I learned how to smile through the pain and tears.

True to his word, he beat me until I passed out from the torment, covered in tears with the smile I'd forced onto my face.

It wasn't the first or last time he'd beat and abused me, but I'd somehow blocked out the rest.

When I outgrew the clothes he'd bought me at six, he called me fat. When I calmly tried to tell him they were simply the wrong size, he beat me, then locked me in my room with nothing to eat for two days.

After that, I started stealing snacks from the kitchen in case it ever happened again. It did, multiple times, but at least I always had something to eat.

At eleven, my father found a love note tucked away in my backpack. He screamed at me, told me I was a "Disgrace who would never be allowed to date anyone" he "didn't approve of."

Then he pushed me down the stairs, and I broke my arm trying to brace for the fall. I wasn't able to write for six weeks.

The doctor and nurses asked me what happened, but my father kept reiterating that he'd simply come home and found me at the bottom of the stairs. He told them I was clumsy, always running into things, bumping into walls, showing up with scratches and scrapes with no explanation.

They didn't seem to believe him, though. They kept looking at me to say something, anything that would allow them to help.

But how could I? He was a powerful senator. And even if I said something, would they believe me?

I had been his punching bag for years. He'd hurt me so many times that I rarely felt the pain anymore. If I opened my mouth, if

I told them what he'd done, what would they be able to do? And how far would my father go to keep his secret?

I didn't know the answer to those questions, but I did know Simon Herrera would do anything to protect his image, and he was capable of grave violence.

I didn't want anyone else to experience what I had, so I simply nodded along, saying I'd been running through the house and tripped down the stairs.

Oddly, my response had given me some reprieve. My father removed me from school, forcing me to learn at home with a tutor, and for a while, the beatings lessened.

Outside of public appearances, he mostly acted like I didn't exist. It was like he'd gotten the confirmation he needed, that I had accepted what I was to him—his doll. A pawn to morph and marionette into whatever he required that day.

That hurt the little pride I had, but there was no other alternative. I couldn't escape from him, not yet, but I would one day. I just had to survive to that point.

By sixteen, I'd become an expert in acting.

In front of others, I smiled, waved, danced at soirees where some men leered at me like a hungry lion dying for a taste. I kept my grades up, excelled at everything my father ordered me to, and sang my father's praises to the masses.

But at night, when it was dark, and I was by myself, I'd let everything fade away except my anger and hatred.

I resented everything my father stood for: the law, politics, government. Sometimes, I was jealous of my mother for dying while I survived only to live a miserable life.

I was certain my father had abused her too. In every photo her blonde hair was in a sophisticated updo. She was always thin, dressed immaculately. The epitome of the ideal wife.

Articles depicted my mother as the perfect hostess at parties and galas, and the first person my father thanked at award speeches. And in every picture, she always had a wide smile on her face—the same one I had been faking for years.

Sometimes I wondered what would have happened if my mother had survived. If my father had been abusing her, much like I suspected he was, would she have escaped with me? Would she have saved me?

I wanted to believe at least one of my parents cared about me. It was the only comfort I had... until I found my mother's diary.

In it, she'd detailed everything. How she'd been forced to marry my father, and that he'd abused her every single day of her life.

From broken ribs to marital rape to constant threats upon her life, she'd gone through it all. My mother's appearance was always flawless, her behavior impeccable, because if she weren't, she would face unimaginable pain and terror.

She'd never had a moment of peace, and any hope she'd carried in her heart of finally getting it had been drained out of her. In that way, we were the same.

But in a little pocket, hidden at the back of her diary, was a detailed plan on how she would kill herself alongside a letter for me. My mother couldn't bring herself to do it while pregnant, but the moment she gave birth, she swore she'd take her own life. And she did.

In her letter, she apologized for giving birth to me, saying she never wanted to bring me into a world with that bastard as my father, but she had no choice. He had her watched nearly twenty-four hours a day.

A baby would make the media see him as a family man. Exactly what he needed for his campaign, and he wouldn't let anyone stand in the way of that—especially my mother.

She hoped that one day I would find a way out. That someone

would save me, or I'd find the strength to save myself. She apologized for being weak, for not persevering for me, for being selfish.

I refused to read the rest, because she *was* selfish.

I understood she didn't have a choice, but I couldn't forgive her. She'd left me with my father. And knew her death would put me in the same situation she had been. Yet she still went through with the pregnancy and her suicide.

Did she know how that would affect me? Did she know I would be called a killer?

Did she care?

I'd been mocked, hurt, constantly reminded that I was lower than scum by my father, and I'd believed it. It was my fault, I killed her. I shouldn't be alive.

But she framed me.

She forced me to take the fall for something she did, forced me to live with guilt and shame that never belonged to me.

That wasn't right. That wasn't fair.

That wasn't *love*.

If I hadn't become the perfect tool for shaping my father's image, I likely wouldn't have made it past infancy.

But I had, and I was determined to survive.

If I had to keep acting, pretending I loved my father and my life, I would. If I had to worship the ground he walked on, or hide his abuse, I would.

I would do whatever I had to survive, and when I was able, I'd leave him for good.

Yes, he was a senator, but he couldn't stop me once I became an adult.

Then I'd escape.

I'd be free.

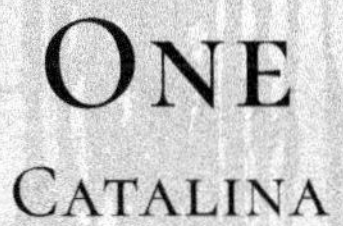

ONE
CATALINA

I went from being an abused doll to a caged prisoner at eighteen.

He increased the guards, forced me into online college, and monitored every message and email I sent.

Had he found out about my plans to escape? Uncovered the jewelry and cash I'd hidden away? Seen my search history? Realized how much I truly hated him?

But if he had, he would've beaten me within an inch of my life.

Then I overheard him telling a guard he had to "keep me separated from others" so I would stay "pure and moldable."

He wanted me isolated.

The bastard.

But I was safe. For now.

No matter how angry I was, I couldn't leave yet. I still needed his signature for everything—bank accounts, purchases—everything I needed to survive.

It didn't matter if I had cash or could pay in full. Companies wanted a legal guardian's approval to cover their ass. So, I waited.

And now that I'd turned twenty-one it was finally here. In one short day, I'd finally be free.

I would have to attend the lavish birthday party my father was throwing for me. Yet another political scheme asking people to fund his campaign while showing me off to someone's rich son. But tomorrow, I'd make him an offer he couldn't refuse.

For years, I'd been asked to do interviews and exclusives, but my father had never allowed it. However, now that I had a degree in political science and economics, the media speculated whether I'd follow in my father's footsteps, and he'd finally permitted me to give them an answer.

I was more likely to burn his house down with his corpse inside.

But I'd convince my father it was the life I wanted.

My plan was already falling into place. I'd donated to the Center of Gentle Love and Hope—a domestic violence non-profit organization—and agreed to set aside time for a tour. Afterwards, I'd ask to visit their other locations far from New York City—and my father—and never return.

It was a simple plan, but it was the only one that would work.

The media knew me. It wasn't like I could just change my name or appearance and disappear. But with my own awards, successes, and PR, the press would be all over me, meaning my father couldn't be.

I'd have to keep up the heroic senator's daughter act a little longer, but I'd be able to go home feeling safe each night, at peace, knowing I'd helped both myself and others.

I stood, checking my appearance in the mirror. My dark-brown hair shined and bounced, the curled ends brushing the top of my ass. My makeup was light—as my father had ordered—

mascara to call attention to my long eyelashes and thin black eyeliner to enhance my dark eyes—but the crimson lipstick I'd chosen was all me. My little act of rebellion.

My long, plum gown of lace and silk highlighted my too-thin body but accentuated my natural curves, the high slit coming to mid-thigh, elongating my legs.

I was a perfect blend of elegance and seduction—my forced role for the night.

I practiced my smile and greetings in the mirror until they were flawless. Then, before the grief of my life could consume me, I shoved it away.

You're almost there. In less than a day, you'll be gone.

My party—more of an art gala with me as the main showpiece—had so far gone off without a hitch.

My father was the picture of perfection in his perfectly tailored black suit, gold watch and cufflinks. Not a single strand of graying, dark-brown hair out of place.

He gave a grand introduction, professing how beautiful I was and how proud he was of me before wishing me all the happiness in the world.

Managing to force a warm smile, I issued a heartfelt thank you. Even shed a small tear, like the Oscar-worthy actress I'd trained myself to be.

I dabbed the tear away with a napkin, and he grabbed my shoulders, kissing my cheeks with a big smile. His blue eyes lowered to my dark-red lipstick and flashed. A warning that I would be punished for defying his orders.

Good. The pain would be worth it for that small piece of control.

His grip on my waist was tight as he nearly dragged me to meet his guests. If I wasn't used to it, I'd have tripped and fallen flat on my face.

When he left to attend a meeting, the vultures descended, trying their best to play matchmaker.

I'd rather die before marrying anyone here.

My rounds finally done, I grabbed a flute of champagne and a few stuffed mushroom hors d'oeuvres before stealing a moment in a secluded corner.

I was exhausted. It wasn't exertion, but something deeper, darker. I'd spent my life holding onto the edge of a cliff, a fingertip away from falling into the abyss, and now, I was starting to slip.

All I had left was myself, and I swore I wouldn't lose who I was to these people, to this life.

But as I looked around the room, rage and hate consumed me. They deserved a taste of the brutality I endured just as much as my father did.

Yes, my father caused my pain and despair, but these people played a part as well. They paid him. They paved his way, bought his every word. Believed his every lie.

There's no doubt my father did and condoned illegal things over the years, and these people knew that. But they didn't care. All they wanted was another dollar sign, another paycheck, another source for power. But what about *my* power? What about *my* voice? *What about my life?*

Why shouldn't I let loose? Rain hell down upon them and show them what years of abuse could do to the heart? To the soul?

I was ruined, destroyed. There were cracks in me that would never be filled. And all I could do was try to cover them and ignore the violence and cruelty underneath. But it was there, festering, waiting to spring free.

Taking a deep breath, I exhaled. In these moments I scared myself, not knowing the lengths I would go for vengeance.

I stared at the champagne, rolling the flute between my fingertips. What would it feel like to break it in my hand and use the shards as a weapon? To experience the same raw, unabashed, chaotic freedom every person in this room but me had enjoyed? How many people could I hurt in the ways I'd been hurt?

Could I kill Malcolm Richards—the man who had been undressing me with his eyes since I was thirteen? Would his wife Cathy cry over his death, or would she use his life insurance policy to take lavish trips with the pool boy she was fucking on the side?

Maybe I could stab Shawn Cruz. He'd certainly deserve it. All he got was a light slap on the wrist after his drunk driving caused the death of a father of three, because he was the District Attorney's son.

None of the people here were innocent, and perhaps, neither was I. But as long as I kept myself under control, I could be better than them.

"You don't seem to be enjoying your party."

The deep voice jarred me and I looked up to find an unfamiliar man gazing at me intensely. He was over six feet tall, with long brown hair that touched his wide shoulders. But it was his eyes that unnerved me the most.

He looked at me like he could consume me, pick me apart, clean to the bone. Like he could see straight into my broken soul. It scared me to think of what secrets he might unearth if I gave him the chance.

So I didn't. Instead, I put on my best smile.

"Of course I'm enjoying it. It's a lovely party. My father truly spared no expense."

The corner of his lip tipped into a smirk before he held a glass of what smelled like brandy to his lips. "You're good. I'm sure you know that. But if anyone here pulled their head out of their asses long enough to pay attention to you for more than a minute, they'd know you were lying."

I almost choked on my champagne.

Mischief danced in the man's rich, brown eyes, and for a moment, I was shocked, until that feeling quickly turned to fear. I glanced around the room, scared that someone—or worse, my father—had caught my mistake.

"Don't worry, no one's looking at you."

He was right. No one had seen my blunder with the champagne nor my shock.

I hated that he'd immediately known what I was afraid of. He was too close, too... accurate, and it knocked me off balance.

His eyes held mine as he stroked his glass with one finger. A slow, continuous caress, as though he had all the time in the world. A sensual touch, something that made my pulse soar.

I took a slow breath, collecting myself. "Why were you?"

"Watching you?"

I nodded.

"Because you're the most gorgeous woman in this room."

His frankness made my cheeks heat, as his finger still stroked his glass. His touch was focused, intimate, as if he were caressing *me.*

I was used to the games, to people trying to manipulate me. I had to be posh, mannered, *cultured*—all things this stranger didn't seem to be at that moment.

I had no doubt he could put on that façade and perform it to utter perfection. He carried an air of mirth and cold calculation, yet was charming and confident, like the beauty of a glacier before it broke apart, causing a tsunami that killed anyone in its path.

He struck me as someone whose every word was purposeful. Someone who had come into their power and could wield it completely. It left me in both awe and envy of him, and it was sexy as hell.

How incredible it must be to have that sort of freedom.

His gaze darkened the longer he stared at me, like he was appreciating me, savoring my presence.

A strange warmth built in my core, and for a moment, I wished I could freeze time. He looked at me as though he *saw* me for who I was, who I had the potential to be.

It left me vulnerable to the cravings of my inner child, to the desire to be *wanted*, to be acknowledged. To be loved as I was, not who I pretended to be.

But I wasn't a child nor a princess. And he wasn't a prince. This wasn't a fairy tale, and I knew better than to be so naïve.

I rolled my shoulders back, ready to play and win whatever game he had up his sleeve. It didn't matter how attractive he was; this man was like everyone else. He was here, after all, which meant he knew my father. And one did not navigate the waters of Simon Herrera without an equally deceptive compass.

But before I could say anything, his phone vibrated. He withdrew his eyes from me, and the loss of his attention made me feel like the air was being sucked from the room.

He sighed. "Unfortunately, I have to take this." The weight of his gaze settled on me for one more moment, and when he spoke again, his voice was a low whisper. "Happy birthday, Catalina. May all your dreams come true."

He turned away, and it wasn't until he slipped out the back door, I realized I'd never gotten his name.

Two

I adjusted the hem on my knee-length, baby-blue chiffon dress and pushed my hair behind my shoulder. It made me seem younger, innocent, *gullible*—the exact image I needed for my meeting with my father. But my eyes were defiant.

It was like my body could no longer contain itself. I listened for every step, flinched at every loud noise, was too watchful, too alert. I barely slept.

I was terrified that, somehow, my father would know. Maybe someone would tip him off. I would forget something, not be careful enough, and suddenly, everything would go to shit.

Naya, the head of the Center of Gentle Love and Hope, had told me multiple stories of women facing the same psychological response when they thought of escaping their abuser.

They'd panic at the notion of leaving, because regardless of the pain, misery, and terror they suffered, they knew their abuser. They knew their triggers, knew their surroundings, and the brain valued that information.

In the known, there was familiarity, a measure of safety, but what waited in the unknown brought nothing but fear. Between that and the possibility that anything could go wrong, it made sense why so many people stayed.

But I wouldn't.

With a deep breath, I stared at my reflection, forcing myself to calm down. Little by little, I smoothed my expression until it morphed into one of a gentle, doting, unassuming daughter. Then I made my way to my father's office and knocked on the door.

"Come in."

I steeled myself, but when I opened the door, I found my father wasn't alone.

Seated in front of him was a large, heavyset man with thick black hair pulled back into a ponytail at his nape. I recognized him as one of the people who had attended the party last night. Someone I'd gone out of my way to avoid.

Being near him made my skin crawl. The air of danger and malice around him was tangible—even in a crowded room.

The rich saw themselves as the elite. They could take whatever they wanted, own whatever they felt they deserved. Everything and everyone had a price. That's what they all believed.

But this man didn't seem like he wanted to pay. Like he'd kill anyone for simply suggesting it.

He acted like the world owed him something, that he had the right to take whatever he wanted by force. And when his brown eyes dragged their way slowly over my body before finally meeting my own, the look in his eyes said it all... he wanted *me*.

"Catalina, this is Fernando Salazar. Fernando, this is my daughter, Catalina."

Fernando made no move to rise from his chair, making sure I had to cross the distance between us to shake his hand. Warning signals fired off in my gut. Something was very wrong.

While my father couldn't care less about me privately, publicly, he always acted like I was his most prized possession. Disrespecting me meant disrespecting him, and that's exactly what Fernando had done. Yet my father said nothing. In fact, he seemed to be completely ignorant of the entire exchange, even though I'd seen him ruin a man for less.

But for now, I was expected to play their game.

I stuck out my hand, donning my most welcoming smile. "It's nice to meet you, Fernando."

Fernando ignored my hand for a moment, his meticulous gaze studying my skin as if I was a piece of art he could critique. Unease filled my veins, but I kept the smile on my face.

Finally, he shook my hand, his grip tight. Squeezing my fingers, expecting me to wince. If it weren't for my high pain tolerance and spite, I would have.

He released his grip, leaving my fingers with a dull ache, then kissed my hand. "It is lovely to meet you, Catalina." His voice was deep with a heavy Hispanic accent.

His kiss felt dirty. Forcing another smile, I pulled my hand from his, the rough hairs of his goatee scratching my skin.

"She's beautiful." He grinned.

"Then you approve?"

I turned to my father, the knots in my stomach twisting tighter. "Approve?"

"Yes." Fernando stood, towering over me.

I gulped at the hungry expression in his eyes. He looked at me like he wanted to crush me, *break* me until there was nothing left. Still, I kept myself calm, not willing to give Fernando or my father the satisfaction of seeing how afraid I really was.

I stepped to the side of Fernando, moving out of his way. But as he walked past me, he grabbed a lock of my hair and brought it to his lips.

Surprised, I instinctually jerked away.

He laughed. "Make sure she looks like this on our wedding day. I want everyone to see how innocent she is before I ruin her."

My father nodded as Fernando left the room.

My mouth went dry, my heart hammering against my ribs as I stared at my father, wide-eyed. "Wedding day? What—"

Without glancing at me, my father tossed a file to me from his desk. "Read over this. I want you ready and prepared."

My chest tightened as I took the file and opened the folder. The pages were filled with details about Fernando—his age; where he lived. "Father, what is—"

"I've arranged a marriage between the two of you. The wedding will happen in three days. You will study this file, which contains everything you need to know including what Fernando expects, and how you will act as a bride and a wife. Do not embarrass me."

Arranged. Marriage. Fernando. Ruin. Embarrass. Arranged. Marriage. Fernando. Ruin. Embarrass. Arranged. Marriage. Fernando. Ruin. Embarrass. Arranged. Marriage—

My fingers shook, then my arms, to my chest. Through my body.

All the work I'd done, the plans I'd made, the abuse I'd taken was for nothing. *Nothing!* My father had transferred the ownership of my cage to that vile, horrible, detestable man.

The file fell from my hand as I threw my head back and laughed, the thunderous sound of my rapid heartbeat and my rage filling my ears. And when my eyes landed on my father, with his blue eyes looking at me in complete disgust, I threw myself over the desk.

My hands reached out to grab his neck, to choke the life from him in the same way he had done to me for years.

Two guards gripped my arms, yanking me back, keeping me

from killing him the way I wanted to, *deserved* to. But I kept trying. I hissed, growled, thrashed like a wild animal.

"I'll kill you! I swear, I'll kill you! You fucking bastard!"

"Enough!" He jumped to his feet then slammed the desk with his palms. "Kill me? *Me*? When I'm the one who has kept you alive this entire time? The one who has fed you, put clothes on your back? Given you everything you've ever wanted?"

I had no idea I'd threatened him out loud. No idea that I'd been screaming and crying, My throat was hoarse, arms held by my sides. I could do nothing but quietly sob.

I broke in front of him.

"You're a spoiled, ungrateful little bitch!" He grabbed my chin, his gaze cold and hard. "The only reason I kept you alive was to serve me. Otherwise, I would have killed you as a baby. That's your *purpose*. You should be *thanking* me for my generosity."

He threw me back like a piece of trash. "Without me, you are *nothing*. You're *worth* nothing." He sneered. "But you will pay me back for the years of money, time, and energy I've funneled into you. I need this deal with Fernando, and he wants you. You will marry him, you will bear him as many children as he desires, and you will do it with a fucking *smile*, or so help me, I will kill you where you stand."

His anger calmed me. It forced me to swallow my fury, carefully concealing it once more, letting it simmer under the surface. Because while I'd rather die than marry Fernando, I wouldn't give my father the satisfaction of killing me.

Instead, I spit in his face and smiled when he was forced to wipe it away.

"You're lucky the media will be circling around this wedding like vultures, or I would beat the shit out of you." He leaned closer to me, his face only inches away from mine as he hissed, "But remember Catalina, I know how to hurt you."

"Do your worst." I went to spit at him again, but a guard hit me on the back of my head, and the world faded to black.

I awoke on the floor of my room with Fernando's file next to me. Remembering the way he looked at me, *touched* me, had bile rising up my throat, and I raced to my trash bin and threw up.

Three days.

Three days was all I had to come back from this, to make a new plan. To gain my freedom.

I wiped away the vomit with the back of my hand, squared my shoulders, then found they'd taken my computer and cell phone. Cutting off all ties to the outside world. Curious, I tried my bedroom door. Locked.

Fine.

I'd slipped up and had finally shown my father exactly what I thought about him, that I'd been acting the entire time. He couldn't trust me, couldn't let me roam around, knowing I'd try to escape the first chance I got. I'd doubted he'd even let me eat today.

But none of that mattered. I needed to survive, to pivot and find a way out of this. And I would, eventually. I *had* to.

A part of me desperately wished that Fernando might be a good person. Maybe he'd actually grow to care for and love me. But I knew that would never happen.

He was a monster, a predator, and to him, I was his prey.

Furious tears threatened to spill from my eyes, but I wiped them away. I didn't have time to cry. I didn't have time to mourn, or grieve all the things I wanted my life to be. I had to fight as hard as I could, and the best way I could do that was to know my adversary.

Taking a deep breath, I tried to keep the mental spiral threatening to send me into a breakdown at bay, then grabbed the file. Huddling myself into a corner on the floor, I opened the folder.

Name: Fernando Salazar

Age: 43

I gulped at the age difference, shook off the fear, then kept reading.

Birthday: October 16th

City and State of Address: New York, NY

Marital Status: Divorced (twice)

What happened to his previous wives? The thought that he might have hurt them sent a shiver down my spine.

Children: None

I flipped the page to photos of Fernando at different parties with an array of people, all of them rich, all in a position of power or authority. There was even a photo of him with the Mayor.

In another photo, he was getting into a black SUV with guards surrounding him. The gun at his waist drew my attention. My father always had guards, but he never carried a gun.

There was no way Fernando was related to a politician then, and I doubted a CEO would need such protection. Maybe he worked in security?

Turning the pages, I realized Fernando had several businesses. Corporations, pharmaceuticals, laundromats, restaurants. He owned half of the port of New York, not to mention countless warehouses.

Each page and photo set off warning bells, but why?

The last page was a detailed list of instructions for me as the bride, my expected demeanor for the wedding, and beyond.

I was to act as a blushing, innocent virgin bride utterly in love with Fernando. The media would be watching, and it was my job to give them the show of a lifetime.

If I failed at any time to make our union look like anything other than joyful and willing, I would face severe punishment from my soon-to-be husband.

Fernando wanted me dressed modestly, nothing revealing. There would be no reception after the wedding and I would be expected to provide him with children as soon as possible. He would tolerate a daughter, but a son was nonnegotiable. Only a male could run his mafia empire, and if I couldn't give him one, I'd cease to be useful.

My heart went into overdrive, chills racking my body.

Mafia.

No. No...

I flipped through the photos again with newfound clarity. Fernando hadn't included the images to show off his wealth or status; he'd included them to make sure I knew the truth.

I wouldn't be able to escape.

If I tried to take a flight out of the state or country, he'd know. If I tried to take a ferry into Canada, he'd know. He had the damn Mayor in his pocket, likely most if not the entire police force.

My vision blurred as tears rolled down my cheeks. There was nowhere for me to go. No plan or scheme for me to grasp onto.

My fate was to become someone else's possession, and there was nothing I could do about it.

THREE

CATALINA

I barely slept that night and was catatonic during my dress fitting.

The room, the people... they all faded away. I lifted my hands when told and turned when instructed, just like a perfect little doll.

My mind was chaotic, broken. My soul crushed to pieces, and yet my body forced me to survive. I breathed, ate when given food, drank when given water, and functioned as though I were on autopilot.

By the next day, the entryways and backyard had been transformed with beautiful arrays of flowers, marble sculptures, fountains, and candles. Chandeliers and draping plants decorated the house in a theme of white, green, and gold. Everything was detailed to perfection.

Any bride would have been overjoyed to get married there if they had been given a choice.

But to me, the sculptures were nightmarish, the rush of the water from the fountains too loud. The plants were thorny vines keeping me in my cage. Each decoration squeezed the walls of my prison around me tighter, suffocating me.

I had two roles—the obedient daughter and the joyful bride—and I was so numb that I went along with both.

But something in me snapped when I heard my father's voice as he walked through the hallway, rattling off commands and tasks to a wedding planner.

What am I doing?

This wasn't me, and it would *never* be me. I couldn't just give up. I *refused* to.

Yes, Fernando's wealth and connections made escaping a monumental challenge. But if others had escaped the mafia, so could I.

I won't be an easy captive. I won't allow them to break my spirit.

When I returned to my room I combed through the file again, looking for anything that might help me. But it only emphasized that Fernando's power was absolute.

But as I read over the page of commands, I smirked.

My marriage to Fernando was inevitable, but if he thought I'd obey all of his terms, he had another thing coming.

I sat on the edge of my bed, the clock ticking loudly, reminding me of the precious time I was losing.

My wedding was tomorrow. The preparations were all in place, exactly as Fernando and my father had wanted. But I wouldn't be.

Fernando wanted a virgin bride, and when I walked down the aisle tomorrow, I wouldn't be.

My plan was dangerous and could go wrong, just like all my

others seemed to. But I didn't care anymore. It was all I had, all I could do. And that small semblance of control was worth fighting for.

The guard who arrived with my dinner was young and arrogant. A man who believed he could have anything he wanted without question, making him exactly who I needed.

"Come in." I held the door open and he placed the plate on the table, but as he turned to leave, I closed the door behind me, blocking him.

The guard opened his mouth, but I bunched the fabric of my dress in my clammy hands and pulled it off.

His eyes widened, taking in my naked form while I swallowed the churning disgust rising within me.

It's okay. This has to happen. It'll be better this way. Just endure it for a little while.

I'd never thought I was beautiful. My father had always said I looked too Hispanic. My skin was too tan, my eyes too dark, my hair easily frizzy and difficult to maintain. But the one benefit I had was my body.

My breasts were perky, my ass round and tight. I had no fat on my body due to the frequent starvation I'd been subjugated to. My waist was narrow, my hips wide, and I had more legs than torso.

Based on the erection in the guard's pants, he found me attractive enough.

"Do you have a condom?" I whispered, my heartbeat pounding in my ears.

"Yeah." His voice was gruff. Slowly, he approached me, like I was his fantasy come to life.

He pulled me into his arms, then angled his head toward mine, but I pushed him back.

"No kissing," I said, my voice quivering.

He smirked. "Fine by me."

He fucked me from behind on my bed as I muffled my small whimpers of pain into the sheets. I stared out the window until the world slipped away, and I no longer felt him or heard our bodies slapping against each other.

When he was done, he rolled off the condom, threw it in the trash, and left.

I walked into the bathroom, turned on the hot water in my tub, and climbed inside. My skin turned red, burning, but I didn't feel it, didn't care.

Tears welled in my eyes, streaming down my cheeks.

I'd taken control. My plan was a success. I wasn't a virgin anymore, and yet the victory cut at my heart and soul.

I'd been desperate for love, for someone to actually want *me*, to make me feel like I was enough. I wanted to have value as my own person, not for what I could do or be but simply because I existed.

I'd held onto the hope that one day, I could finally grasp the love I'd always wanted. But I'd never gotten that.

It was time to accept the truth. And even though the alternative would have been worse, even though I'd done the right thing, I grieved for everything I'd lost.

It wasn't just my virginity; it was my hopes, my dreams, my life, *me*. My heart was broken, dead, nothing more than an empty shell.

I sobbed into my arm, biting hard, trying to dull the anguish and sorrow threatening to consume me. But this time, it didn't work. And when it failed, I covered my mouth with my hands and screamed.

I screamed and screamed until the water almost overflowed.

I shut off the faucet, sitting there until the water, and my body, became numbingly cold.

I let myself feel it all, because this would be the last time I could. When I walked down the aisle tomorrow, I would have to do so as a warrior, prepared for battle. There would be no room for regret, self-pity, or any foolish emotion ever again.

My wedding day would mark the beginning of my resistance, and I would be ready for it.

My bedroom door flew open, the loud sound startling me awake. A cheery young maid pulled open the curtains, then placed a meal on my table. "Wake up, miss! Today's the big day! You must be so excited."

I'd rather walk through fire. Although I suppose that's exactly what I'm about to do.

The woman had left by the time I forced myself out of bed and reached my table. My stomach was in too many knots to eat much, but I managed to drink the soup, eat a piece of bread, and swallow the fruit before my stylist, makeup artist, hairdresser, and their assistants barged into the room. I endured being poked and prodded until they transformed me into the image of bridal perfection.

The women cooed over their work, complimenting me on my beauty, but I ignored them. They might not know the full scope of what was happening, but I couldn't help feeling they were complicit in the worst day of my life.

Once they left, I stood in front of the full-length mirror, barely recognizing the person staring back at me draped in ivory satin, tulle, and lace.

The clock tolled, the sound slicing through me like the blade of a guillotine.

It's time.

A guard led me out of my room to the base of the stairs where my father waited for me with a sneer. "Don't mess this up, Catalina."

I held his gaze. "You're forgetting that after today, you will no longer hold any power over me. My fiancé clearly has you by the *balls*, Father. So keep your threats to yourself."

His eyes narrowed, but before he could speak, the music started.

He huffed, then forced my hand into the crook of his arm, turning us to the double doors leading out into the backyard, where the new chapter of my nightmare was waiting to begin.

As we stepped into the bright sun, I scanned the crowd, unsurprised to see my father's donors and colleagues on one side and what I assumed to be Fernando's mafia organization on the other. Their all-black suits and dark auras permeated the air.

Finally, I looked toward the altar where Fernando stood in a tailored black suit. His grin reminded me of a cat that had finally caught its mouse. It ignited a fire in my blood, and for once, I didn't have to worry about what would happen if I didn't contain it.

With a smirk, I stuck my foot out and tripped my father, pulling my foot back just in time to ensure he didn't take me down with him.

A chorus of gasps erupted from my father's guests while Fernando's people snickered. Not a single person moved to help him, much to my delight.

My father had spent years buying the people around him, and now that he was down, no one bothered to help him up. If that wasn't karma, I wasn't sure what was.

Ignoring the patrons, I left my father there and marched toward Fernando, who sneered at me.

We were to meet a few steps before the priest and the altar, where my father would hand me over to Fernando, and we would take the last steps together. However, when Fernando extended his hand to me, I ignored it, continuing the last few steps on my own.

The priest's eyebrows nearly shot off his head as he glanced between us. Eventually, Fernando joined me at the top, a small tic in his jaw.

I blocked out the priest's prayers and blessings. It had been a long time since I'd believed in God, and as I stared at the man across from me, it cemented that either the primordial being didn't exist, or he hated me.

The feeling was mutual.

When it came time for me to say the two words that would lock me into my fate, I hesitated. For a moment, I fantasized about finally telling the truth. What would happen if I admitted I was being forced into this marriage by my abusive father who had threatened to kill me just days before? What would people think if they knew they'd supported such a monster?

But what was the point?

At best, they'd remove their donations quietly, then distance themselves to avoid any possible backlash. At worst, they'd believe I was lying, and the wedding would go forward in a less public location where I would be bruised, bloody, and have no voice of my own.

Even if they did believe me, much like they'd refused to help my father, they would refuse to help me. Especially if it meant acknowledging they'd made a mistake with the man they were in business with. Still, this moment with my small power of choice gave me joy.

I didn't know Fernando well, but it was clear he was a man of few words in public. He seemed to believe speaking to someone who couldn't benefit him was beneath him, using his guards, his size, or his presence to intimidate people.

That was why he hadn't pulled me back and forced me to go up the stairs with him. He didn't have to. No matter what tricks I played, everything would go according to his plan.

But making him sweat, irritating him, being anything other than the obedient wife he wanted gave *me* power, and I would continue to be a thorn in his side until I set myself free.

Fernando's grip on my wrist tightened. I'd have bruises come tomorrow morning, but I still waited a little longer, relishing in the growing impatience in his eyes.

"I do," I finally said, swallowing the bitterness on my tongue.

Fernando reached for the rings, but I grabbed them and shoved them on myself to make a point. He would never fully control *me*.

His nostrils flared and his neck corded.

Good.

When the priest turned and asked him the same question, Fernando's grip tightened around my hand as he snarled, "I do." He pulled my hand to his, forced me to take his ring, then squeezed until I finally slipped the band onto his finger.

"With the power vested in me, I now pronounce you husband and wife. You may kiss the bride!"

The finality in the priest's words echoed in my ears. Fernando leaned in to kiss me, but I turned my head at the last second, making him kiss my cheek.

"You'll pay for that, *wife*," he growled in my ear.

I turned my head and glared. "You should be happy you even got my cheek. Otherwise I would have thrown up on you on the spot."

Fernando glowered, leaning in close. "Don't forget who you're speaking to, Catalina."

I forced myself not to grind my teeth, taking a deep breath instead. "You may be the boss of the mafia, but that's as far as your leadership extends. If you wanted an obedient wife, you should have picked someone else." I flicked my eyes to our audience. "Now, in case you haven't noticed, the people are starting to stare, and I believe that goes against your idea of a perfect wedding."

His eyes narrowed. Then he stood to his full height, pulled me to him, and forcibly tucked my hand into his arm.

I ignored the congratulations and happy smiles of the guests. Ignored everything until we neared the exit where my father stood.

My father reached out to Fernando, grasping his hand with fake tears shining in his eyes. "Welcome to the family, Fernando. Please take care of my baby girl."

I glared at him. *Putting on a performance, even at the end.*

Fernando grimaced, but quickly forced a smile. "I promise."

The exchange spoke volumes. Fernando had the power here, but they were partners in something that required an appearance of companionship.

I doubted it had much to do with money, Fernando probably needed my father's status to access something. If my father was still playing the role of doting father, then I wasn't just Fernando's wife to breed, but a link between our families.

I smiled, the first real one I'd had in longer than I could remember. Fernando might abuse me, but he couldn't kill me as long as he needed Simon. And my father couldn't hurt me and risk angering Fernando for injuring his new possession. Without meaning to, they'd given me leverage.

Fernando could only know what my father told him. And since I'd fooled my father for years, that information was likely inaccurate. Which meant I had a higher chance of escaping with Fernando than my father. It would take time, but it *would* work.

There was nothing but hatred in my father's eyes as he turned to me, his arms outstretched for a hug.

I stepped into his embrace. "Goodbye, Father. I hope the next time I see you is at your funeral."

A vein throbbed in his forehead, and he looked ready to strangle me, but he couldn't, and it made me feel like I was flying.

The feeling continued. I was exhilarated, like I'd just jumped from a skyscraper. I laughed in glee as Fernando yanked me outside, done playing the loving groom.

He threw me into the limo, making my head hit the glass hard, but even that couldn't wipe the smile off my face. For a moment, I closed my eyes and simply basked in bliss. Yes, I'd left the lion's den for the devil's lair, but at least I'd left.

"You're in an awfully good mood for someone forced into marriage, Catalina. I hope you keep that up for our wedding night."

The threat in his tone chilled me, but I refused to show it. Tonight would be another battle, and no matter the consequences, I would win.

Four
Catalina

Fernando's mansion screamed wealth—the immaculate landscaping and pristine marble facade, the towering columns with gold accents. It was more a looming palace than a relaxing home. The perfect temple for a sadistic, power-drunk man—and my gilded prison.

Fernando exited the limo, issuing low orders to two nearby men. And by the time I maneuvered myself and the ridiculous weight of my gown out of the car, he was gone.

Thankfully, neither man tried to assist me. I needed to be careful around them. They looked at me much like Fernando did, as if they owned me and could take me whenever they pleased.

Refusing to show my disgust, I straightened my shoulders and lifted my chin, waiting for them to address me or move.

"El jefe se consiguió una puta bonita, ¿no?" one guard chuckled. *

---

* The boss got himself a pretty whore, didn't he?

"¿Crees que el jefe nos dejará follárnosla?" the other said, licking his lips. *

"Sí, si ella todavía le queda algo de espíritu por romper." †

They laughed, one slapping the other's chest, cheering each other on.

My heart thundered in my chest.

Publicly, my father had all but disowned his Hispanic heritage, wanting to appeal to the rich white men and women who would get him elected. But privately, he demanded I learn Spanish.

I knew *exactly* what they said.

Fernando would do whatever it took to fuck me, and according to his guards, he wasn't above passing me around.

I had to survive. I would fight Fernando tooth and nail to keep myself safe. But as the guards led me through the heavy wooden doors, I found nothing I could use as a weapon.

The foyer was lined with statues secured into glass arches, followed by artwork any museum would be jealous of. He even had a rare Fabergé egg.

Fernando appeared to be a collector of whatever he deemed beautiful, caging it away behind glass, only taking it out when he wanted it to be put on display—myself included.

The corridor ended at a large fountain, which appeared to be the heart of the mansion. Turning to the right, the guards took me up a grandiose staircase, then down a hallway. I counted doors, windows, but no additional guards save the men beside me. It made me even more wary. Fernando had something sinister planned to keep me here.

Eventually, we stopped at a pair of large, dark wooden doors.

---

*   Do you think he'll let us fuck her?
†   Yes, if she still has some spirit left to break.

One guard pushed inside while the other looked over my body with darkened eyes.

I didn't acknowledge him and instead focused on trying to calm myself down. I didn't think Fernando was in there, nor did I think he'd let his guards have me first. But if I was wrong and I let my panic overtake me, I wouldn't be able to defend myself.

When the guard returned and nodded to the one beside me, I was shoved inside, flying forward. My gown's weight tangled around my legs, and I fell.

They laughed again, closing the door behind them, muttering about how stupid and weak I was. But I couldn't let their words get to me.

The moment the heavy lock clicked behind me, I sprang into action, taking stock of my surroundings.

The large room boasted a king-sized bed, dresser, tables, and chairs. Everything was in its place, in complete immaculate opulence. Even the three doors were ornate, especially the one leading to the balcony.

Fear clawed at my throat, but I pushed it back. I needed something to arm myself. Fernando was too large for me to fight head on, but if I could surprise him, I might have a chance.

I scoured the dresser and the nightstand. Nothing. I tore through the closet, flinging his neatly folded clothes everywhere.

I needed to find a knife, a screwdriver, even a letter opener, anything small enough to hide but sharp enough to do damage, but there was nothing.

Running toward the other nightstand, I nearly tripped on my gown.

Ahh! I can't fight like this. I need to get this stupid dress off!

With shaking hands, I twisted and bent my arms until I found the buttons. One by one, I slipped them through their closure until I was almost free.

Then the door unlocked.

Move. Move. Move! But I couldn't. My breathing was ragged; my body trembled, fueled by adrenaline.

It was too late.

"There were a lot of things I expected to find when I walked in here tonight, Catalina, but you getting undressed for me wasn't one of them." Fernando smirked. "I didn't think you'd be so *excited* for me to stuff my cock into you."

I choked on the bile rising in my throat, forcing it back down. But I couldn't keep myself from shaking. "The thought of you touching me makes me sick."

"I'm going to do more than touch you." He shrugged off his blazer, letting it drop to the floor. "I'm going to fuck you, and when I take your virginity, I'm going to make it hurt. Punishment for the way you disrespected me today."

Bitter rage boiled over, burning away my fear. *I disrespected him?!* What about the way he'd traded me like an object or planned to use me like a slave? What about his guards? What about that bullshit wedding?

You haven't even fucking seen disrespect.

"Oh, it seems you're confused." I smirked, my voice deceptively calm. "You see, I gave away my virginity yesterday." The smirk faded as my resolve hardened and my voice turned razor sharp. "There's *nothing* left for you to take."

Fernando's face turned a deep shade of red, twisting in anger. He lunged at me and I dodged him, but I couldn't keep it up for long.

He reached for me again, and I slipped away, evading him until a painful yank at my scalp stopped me. Fernando began dragging me back by my hair as I fought to break free. Then he slammed me against the wall.

Tears blurred my vision as he began ripping off my gown. I

kicked and screamed, but it was no use. He was too strong, too big. His laugh, a cruel, mocking sound, wrapped around me as if he'd already won.

He leaned in to kiss me, and I bit his lip, hard, drawing blood, and it tore as he pulled away.

He howled in pain, blood gushing down his chin as he reared back to hit me, but I kneed him in the balls, making him double over. Stripped down to meager pieces of my torn gown and underwear, I ran.

I made it to the bedroom door, but it was locked. I frantically searched the room. Then I saw it, my only way out—the balcony.

Would I survive a fall from the second-floor? Even if I landed on my feet, I'd probably break something. And what about Fernando's guards? What other traps had he set to keep me in line? Dogs? An electric fence?

What about his gun? He had to have it on him. He hadn't used it yet because he thought he'd beat me. This was just *foreplay* for him. But if I escaped, would he shoot me?

It doesn't matter!

The fall, the consequences, none of it mattered. I'd rather die than let him touch me, even if it meant taking my own life.

I sprinted toward the balcony. Fernando lunged toward me, but I leapt onto the bed.

Jumping off the mattress, I was almost free when he grabbed my ankle.

I fell, catching myself before my face slammed into the floor. Fernando crawled on top of me, forcing me onto my back.

Using every ounce of strength I had, I fought, screaming, growling, thrashing like a demon being dragged back to hell. But he'd pinned my legs with his own, rendering my kicks useless.

I raked my nails across his face, scratching his eye, before punching him. He yowled in pain, but it didn't faze him. Fisting my hair, he pulled my head up, and slammed me back down.

The world spun, stars burst before my eyes, and blood pulsed in my ears. He did it again and again until my body went limp, my vision hazy. Finally, he let go of my hair, ripping the last of my clothes.

No! Move, move, move! Please!

A whimper escaped me as I begged, *pleading* with my body to respond. My limbs were heavy, the room spinning. Still, I fought to push or shove him away, but it was no use.

"Look at you, so vulnerable, completely defenseless." He sneered, his hands gripping my hair again. "Beg, Catalina. Beg for me to not do this to you. Whimper. Cry for me."

His laugh echoed through the room.

I couldn't stop this. There was no way out. No escape. He was going to rape me.

In the end, it didn't matter how hard I tried, how hard I fought. This was always going to be the outcome. He was going to win.

My eyes closed, my body ready to give up...

No. No!

Opening my eyes, I moved my hands to fight him again. But Fernando pinned them above my head, grinding his hips against mine, his erection pressing against me.

"That's right, keep fighting me," he growled, tightening his grip on my wrists with one hand, while his other pulled down the zipper of his pants, releasing his cock.

I wiggled my hips, trying to stop him from removing my panties. His grip loosened, and I got my hands free, but he pinned them down again, my shoulder bumping the edge of a table.

Yes! If I can just—

I hit the table again, but it didn't budge. Fernando reared back to punch me, and I braced for the blow.

Thunk.

His face went slack. His smile vanished, his eyes glazed over, and he collapsed on top of me.

Unable to breathe under his weight, I shoved at his shoulders, kicked at his legs, gasping for air, until finally I pulled myself from under him.

I blinked rapidly, trying to clear my blurry vision. There were four versions of Fernando spinning on the ground, but they were all still.

Is he dead?

I pressed on my chest, then hit it several times to calm myself down and think clearly.

What just happened? I did my best to scan the room, and while it was in shambles, none of the doors or windows were open.

I tried to stand, but the room spun, and my body shook uncontrollably. Slowly, I crawled around Fernando's body, inch by inch, until I found a vase with blood on its side.

My savior was none other than one of his prized pieces of art —a heavy, bronze antique vase.

I slumped against the floor, relief flooding through me as tears filled my eyes. Then reality set in and panic gripped me again.

Fernando's guards were still in the mansion. Clearly not close enough to hear, but I was sure they'd notice me if I ran into the street in my underwear.

And if Fernando was still alive, eventually, he would wake up and rape me.

I have to do it.

I had to be the one to end his life. But could I? I'd imagined someone's death plenty of times in the darkest corners of my mind, but to actually carry it out...

My hands shook, a tremor of fear and dark excitement. I gripped my wrist hard, using the pain as a reminder of what was at stake.

I thought back to the party, to the years of manipulation and abuse.

My view of morality was skewed. I wasn't a good person and would never claim to be. But I'd always believed there was a line I wouldn't cross, one that kept me human or at least made me better than my father. But as I stared at the man who planned to make my life a living hell, that line seemed to blur.

I didn't want to be a monster. I didn't want to be evil like Simon, Fernando, or their co-conspirators. Yet here I sat, contemplating doing something unforgivable: taking Fernando's life with my own hands.

But then I thought about today, everything I'd witnessed, even the folder Fernando had prepared. He had everything I'd ever wanted—businesses, money, influence, *power.* He was untouchable, but as his wife, if I killed him, it would all become *mine,* and why shouldn't it be?

I thought back to the wedding, how someone could have helped me, asked a question, *cared.* But they hadn't. They'd turned a blind eye because it didn't fit their narrative.

Why couldn't I do the same?

If I killed Fernando and his guards, I wouldn't have to run anymore. I wouldn't need to look over my shoulder anymore. I'd finally have complete control over my life through the mafia, and no one would be able to take that away from me again.

I'd save myself and claim his power as my own.

But first, I'd have to kill him, and I'd kill anyone else who *dared* to get in my way.

I dragged myself and the heavy vase closer to him. My hands trembled, but I clenched my teeth in resolve. I raised the vase above my head, then slammed it down with all my strength onto Fernando's skull.

My first two attempts missed, but on the third strike, I hit him. The sound was sickening, but I didn't let it deter me. I hit him, over and over, until blood pooled around him and onto the floor.

I'd hoped that was enough, that he was finally dead, and my nightmare was one step closer to being over. But as I reached down to check for a pulse, I found the bastard was still alive.

I didn't have the strength to keep hitting him, but there was no room for me to fail. Determined, I searched his body for the gun I was positive he kept on him, and found it and an extra clip at his hip.

It was heavier than I thought it would be, but once I found the small safety switch near the barrel, I flipped it off.

I grabbed a nearby pillow, hoping it would muffle the sound like it did in the movies. Pressing the gun against the back of Fernando's head, I squeezed the trigger.

The gun jerked in my hand from the recoil, and the smell of burnt gunpowder filled the air as it seared my skin. But I focused on the task at hand.

I fired two more shots for good measure, making sure he was truly dead. And when his guards finally appeared, looking for their deceased boss, I'd shoot them too. Then the empire would be mine.

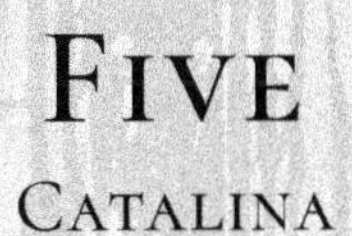

FIVE
CATALINA

Forty hours later

I clenched my shaking hands and took a deep breath.

Calm down. You can do this. You have to do this. You can pretend like you always do.

I'd handled everything: shot and killed Fernando's remaining guards from behind, found the police he had on his payroll and made them deal with the bodies, then submitted Fernando's death certificate for the insurance company. Now it was time to deal with his men.

I studied each man's face as they arrived from my office above the meeting hall. Some seemed confident, others slack. Some joked, clearly friends with other high-ranking members.

They had no idea that their boss had been brutally replaced by me.

On the other hand, I knew each of their names, their families, children, girlfriends, even their mother's favorite color. I'd investigated and memorized everything. And it was because of those efforts that I was certain I'd get exactly what I wanted: recognition.

As the new Doña of the Salazar Familia, this would be my first address to the capos who had previously reported to Fernando. I expected they'd challenge my authority. In fact, I was ninety-nine percent sure who would be the first man to say it was all bullshit.

I was a woman, and in all my research, there had never been a single woman named the head of a mafia family. Some even considered it bad luck. However, while Fernando ruled through fear and violence, I aimed to gain true loyalty, not submission. Of course, that depended on how the men acted today.

If they were willing to give me a chance and respect me, we could be on equal, solid ground. I promised myself, and the people I was now responsible for, this power would not go to my head. I would make choices for not only my survival, but theirs as well.

However, if they berated or disrespected me, much like I unfortunately believed they would, my hand would be forced, and they would suffer the consequences.

As the men glanced around, confused by the empty chair at the head of the table, I smoothed the wrinkles that didn't exist from my black, satin blouse and pleated trousers, checked the heels that gave me a much-needed boost of height and confidence, and made sure the gun beneath my blazer had a full round and another clip, just in case.

Truthfully, I wasn't any good with it yet. I needed time, training, and to put on muscle so my arms didn't shake when I used it. But I didn't need to be an expert if someone was at close range. All I needed was the element of surprise, and there would be plenty of that today.

Squaring my shoulders, I descended the curved staircase then stepped into the room. The men's eyes flickered my way, some with interest, before glancing behind me, clearly searching for Fernando.

I strode to the head of the long table, then sat in my new, comfortable, leather chair. "Gentlemen, thank you for coming. I'd like to—"

Juan jumped up. "What the fuck do you think you're doing, huh, puta? Get the fuck out of that chair—"

Bang!

I sighed gently, sliding my gun to the left, crossing my legs at my thigh, waiting for the men to come to terms with their new reality.

Juan was who I'd guessed would be the first to question me, although truly, I'd wanted him to prove me wrong. He would have been a good capo. But now his dead body was slumped over the table with blood pooling around him.

Faces morphed. Those who held smiles when Juan opened his stupid, little mouth, now, held nothing but horror. Those who had looked at me with disgust as if I were nothing more than a cockroach had eyes now bulging out of their heads. Shock. Disbelief. Then, finally, fury.

Before someone else opened their mouth, forcing me to kill yet another person today, I held up a hand, commanding silence. "I know this is a shock for all of you, but I would advise you to be careful about what you say. I am more than willing to be understanding and work with you, but the one thing I refuse to tolerate is *disrespect*."

Antonio jumped to his feet. "You just walked in here and killed Juan. Now you want us to respect you? We don't even really know who you are!"

I'd been correct again. It was disappointing that two big, bad, ruthless mafia men could be so ridiculously predictable. "Yes, I do, for the reason you just mentioned. You have absolutely no idea who I *really* am and what I can do. But I know everything about you, Antonio Perez. I'd like you to make it home to Marie and your baby girl she's carrying, but that all depends on you."

He froze.

I smiled as my eyes touched on every man in the room, knowing I had them fully ensnared in my carefully casted web. "I know everything there is to know about every single one of you. If you're married and to whom, how many children you have, who your parents are, even the street you grew up on and the hospital you were born in."

I twirled my fingers in the air. "In this room, *I* have the power. Every single *glorious* drop of it. And if you'd like to learn why and how that will affect you for the rest of your hopefully long lives, I suggest you sit down and shut up." I sneered, sliding my finger to the trigger. "Or will I need to shoot someone else today?"

Antonio slowly slid back in his chair, and a quick glance told me the rest of the men were either afraid, shocked, or angry. All things I'd expected and could deal with accordingly.

"Thank you." I carefully folded my hands in my lap. "My name is Catalina Salazar. A few days ago, I married Fernando. Some of you and your guards were at the ceremony. Fernando Salazar is no longer with us."

Gasps echoed around the room.

"Who did it?" someone shouted.

"Who killed him?" another one of my capos yelled.

"I'll get that son of a bitch!" Eduardo shouted, slamming his fist on the table as his large body shook.

"That would be me."

The room fell silent, the men looking at me like I'd grown a second head. If this wasn't such a serious meeting, I would have laughed.

"*You...* killed Fernando?" Luis asked.

"I did. I also killed his guards, Alfonso and Benito. You see, I don't take *kindly* to men who believe women are beneath them or men who don't understand the definition of the word, 'no.' I'm certain I don't need to explain it to you, correct?"

Slowly, they all nodded, some unable to meet my eyes.

"Good. Now let me explain how things are going to go. As Fernando's widow, I now own everything he had. Every asset, every responsibility. The entire Salazar Familia. Effective immediately, I will be taking over all operations here and rebuilding the connections needed to keep this family, *my* family, safe."

Eduardo opened his mouth, but I narrowed my eyes at him, and he promptly shut it. He was one of the few men I hoped to eventually win over. He was loyal, fiercely protective of this familia, and to him, Fernando had been a mentor and friend. I was certain that he saw me as the enemy, and he wasn't the only one.

"I understand that I have a lot to learn here, and that you all have concerns. There has never been a woman leading the mafia on her own nor someone not explicitly trained in your day-to-day functions." I looked around the room. "Let me assure you, I will do what needs to be done. As you can see"—I waved a hand at Juan's body—"I have no issue with violence and I'm not afraid to get my hands dirty."

Lifting my head, I sat up straighter in my chair. "I would like to offer each of you two options. First, stay here, cooperate with me when necessary, do the job you've been doing and do it well, and continue to reap the rewards you have been. Or leave."

Several of the men drew back while some leaned forward, interest written all over their faces.

"Should this be too much for you, I'm offering you a chance out. Leave this room now, and you leave the familia, with one small caveat. You will never share what you've learned about the Salazar Familia with anyone. Break that rule, and I will *break* you.

Threaten my family, and I will destroy yours," I hissed. "Make your choices, men."

I leaned back into my chair, silently watching them. From what I'd been able to find, I doubted most of the men would leave.

The mafia lifestyle was similar to that of a celebrity. It was grand. The thrill of power was infectious. Working up the ranks created a sense of pride for many, and the money and perks were just as addicting.

But it all came down to whether or not they could listen and learn to take instruction from me.

After a few minutes, I was pleased that not a single man had gotten up to leave. They may, later. They might be difficult with me, disrespectful, or even try to kill me one day. I was aware of all of that. I didn't trust a single person here, and I doubted I ever would. But, for the moment, they at least had the decency to hear me out, and that was enough.

Six

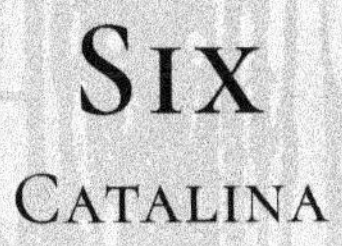

Catalina

Six months later

I flipped through the financial reports my assistant, Olivia, had prepared. Our numbers were impressive.

"The profits from the shipping company exceeded projections again," Olivia said with a smile. "At this rate, we'll triple our revenue from last year."

I hummed in satisfaction. "Good. What about the casino and nightclubs?"

"Also exceeding expectations. The new security measures seem to be working, and there haven't been any issues."

I leaned back in my chair, interlacing my fingers. "Excellent. Schedule a meeting with our capos to discuss expanding into new territory. I think it's time we looked into opportunities on the West Coast."

Olivia made a note on her tablet.

"What about the clinic?" I asked.

"Construction is complete. The interior designer has a

meeting with Naya at the Center of Gentle Love and Hope today to go over color schemes and furniture."

I suppressed a small smile. I didn't have any friends, but I spoke with Naya often. Building the clinic for her foundation was a huge step forward in helping the women who had nowhere else to go. But she worried that I was doing far too much for the organization and could be stubborn. I was sure I'd have a voicemail about the meeting later.

Olivia's brown eyes hardened for a moment, her demeanor shifting. "Your father called again. I've taken care of it."

I clenched my fist underneath my desk. I meant it when I'd told my father the next time I saw him would be at his funeral, but he'd started calling me frequently after the news of Fernando's death. I didn't have the energy or time, and refused to spare any to deal with him.

Luckily, my efficient and take-no-bullshit assistant handled the issue for me. "Thank you."

Olivia nodded. "I've also scheduled your meeting with Ruth Aguilar today at three. Do you want me to add anything to the agenda?"

"No. I'll be out for the rest of the day."

"Please let me know if you need anything else, Doña."

Olivia slipped out the door and I sat back in my plush leather chair. So much had changed in the last six months.

My body no longer felt weak. Thanks to the nutritionist and personal trainer I'd worked with, I was no longer malnourished.

I'd thrown myself into kickboxing, judo, karate. Learned to become proficient with guns, archery, and throwing weapons under a Navy SEAL. I was a competent fighter who could beat most of my men in hand-to-hand combat.

I'd also legitimized myself in The Underground repairing

some of the damage Fernando caused to the Salazar Familia's reputation.

There was still trouble, though. Many mafia heads believed as a woman, I couldn't lead alone and would do better married, preferably to one of them.

But I simply fielded their calls through Olivia unless they stepped out of line. Then I spoke to them in the only language they could understand—violence.

I'd castrated several men and mailed their ball sacs to their bosses with a note they'd be next. I'd even sent a mafia boss the severed fingers of six of his capos last week.

Internally, I'd had to kill a few of my own men as well, but the rest had begun to respect me. I'd fostered those relationships by investing time in getting to know their loved ones, hosting recurring meetings with wives, mothers, and whoever else they cared about until I had their trust and support.

It was a lot. I worked excessively, always stayed busy. I had to. It was the only way I could calm my mind and keep my past from overwhelming me.

A knock on my door interrupted my thoughts.

Olivia poked her head inside. "Your car is ready whenever you are."

"Thank you, Olivia. Please let Ruth know I'll be there within the hour."

Olivia nodded and closed the door behind her.

Grabbing my purse, I made my way downstairs, where my driver awaited me.

At my approach, he opened the door. "Doña."

One day, I'll get used to people calling me that

"Thank you."

The driver gave a curt nod, and I slid into the backseat. Then I began working, skimming over emails, and scanning our surroundings every time we came to a full stop.

As the town car approached Ruth's modest single-story home, I took in the well-kept lawn and vibrant flower beds lining the walkway.

A smile tugged at my lips. Even at eighty-four years old and a grandmother to six, Ruth refused to let age slow her down.

The driver opened my door, and I made my way up the paved steps.

Before I could knock, the front door flung open. "Catalina, mi amor, it's so good to see you!" Ruth took my hands in hers, a warm smile brightening her face.

I squeezed the silver-haired woman's hands with a chuckle. "It's good to see you, too."

"Come in, come in." Ruth guided me to the kitchen and I took a seat at the table while she prepared two mugs of fresh tea.

When Ruth settled beside me, she launched into everything that had happened since my last visit a month ago—her granddaughter's first steps, a new Telenovela she'd become obsessed with, the latest neighborhood gossip, and finally, information about her son Joseph.

Joseph was one of my capos and an obedient but quiet man. He was the first to follow me and I was grateful, but still cautious. I was considering bringing him in on some of my more important dealings, but I needed to speak with Ruth first, to gain more background on him. And no one knew Joseph like his mother.

"Joseph tells me you're doing well, that this familia is better now because of you, and I agree."

Even though her words were kind, something was off. She seemed nervous, and that wasn't like Ruth.

"I have to admit, I had my doubts. In my time, a woman in your position was unheard of, and with how the men treated us here..." Ruth trailed off; she didn't need to say more.

"I understand. I remember how things were when I married Fernando. He and his men treated women like toys, and I'm certain some of them are still prejudiced. However, this organization will continue to change and get better for as long as I'm here."

Ruth scanned my face. She swallowed hard, her hands trembling around her cup as tears pooled in her eyes. "You've already made such a difference. But there are things... things you don't know, things I fear you won't be able to fix, and we'll never be whole without them."

I leaned back. Ruth always spoke her mind. She was blunt, tough, and strong. For her to hold back, or admit fear, was entirely unlike her. My questions about Joseph could wait until later—this was more important.

Reaching out, I squeezed her hand softly. "It's okay. I value your opinion, so please tell me and I'll do what I can."

Ruth took a deep breath. "Fernando was a cruel, cruel man. He had unforgivable ways of keeping us in line."

The pain etched on her face as she tried to share her past was all too familiar to me, and I gently ushered her to sip her tea.

After a few minutes, her eyes met mine. "He threatened to take our children."

Everything stopped. I couldn't hear my heartbeat or feel the sun's warmth on my skin. The words echoed endlessly in my skull until it ached. The air thickened; it was nearly impossible to breathe.

"What *exactly* do you mean by *take*, Ruth?"

"If we didn't follow orders, if we questioned him, he'd take them. At first, it was just our sons at fifteen or sixteen. He'd put them to work for him. It's what he did with Joseph. He had no use for little girls, so we thought they were safe... for a while. But then he started taking them too."

My nails dug into my palm containing the rage, the revulsion. "Do you know what he did with them?"

Ruth shook her head. "I just know they never came back. I held their mothers as they cried their hearts out. Some fought and were killed. And those that survived, died inside. That hijo de puta got whatever he wanted, no matter who we asked for help." *

"How old were the girls he took?"

Sadness clouded Ruth's face. "As young as three, as old as thirteen."

Fuck.

I'd uncovered a lot about my familia, but so much remained unknown. Fernando was secretive. He didn't share details even with his closest men.

There were no records of minors working for Fernando. His staff was always women over nineteen from outside the familia. Fernando was a greedy pig, so I doubted he killed the kids. But the alternative sickened me.

Trafficking was a lucrative business. There were substantial financial gains I couldn't track, hundreds of millions of dollars' worth. To my horror, it made sense *they* were the money's source.

I was furious. If I could, I would bring Fernando back from the dead and kill him all over again. But this time, I'd do it slowly. I'd keep him alive for as long as possible while I tortured the truth out of him.

A part of me was mad at Ruth for not telling me sooner. But

---

* That son of a bitch, got whatever he wanted, no matter who we asked for help.

deep down, I didn't blame her. I'd never said a word about my abuse, because I knew no one would ever believe me.

But for the mothers who lost their kids? They'd tried and gotten nowhere. Why would they open up to someone, especially after so long? That Ruth had said something now was a show of utmost faith and trust.

She gripped my hand tightly. "I have no right to ask, Doña, but I believe in you and that you want what's best for us. If you can, please find out what happened to the children. Give us the peace we've never had."

"I will." I squeezed her hand just as tight. "I'll give this familia the answers it deserves. I won't rest until I do."

My hands gripped the steering wheel tight as I stopped at the electronic gate of Fernando's mansion. I took a deep breath as I entered the code, trying to settle my nerves.

I hadn't set foot in this house since the day he died. Everything about this place filled me with dread and nightmares.

He's dead. He can't hurt you. You're strong. You beat him, I told myself, but the words of encouragement didn't make me feel better.

I entered Fernando's office on trembling legs, forcing myself to focus on the task at hand. My familia was counting on me to find answers, to locate any records of the children stolen from them. I couldn't do that if I had a mental breakdown.

He's dead. He can't hurt you. He's dead. He can't hurt you.

I repeated the words over and over until I believed them and began systematically searching his office. I pulled out every drawer, even searched within the furniture for hidden compartments. I moved the heavy pieces to check for loose floorboards, and hidden safes behind the walls. I pulled the frames off paintings, checking to see if paperwork had been hidden beneath them, and turned books inside out.

Fernando had a habit of hiding things in odd places. It was the only reason I hadn't sold the mansion, or several other houses and buildings he owned. He kept records behind glass photos, USBs in vases. It was random, but it made sense in this line of work.

He had to have records somewhere. But the truth was it could take months, even *years,* to find a single piece of evidence tying him to human trafficking, much less find the girls he'd taken.

This wouldn't be easy. I had no point of reference. Alfonso and Benito had been Fernando's right-hand men, so when I'd killed them, I'd killed anyone who could tell me his secrets.

After several hours of searching and finding nothing, I hurled the book I was searching through, yelling in frustration.

The book crashed into a stack I'd looked through and discarded, but the loud, chaotic bomb of noise catapulted me back in time.

Suddenly, Fernando was there, his ugly, depraved face with a wide, cruel smile as he pinned me down. His heavy weight pushed me to the ground, leaving me unable to move. His fat fingers twisted in my hair, lifting my head, slamming it down, triumph shining in his eyes.

I panicked, unable to breathe. I tried to scream, but nothing came out. The world tilted as I crashed to the floor, gasping for air. I was stuck living out this nightmare until he was unconscious, then I could finally pull myself free.

When I came to, tears poured down my face. The room spun as I crawled under the safety of the large wooden desk. I wrapped my arms around my knees, curling into a ball.

"He's dead," I whispered, trying to pull in air, trying to calm myself down. "He's dead. He's dead. He's *dead*!"

I screamed the words over and over until I finally stopped shaking. Then I wiped my eyes and bit my lip in anger over being so weak.

Why? Why after everything that I'd gone through, after all the trauma I'd endured, did I keep having these flashbacks? Why hadn't they gone away? It had been six months. I'd achieved so much, so why couldn't I let that go? Why was I stuck reliving that nightmare?

I gripped the edge of the desk, using it to help me as I slowly stood. The answers to those questions didn't matter now. I had to shove them back, into the deepest parts of my mind. People were counting on me.

I won't fail them.

In the end, I was the victor here. I was in control. I had escaped my father, survived Fernando, and I'd built a new life. Like a phoenix, I'd risen from the ashes, and I refused to let anyone hold me down, including *myself*.

Taking a deep breath, I looked around the office. I'd need to come back to continue the search. But that was enough for today.

I'd go home, recollect myself and think things over. Maybe there was a simpler way, a connection somewhere that could lead me to the information, or perhaps I could make a new connection myself.

I'd need to see what other mafia familias had ties at the borders and overseas, but the important thing was I would succeed. No matter how long it took, I would find them, whatever the cost.

Seven

Marco

I settled into the plush leather seat of my private jet, awaiting take-off. Italy took longer than expected, but I was finally heading home. After we ascended, I pulled out my cell phone and opened the email in my inbox.

A picture of Catalina filled my screen. Smiling in predatory delight, I traced the outline of her wind-blown hair, gorgeous face, deep brown eyes, and cute nose to her beautiful lips that I longed to taste. My finger followed the graceful curve of her neck and I let myself get lost in the fantasy of what my hand would look like wrapped around it.

I imagined how her golden, tanned body would feel beneath mine, the face she'd make writhing in pleasure. What her moans sounded like, the way she'd come. Would she be quiet, lost in her throws of ecstasy, or would she scream?

I wouldn't be doing my due diligence if I didn't keep her coming until she did.

I shifted in my chair, fixing the erection in my pants.

I remembered the day I first laid eyes on her. She stood beside her father, her hand raised in an expected princess wave that didn't quite reach her eyes.

To the crowd, she was the fortunate daughter of a powerful man, but to me, she was so much more.

My mother was a De La Rosa, a tight-knit family known to practice witchcraft and mediumship in The Underground. They had an uncanny way of protecting their own, believed everything happened for a reason, and their visions were *always* right.

As a child, my mother had taught me to trust my intuition. She promised I would need to, especially as heir to the Torrino Mafia Famiglia. It was those instincts that told me to look closer at Catalina, to truly try to see through her façade.

I studied her, observed her. There was no denying her beauty and intrigue. But her intelligence was unmatched. She was determined, far stronger than the fragile thing her father presented her to be. And wild like a tempest, capable of great things and destruction.

But more than anything, she was meant to be *mine*.

When the invitation to her twenty-first birthday arrived, I didn't hesitate to respond. The party was extravagant, but it couldn't touch her radiance. That was what her father was trying to control until it withered away and died, and I refused to let that happen.

I wanted to free her from him, to show her a life where she could be her true self. I was willing to pay anything, *do* anything to save her, and I had been so close at the party, until I found out my cousin had been shot by a rival famiglia.

The news of her marriage to Fernando had been a tremendous blow. It was suspicious that Simon had called so many mafia leaders to the party, but I didn't know he was bartering Catalina. If I had, I would have stayed. I would have done anything to win, even if that meant killing every other family in New York.

I'd failed her, but she didn't need me to save her.

At first, no one believed she'd murdered Fernando or other members of the Salazar Familia. She was five foot four, one-hundred pounds soaking wet, and by all public accounts, docile, obedient, and easy to keep in line.

But I knew she did it. She had teeth and when forced into a corner, she'd use them. Where others saw docile, I saw patience. Where they saw obedient, I saw carefully manipulative. Catalina was a mastermind at what she did, and it was only a matter of time until others saw and recognized it as well.

Now, The Underground knew her as Señora de la Muerte, Lady of Death. She'd survived those that tested her, leaving over a dozen bodies in her wake, all within a couple of months. The way she carried herself excited me, but I would need to change my plans if I ever wanted to win her heart.

Catalina never let anyone close, especially men. Much less one from a rival family.

She was cautious and she needed to be. She was a queen in her own right that would bow to no one. But most men would want her too.

Convincing her I did not would be a long and difficult journey.

But I preferred a challenge, and winning over Catalina would be the sweetest reward. The smile on my face deepened.

I would take my time, seduce her, show her my respect and loyalty. Earn her trust, her love. She would be my ally, my partner, my wife. It was destiny, a fate that nothing and no one could change. I wouldn't allow them to.

Excitement coursed through my veins as I traced her lips once more.

Soon, Catalina. Soon.

Catalina exited the Salazar mansion, and I drummed my fingers on the steering wheel. Something was going on.

I'd been tracking her movements either personally or through my men, and over the last six months I'd been in Italy, she'd never come here on her own. Yet today marked the fifth day in a row. She was also leaving the office more often, frequenting warehouses and other establishments she normally didn't, pushing back several of her routine appointments to later in the day.

What are you doing, Catalina? What are you trying to find?

Perhaps I could position myself as an ally in her search. This could be the perfect opportunity to get close to her, and I would not let it slip through my fingers.

I tailed her, staying several cars behind, then turned left into a gas station when she turned right toward her office.

I pressed the Bluetooth on my car. "Call Anthony."

"Yes, boss?"

"I need you to confirm when Catalina arrives at her office."

"It concerns me that you've been stalking this woman for a year. If she has you this wrapped around her finger when she doesn't even know your name, you might die by the time you finally win her over."

The laugh in his voice irked me, but the fact that he might be right pissed me off even more. "Anthony." I warned.

"Yes, yes, I know, I know. Even though I'm your second in command and your favorite cousin, you'll kill me if I keep talking, yada, yada, yada."

"And yet, you still continue to speak." I huffed. "Just let me know when she gets there."

"Fine," he scoffed.

I hung up. After a few minutes, I checked my text messages. Nothing.

Another minute went by, and I glanced at my screen again, but there was still nothing.

I sighed.

While I knew Anthony was joking, he was serious when he said he was concerned, and I didn't blame him for being so. I was obsessed with Catalina, and this was the only time I'd ever used my men for personal business. They didn't know what she meant to me, but they knew how I normally went after something I wanted, and this wasn't it.

I understood how odd my behavior was, especially to Anthony. But she was worth it.

Catalina wasn't just some woman. She wasn't an itch I was trying to scratch or someone I'd lose interest in once I had her. She was my *everything*.

My phone chimed with the message I'd been waiting for.

ANTHONY

She's arrived at her office and is
heading to the top floor

I put the car in drive and sped off, trying to ignore the way my heart raced at the thought of being near her. I didn't just want to see her again, I wanted her to acknowledge me, to *see* me, and *finally* she would.

Pulling into a parking spot, I checked myself in the mirror, smoothing my ruffled long brown hair. I made sure the collar of my shirt was perfectly folded and adjusted the cuff of my blazer before leaving my car.

I stepped into the building, thankful for the cold air blasting my face, then used the security card my hacker made for me and took the elevator to the top floor.

Crossing the threshold, I saw her assistant, Olivia. Like Catalina, she was incredibly proficient and not one to be trifled with.

Putting on my most professional smile, I stepped up to her desk, and leaned against it. "Hi, I'm here to see Catalina Salazar."

Olivia barely spared me a glance before checking something on the computer. "Do you have an appointment?"

"No, but I have urgent information I need to discuss with her."

"I'm sorry, but without an appointment, I can't let you through. Ms. Salazar's schedule is fully booked for the next several weeks."

I glared at her. Olivia's tone was as frigid as the Arctic Circle, and she was full of shit. There was no way Catalina was that busy; Olivia was stonewalling me.

"I understand and I won't take much of her time, but this *is* important. I need to speak with her *immediately*. If you could just squeeze me in—"

"As I said, she is fully booked." She glanced toward a clipboard on her desk. "You're welcome to leave your contact information and I can pass along the message to her."

Don't shoot her. Do. Not. Shoot. Her. Catalina won't like that. A muscle ticced in my jaw as I clenched my teeth and bit out, "Then I'll wait."

"Sir, that will not be possible. You can either pass along your contact information to me and leave, or I will be forced to call security."

Good. Them I can shoot. "You do that."

I turned just as a door opened and my heart stopped.

Catalina.

She snapped a binder closed. "Olivia, could you—" She froze. And for a single moment, neither of us took a breath.

"You," she whispered, and the single word hung between us, tethering us together.

The air charged. Every hair on my body stood up at her attention. She was a vision in a black satin blouse and red pencil skirt. Strands of her hair gently flicked over her neck and shoulders, and her dark brown eyes were dilated.

Pleasure soared down my spine that she'd responded to me, *remembered* me. I'd caught her off guard and she hadn't been able to hide it. I was honored.

I held her gaze, then smirked. "It's been a while, Catalina."

EIGHT
CATALINA

I couldn't move.
Breathe.
In and out. In and out.

My heart pounded so hard it was all I could hear. Seeing him reminded me of the night of the party, and I felt everything—anger, frustration, even a hint of fear.

But it wasn't just that. This man was uniquely capable of getting under my skin. He saw things I didn't want him to, things it wasn't safe for anyone to see. I had to keep them hidden, especially in this line of work, and even more so if he was working for my father.

Something in me said he wouldn't be the type. With his shoulder-length brown hair and tattoos peaking under the collar and cuffs of his shirt, he seemed like someone who would play the long game until he got what he wanted. Then he'd kill you.

But while I trusted my gut, there was no other reason he would have been at that party except to meet my father, which meant his presence was a threat.

"It's nice to see you again. I hope your dreams came true." His voice was deep, but warm, as though he truly meant it.

I turned to my assistant. "Olivia, cancel my schedule for the rest of the day, then head home." I turned back to the man. "And you, follow me."

I could *feel* him behind me. The hairs on the back of my neck stood at attention as the static electricity arched between us. I was hyperaware of him and I hated it.

The elevator doors opened, and when I stepped inside, he followed. The moment they slid closed, I spun around, pinning him to the wall, my knife against his throat.

His eyes widened for a fraction of a second, but he didn't make a move. He relaxed, his dark brown eyes somehow growing even darker, then he smirked.

Is he enjoying himself right now? He's fucking crazy.

"Why are you here?" I hissed.

"To meet with you, of course. Although if I would have known this was the reaction I'd get out of you, I would have come a lot sooner."

Yep. Crazy.

But based on his reaction, a fight wasn't what he wanted, which meant I wouldn't need to kill him. *Yet.*

The elevator reached the ground floor, and I moved to step outside to the patio area, but he grabbed the door before I could.

I glanced up at him and he had another infuriating smile on his face.

He was playing with me, and I was letting him.

Control yourself. The faster you find out what he wants, the sooner he leaves. Take a deep breath and deal with him the same way you would anyone else.

We walked in silence to the boardwalk encircling a glistening lake with a water fountain in the middle. I listened to the small chirp of birds and let the rays of the sun warm my chilled body. Then I turned to him and asked again, "Why are you here?"

"I meant it when I said to meet with you." His tone was gentle, casual, as if it was the perfect explanation when it made no sense at all.

"If you wanted to speak with me, you could have just called the office or sent an email. I am a busy woman."

"I know. Your assistant said the same thing. But seeing you in person provides benefits that a phone call and email wouldn't."

"Why don't you cut the crap and just tell me what you want?" I glared at him, but his grin only grew.

"Are you always this dismissive?"

"Do you always assume a woman will bend over backwards to your every whim and be flattered if you pay her a sliver of attention?"

He was silent for a moment, then threw his head back, clasped his stomach, and laughed. The sound was deep, rich, *real*, and I was speechless.

His eyes crinkled at the corners, his smile so wide that for the first time I noticed he had dimples, and the way the sun shone over him, as his shoulders shook with each chuckle, had me transfixed.

I was both enamored and envious of his ease with me. And I was even more infuriated, that after everything I'd been through, I still found him attractive.

You're a woman. You have eyes. Of course, you'd find him attractive. Admitting that doesn't mean you'll act on it.

I gave myself a small, mental nod. The friend of my enemy was my enemy as well, and that included this man. I turned back to the lake, waiting for him to sober.

He was still chuckling as he said, "Not everyone bends over backwards for me, but I do normally have an easier time. That assistant of yours is a handful."

I imagined Olivia dealing with him and had to suppress a smile. "You might have had an easier time if you were a woman."

His eyebrow arched in question.

"She's gay."

The man looked like he was barely holding back another full-blown laugh. "And what about you?"

"What about me?"

"Well, you're not bending over for me right now, although I promise if you did, I'd make sure it was *extremely* pleasurable for you."

I smirked. "That's because I'm simply not interested."

He settled the full weight of his unnerving gaze onto me, searching for something I refused to give. Then he turned serious. "The night we met, I never formally introduced myself. The reason I came here to see you was to make up for that. My name is Marco Torrino."

His name hit me like a ton of bricks. He was the leader of the Torrino Mafia Family, one of the most intricate and feared in this city.

New York had almost twenty-five different families living or working within it, Hispanic, Italian, Irish, Russian, and Japanese, and most were enemies. We were all out to protect our own, and it only took one person to step over that line to start a war.

It's why I'd done my best to sort through and memorize each of the leaders' names, but keeping up with their day-to-day activities, as well as their immediate families' was a full-time job and time I didn't have.

Fernando didn't keep tabs on other families, only struck deals or threw cash at them, so I had almost no information about the Torrino's boss, besides his name. But it shocked me to believe it was the carefree man in front of me.

Marco wasn't crazy, foolish, or at ease. He was *dangerous*.

I straightened my back and asked in a cold tone, "When did you get back to the country?"

He touched his chest. "I'm honored that you looked into me."

"Of course, it's only natural that I keep an eye on my enemies."

"I'm not your enemy, Catalina," he said, his voice low. "I'm your ally."

I scoffed. "As the head of another family whose borders are near my own, yes, you are. And anyone who was invited by my father that night was someone he believed could be an ally to him. An ally to my father could never be one to me."

"I am not your rival, nor your father's ally." Marco sneered, clenching his fist around the metal railing.

Why does he seem offended? Did I touch a nerve? "Then why were you invited?"

"Likely for the same reason Fernando was." His voice turned hard and flat. "To barter a deal."

Ah, yes, of course. I'm always the trophy, a prize to be fought over, then sold, never a person with value and worth.

I bristled under the heavy reminder of my past, the air suddenly as frigid as Marco's tone. It cut into me like a knife, breaking the glass jar I kept my emotions buried behind.

The truth hurt. It shouldn't have, but it did.

It wasn't as if I'd grown stupid enough to believe my father cared about me, or that if I could go back in time, I would have been able to escape my arranged marriage. But somehow, knowing that if Fernando had said no, my father would have offered me to Marco instead, made me sick.

How many people had my father invited that night for his deal? Was Fernando the first on the list, or did he have an entire roster?

Was that part of the reason I was constantly hounded by bosses thinking they could marry me and claim my empire?

Were my father's decisions still affecting my life and success today?

When will it ever stop?

I'd been ignoring my father because I couldn't figure out how to deal with him. I couldn't kill him, it would be a PR nightmare, and as his next of kin, it would bring unwanted attention to my familia.

I had no idea if he was in bed with other families, and while I had power now, I was only one person. It was what held me back trying to find the people Fernando trafficked, and it was what was holding me back now.

I leveled my gaze at Marco but couldn't keep my sadness out of my tone. "Would you have made the same choice?"

His body trembled, nostrils flared, eyes narrowed, the vein in his neck engorged. But it was his face, the cold, absolute fury that came over him, that shocked me.

He looked like death, like someone who would destroy anyone and everyone in his path. For the first time since I'd met him, he looked every bit the killer I knew he was.

"If you wouldn't have killed Fernando, *I* would have. Do not *ever* compare me to that bastard again," he growled.

My throat went dry. I couldn't speak, and even after I swallowed, I still couldn't utter a single word.

I didn't trust anyone, especially not men, but I *believed* what Marco said. I may have not trusted a single other word he'd spoken since the moment I met him, but I knew, without a doubt, he would have killed Fernando for me. His reaction had been far too immediate for me to think otherwise.

I didn't know how to handle that, how to accept that there was someone, a complete stranger, who would have come to my aid. So I asked the only other thing I could, the only thing that felt safe. "What do you want from me?"

His eyes softened, his tone gentle. "There's something you need. Let me help you find it."

His words were a caress on my skin, but instead of calming me, it raised my hackles. "Have you been watching me, Marco?"

His lip lifted in a small smile. "I wouldn't be good at collecting information if I wasn't."

"Tell me then, did you know Fernando was trafficking children?" I hissed.

The thought that he might have found out what Fernando was doing, perhaps had even allied with him in the past and that was why he had approached me now, filled me with disappointment and disgust.

The mafia did illegal things all the time, but there were limits. If nowhere else, then for those in our own familia. It was our job to provide discipline, protection, and order, not to sell our members and treat them as cattle.

I had a firsthand experience of what that felt like, and even though I might need it, I could never accept the help of anyone who would do the same, especially in their own familia.

Marco stood to his full height, and I realized he'd angled himself so I wouldn't have to crane my neck to look at him. He'd been respectful, even when I hadn't been.

A thread of guilt twisted my gut.

You don't owe him anything, least of all respect. To some level, that was true. He had shown up on my turf, unannounced. I was certain he'd given Olivia a hard time. And while I still didn't know what his plans were, I was one-hundred percent certain they were far from innocent.

"Have you ever seen the ramifications of a mafia war?"

His question cut through my thoughts, and the intensity of his gaze stole my breath.

"No."

"When a mafia head is removed internally, it shakes up their entire organization. I'm certain *you* have some experience with that." His gaze hardened. "But when they're removed by another family, it's different. If both sides are not aligned, they will go to war, and that means they will risk *everything*, not only their lives, but the lives of those under them." He clenched his jaw so tightly that a tic started in his teeth. "I've seen innocent men, women, and children killed by stray bullets and assassinations all for power. A mafia war covers the streets in *blood*," he cursed.

I steeled my breath. "Why are you telling me all of this?"

Marco leaned onto the railing, and although the stance seemed casual, the tension in his shoulders said otherwise. "I have always hated Fernando. I hated the way he did business, how he ran his *familia*, and the person he was. He was an asshole who cared about no one but himself and thought he could buy anything he wanted in the city, and did, *frequently*," he bit out. "But if I would have known he was trafficking children, I would have started a war, regardless of the expense it would have cost me. I've seen people who have gone through that, how it affects them. How it *breaks* them, and I would never stand for it."

I gulped. I wanted to question him, to ask if he would really go that far for the freedom of someone else, but when he turned his head and I met his eyes, absolute certainty shone through.

"I'm not the only one who would have either, Catalina. Some sections of The Underground operate differently, but the Spanish are forbidden from trafficking or slavery within the *familia*. Our people came to New York to get away from those things in their own countries, and that was one of the rules we all agreed on."

"If that's the case, then how did Fernando get away with it for *years*? Someone should have caught him."

He nodded. "That's what I'd like to help you find out."

I angled my head up to him, observing him in the same way he often observed me. "And what do you want in return?"

"A favor."

I crossed my arms. "Are you going to expand on that?"

He smirked. "When the time is right."

A small, hollow chuckle escaped my lips. "I'm pretty sure that's the oldest trick in the book, Marco. Why would I agree to that?"

"Because you need my help. My specialty is gathering information, and you'll find no one better than me in the entire Northeastern United States. I also have ties to Italy. If anyone has been trafficked out of New York through Spain or Italy, I'll be able to find them in time."

I bit my lip to keep myself from scowling. He was right.

"And if that's not enough, I can teach you about the other families here."

My head snapped up, and I glared at him. "What—"

"I'm not insulting you," he said gently. "But I know how much there is to learn about this world. It took me years to understand the ins and outs, and you've only been in this for six months. You've done an amazing job in that time, better than I or anyone else could, and you will continue to, even without my help. But why not use me for all I'm worth? I have knowledge you won't be able to find anywhere else. Let me help you fill the gaps you have."

He took a step closer, and I studied him. His dark hair blew around his face, but his deep brown eyes never left mine. An air of ease and certainty seemed to exude from him, wrapping around me. Yet he didn't seem cocky; he seemed genuine.

Still, I had to ask. "Why?"

"Would you prefer me to lie to you or be honest, even if it will make you uncomfortable?"

I raised an eyebrow. "I'd prefer honesty if you can manage it."

He chuckled, taking another step closer until the tip of our shoes touched, and my heartbeat raced in my chest. "Because I want to see you succeed. I went to your birthday party, not because your father reached out to me." He leaned in, his voice a dark, hushed whisper. "It was simply an opportunity."

I tried to shrug off how breathless I was. That anything about him could affect me even in the slightest was something he could never know. If he did, he'd use it to his full advantage. I was sure of it. "For what?"

"To meet you."

"You can't honestly expect me to believe that."

"It's fine if you don't. But I saw potential in you that night and I see it now. You could have ruined your entire familia. Instead, it's running better than it did even when Fernando was alive." He stood to his full height once more. "You have skills and a mind that most don't, and anyone else would have failed where you have succeeded. There are no limits to where you can go, what you can achieve, and it would only make sense for me to ally myself with you and stay along for the ride."

The small part of my heart, the piece that had always wanted to be enough, do well enough, be praised for my accomplishments, fucking *danced* at his words, and I *hated* it.

"You know, your ability to be so smooth and find the right words to say is only going to make me not trust you more."

He shrugged. "I told you my honesty would make you uncomfortable. But does that mean you're going to turn down my offer?"

I wanted to, but I couldn't. He had more knowledge than I did and contacts outside of the country, and I needed that. And he was offering to share the information he had on other families with me, which would only aid my familiarity with this world.

I couldn't trust others. I had no one in my corner. But now

this incredibly frustrating man was attempting to give me everything I needed for something as simple as a favor.

"I have conditions."

He grinned so wide, his dimples showed. "Name them."

"You will not attempt to hurt or kill me or my familia. Nor will you try to ruin us in any way."

"You have my word."

"And you will also not try to usurp me from my position as head of my familia nor try to undermine me or my power."

"Is that all?" His eyes twinkled. "I can even write up a contract if you'd like."

He looked thrilled, like he'd won something, and it irked me that I didn't know what it was. Still, I had no other stipulations. This deal was incredibly sided in my favor. He didn't have to concede to anything I wanted, yet he was still willing to.

I sighed. "Yes."

"Then I'll have the contract drawn up and sent over to you within the hour." He stepped back and held out his hand. "I'm excited to be working with you, Catalina."

He said my name as if he was savoring it, like a snake who had just caught the prey of a lifetime. It unnerved me, but I wrapped my fingers around his hand and shook it anyway. "Same to you, Marco."

He hummed, his fingers adjusting around my own and, with a firm grip, he bent down and kissed the back of my hand.

A bolt of electricity zipped to my shoulder, and I bit my cheek to keep from gasping at the small touch. But when he looked at me, his eyes were full of heat and mirth.

Dropping my hand, he stepped back. "I'll be seeing you soon, Catalina."

He walked away, but the feeling of his lips on my skin stayed behind.

What did I just get myself into?

NINE
Catalina

I grabbed my purse and stood to leave my office, just as my phone buzzed with a new text.

I sighed.

I glared at the screen. The audacity of this man, assuming I would drop everything for some lavish dinner. *But...*
Am I actually considering this?
Le Jardin de Nuit was a small restaurant that I'd heard was

absolutely divine. They used only the finest, freshest ingredients and were renowned for their unique spin on French cuisine. I'd wanted to go for a long time, but I'd been too busy.

My phone rang, and I rolled my eyes as Marco's name flashed across the screen.

"I take it you're about to tell me off?" There was a hint of a smile in his voice, and I huffed.

Damn it. He was right.

"Our alliance is to share information about the trafficking and mafia leaders, not have dinner dates," I said sharply.

"I agree completely," Marco replied in a nonchalant tone. "But we should get to know each other first, don't you think? You said you wanted to keep an eye on me when you thought I was your enemy. Now that we're working together, I'd assume you'd want to learn even more. How else will you know what to expect from me?"

I ground my teeth. He had a point.

"Plus, if I'm supposed to provide you with information, we'll need to discuss what you already know so I can fill in the gaps. That would be so much easier over a nice meal, no?"

I *hated* how often this man was right. "Fine."

"Would you like me to send you a car?"

"Would you like me to blow it up?"

Marco laughed, and the sound rolled through me, soothing a bit of my irritation, which only made me despise him more.

"I do always enjoy a good explosion."

"Goodbye, Marco." I hung up.

I opened the file I'd started on him. There was barely any information. Marco "The Devil" Torrino was thirty-two, eleven years older than me, born to an Italian father and Hispanic mother. Both died in an unsolved car crash when he was eighteen.

From what I could find he'd been running their branches in

the States and Italy flawlessly ever since. He was charming, had the logic to twist and use my own words against me, and was determined, observant, and ruthless.

I didn't want to go to dinner with him. I'd done so with mafia heads before only for them to try to get in my pants, or offer a 'deal' which would cost me my familia.

Unfortunately, Marco, thus far, was unlike anyone else I'd ever met. He never reacted the way I expected him to, and could guess my next move before I'd made it.

Our alliance might put us on common ground for now, but he was still, and would always be, my enemy. Which meant his ability to read me was incredibly dangerous.

But that wasn't the only reason I was afraid. While I wasn't under my father's thumb anymore, I was still scared of being seen, of my mask falling away and revealing just how weak I truly was.

The brick walls I'd built around myself kept me safe, and Marco's ability to view me through them was intrusive. Like he was breaking me down little by little, making his way inside, through vulnerabilities I didn't even know I had. And that made our little 'partnership' incredibly one sided.

I had to go to this dinner to learn about him, to understand the man underneath, and peer into him in the same way he did into me. Which meant I had to check my prejudices about men, about *him* at the door. That's the only way I'd learn who I was in bed with.

It would not be because I was curious about him, or because —as much as he annoyed me—I enjoyed our banter and how he kept me on my toes. It would not be because a part of me loved the attention, or that no matter how much I pushed him away, he always came back for more.

No, it wouldn't be for any of that at all.

The restaurant glowed softly under the streetlights. The evening air was crisp, and I was grateful for the chill. It helped calm my nerves.

Marco stood at the entrance, waiting for me. His black suit fit him perfectly, with the collar and first button undone.

My eyes fell to the little expanse of his chest, drawn in by the tattoos I could only see the tips of when his shirt was fully buttoned. A single strand of hair blew against his cheek and I had the strangest impulse to brush it away.

It's just the atmosphere. Nothing else.

Marco's smile softened his face. He looked pleased, as though he thought I might have stood him up. It made him seem younger, boyish almost, even with his neatly trimmed beard. It was an odd contrast to the infuriatingly confident man he'd showed me thus far, and it made me more amenable to him.

His hand came to my back as he reached beside me to open the door, and I tried to ignore how large it was, how his warmth seeped through my silk blouse.

The restaurant was just as beautiful as I imagined it would be with large arches, curved windows, and a glass ceiling that made the interior blend seamlessly into the outside world. Yet it was also intimate, decorated with tall white pillar candles, fresh flowers, and dim lighting coming from the chandeliers.

The hostess led us to a table and the entire time, Marco never moved his hand from my back, nor did he once fall out of step at my side.

It should have been awkward, but it felt strangely natural.

When we arrived at our table, Marco pulled out my chair.

"Thank you."

"You're welcome." He pushed in my seat as I sat, then took his own across from me.

"Would you like some wine?" Marco motioned to the list.

One glass technically couldn't hurt, and it would be out of my system by the time we left.

"All right."

His lip tipped at the corner, showing a hint of his dimples. "Do you prefer red or white?"

"Red."

He made a gesture with his hand, summoning the server, then ordered the most expensive bottle off the menu.

The man dashed off to retrieve it, while I blinked several times to see if I'd read the price correctly. "Marco, are you trying to go bankrupt on this dinner? That was a fifty-thousand-dollar bottle of wine."

"Don't wound my pride like that, Catalina. I have enough money to buy this restaurant and the entirety of Manhattan twice over." His voice dropped to a whisper. "And if it would please you, I'd spend that and so much more. You're worth it."

It was a line. A simple, stupid, insignificant line, but it got to me. My heart began to race. *I need to deflect.*

"Are you like this on all of your dinner dates?"

"Honest, you mean?" Marco stroked the stem of his wineglass, his eyes twinkling in mischief.

"No, terribly flirtatious." I sipped my wine, letting the hints of vanilla and cocoa and the silky finish soothe my frayed nerves.

He grinned. "No. I don't go on dates with mafia heads, and I haven't been on a date with a woman in a very long time."

I twirled my glass slowly. "Ah, yes. I can see how that might be the case with the whole women-falling-at-your-feet thing."

He chuckled.

I took that moment to make my final decision on what I'd order, and when I set the menu to the side, he called over the server once more.

Once the eager man left, I leveled with Marco. "You invited me here today for us to get to know one another, correct?"

He folded his hands in his lap. "Yes."

"Is there anything I'm not allowed to ask you?"

"That would defeat the purpose of you getting to know me, and I want you to know me *very* well. I'll be happy to answer anything you ask. Are you willing to do the same?"

No. I wasn't sure what he might ask me and if I wasn't careful, I might reveal something I shouldn't.

His shoulders were at ease, his body mostly relaxed apart from his straight position. He was careful, watchful, pensive almost.

Remember why you came here.

Marco had this air of mystery about him, like he could reveal all his secrets and somehow it still wouldn't be enough. And that's what I wanted. Not his charm, or half-truths. I wanted the man behind it all. To look beyond his mask the same way he did mine.

I rolled my shoulders back and nodded.

He hummed low in his throat. "Good, now what do you want to know?"

"Why are you always like that? Flirtatious, at ease when you're around me? Is it because you don't see me as a threat?"

He chuckled. "Absolutely not. I am fully aware of your capabilities and violence." He took a sip of his wine. "It's one of the things I like about you. Your strength is impressive, and I find it admirable."

I was suddenly grateful that my skin was more golden and tanned than white, or else he would have been able to see me blush in the dim lighting.

"Then why are you always at ease around me?"

"Because I want you to feel comfortable with me, and I hope to eventually earn your trust."

I tilted my head to the side. "And have I earned yours?"

"Yes."

"But you barely know me."

"It's my job to gather intelligence about the people I'm working with. And what I've learned about you, I like *very* much."

The server arrived with our main dishes, providing a much-needed distraction. I swirled a bit of the creamy pasta around with a small slice of chicken and shrugged off his words. "Tell me about the other side of you, then."

He cut a piece of his filet mignon. "The other side?"

I bit into my meal and was immediately ejected into the stratosphere. It was sensational, the perfect amount of chew and softness, with hints of garlic, parsley, and thyme.

My relationship with food was still damaged, and I often had a difficult time trying something new. But this was damn good. I could barely keep myself from happy dancing in my chair.

Marco noticed. He didn't even try to hide his smile and the warmth in his eyes.

I averted my gaze and circled back to my question. "Yes. You're clearly a flirt." I cut into the chicken with a little too much force. "But you have an edge to you as well, one that you rarely show, at least to me, but it's there. How else could you successfully run both your branch here and in Italy?"

His grin grew wider. "It makes me happy you believe I'm capable."

"Of course I do. I would be a fool not to. But what I want to know is if it's difficult for you."

His eyes hardened for a fraction of a second. "I've gotten used to it, but it has its challenges."

I wanted to ask him more. But I also didn't want to make him too uncomfortable.

He took another sip of wine. "When I went to Italy, it was because a rival famiglia shot my cousin and almost killed him. He was hospitalized for several months."

My eyes widened. "I'm so sorry to hear that."

Marco shrugged. "It's fine. It's an unfortunate part of the job, but I dealt with it."

"How?"

He stared at me and I could almost see the wheels in his mind turning. I set my fork down and met his gaze.

I wanted his ruthlessness, to know if it matched or exceeded mine. There was truth in that, an honor in cruelty that could never be matched, and that was the only version of Marco who could help me.

"Do you truly want to know?"

I was thrilled by the edge in his voice. "Yes. It won't ruin my meal, if that's what you're asking."

He hummed. "First, I made sure that we weren't in the wrong. You've been cleaning up Fernando's messes, so I'm sure you know what I mean."

I nodded. "And were you?"

"Not in the slightest. They were upset that we owned a particular piece of land and wanted to encroach. They came to my cousin with a deal. We both told them no, but they figured since I was in the States I didn't truly hold any power in Italy. Obviously, they were wrong."

I leaned back in my chair, giving him my full attention.

"I found the man who shot my cousin, tortured him for information, chopped him into little pieces, then served him to their leader in a restaurant not as nice as this one." He motioned around us. "The face he made when he saw the eyeball was priceless."

I laughed. It came out as a bark so sudden it startled me, but I couldn't stop. I kept laughing until I wheezed and my eyes blurred with tears. When I finally sobered and wiped my eyes, Marco looked like a blind man who had just seen sunshine for the first time.

I'd never seen anyone look so delighted.

"I was wondering what it would take to make you laugh. I didn't expect torture to be the answer."

I was still chuckling as I dabbed my eyes with the napkin. "I'm sorry. I pictured his face in my mind and—"

"Don't be. I'm honored I got to see this side of you. I don't think you let it out very often."

He wasn't wrong. I shifted in my chair.

He cut another piece of steak. "How is mafia life treating you?"

It was tough. But I loved it. "It's good. It's very different from the life I had before."

"I didn't get the feeling you liked that life."

"You're worthless. Ungrateful. Nothing but trash. I should have killed you when I had the chance—"

Taking a deep breath, I locked the memories of my past back where they belonged.

"No, I did not. Every day was torture, but now I have my freedom."

"I'm sorry for what you went through, and I'm sorry that you went through it alone."

Marco's eyes filled with longing and sorrow, sparking a connection between us I couldn't deny.

For a while, when I would get lost in the silence at night, my misery would suffocate me. Sometimes, no matter how hard I tried, I could still feel its fingers around my throat.

But I wouldn't allow that here, not now, in front of him.

Those were the demons I hid, my broken pieces I refused to let anyone see.

"Thank you," I whispered softly.

"Of course." He nodded. "Do you find this life difficult?"

"It has its challenges."

"Do you experience those challenges with your own men? I never see you with anyone, any guards, or your own team."

I glared at him. "Well, I don't see you with yours, either."

"Yes, but I imagine it's harder for you."

I raised an eyebrow. "Why? Because I'm a woman?"

"Exactly. I'm not saying that you can't defend yourself. I'm fully aware that you can, but there are plenty of people in this business who see women as less than." His grip tightened as he cut his steak. "I can't imagine how often you have to deal with that. And I would hope you wouldn't have to deal with it within your own familia."

I swirled my wine because I didn't want to admit that I had and that I couldn't trust my own men. But if he was willing to be honest with me, then I needed to hold up my end of the bargain as well, at least somewhat.

"My men were loyal to Fernando. Now they're learning to be loyal to me."

He frowned, and it grated on my nerves. Was that answer dissatisfactory to him? Did he now see me as someone less than? A failure who hadn't won over her empire in its entirety?

He put down his utensils, then gently dabbed the corner of his lips with his napkin. "I come from two separate families. One is the Italian side, the Torrino Famiglia from my father, and the other is my mother's Hispanic side, the De La Rosa Familia." He took a deep breath. "When my mother married into the family, she had her own way of doing things. She was a bruja and people within the Torrino Famiglia believed she couldn't be trusted. Not only was she not Italian, her family was dying out and their power was dwindling here in the States. Some people believed she put a hex on my father or bewitched him in some way, because there was no other reason for him to marry her."

Without meaning to, I folded one hand under my chin and leaned in closer, enraptured by his story.

"My father protected her. He loved her more than anything in the world, but she never cared about following other people's conventions."

"What do you mean?"

"She didn't care to win over his family. She didn't care if they never trusted, respected, or honored her, and she made my father promise to never force their hand." His lips curled into a small, soft smile. "All she wanted was for him to be happy and safe, and she knew if he tried to force his men to accept her, it would only breed resentment and eventually lead to his downfall."

"It took years for people to finally accept her, but it happened organically. They grew to love her for her ideals and the way she loved us, and them." His voice grew quieter, tinged with deep, immense grief. "They loved her so much that they mourned as much as I did when both she and my father were killed."

My heart ached for him. "I am so sorry for your loss."

"Thank you," he whispered, then straightened in his chair. "I told you all of this not to upset you, but because I believe you too have your own way of winning over people. And you will do so at any point in time you need to." His gaze met my own, the intensity almost robbing me of my breath. "When I look at you, I see a woman capable of claiming the entire world. A world where everyone would bow down at your feet if you wished them to."

"And would you bow to me as well?"

Gently, he took my hand and brushed a single kiss on my

knuckles. "I will gladly get down on my knees for you. Anytime, anywhere."

"I had a wonderful evening, Catalina," Marco said in that low, sultry tone of his.

I tried to ignore the way my heartbeat sped up from it. I was still getting used to how frequently he flirted with me.

I gave him a small smile when he held open the restaurant door for me. "Thank you for dinner, Marco. It was very enlightening."

He fell into step beside me. "Whenever you'd like to learn more about me, feel free to let me know. I'm an open book to you."

"Mhmm, I'm sure you are." I hummed.

He chuckled and held his hand to his chest in mock injury. "I'm hurt by how much you don't believe me."

I patted his shoulder. "Aw, I'm so sorry. Did I bruise your incredibly massive ego?"

His eyes darkened as he leaned toward me. "That's not the only thing massive about me."

A shiver ran down my spine, and I had to bite back a curse. *This is ridiculous!*

I'd been around men before, I'd been *with* a man before, but I had never had such a hard time getting my body to listen to me.

I forced a smile. "You're right," I started counting on my fingers. "There's your massive amount of self-inflated confidence, levels of delusion, and belief that you're a gift to women everywhere. Should I continue?"

He laughed. It transformed his face, and I lost myself in it for just a moment. The sound was infectious, and it had me chuckling softly as we walked to my car.

I pulled out my remote and unlocked my door, but before I could open it, he grabbed it for me.

"Absolutely not."

I slid into my car. "I am actually capable of opening doors, you know."

"I know," he said as he rested his chin on the top of the door with a serious expression. "But just because you're capable of something doesn't mean you have to be the only one to do it." Then he stepped to the side. "Drive safely, Catalina."

"You too," I murmured before he closed the door.

Marco waited for me to back out, standing with one hand in his pocket and the other in a wave goodbye, which I returned. But even when I could no longer see him, I couldn't get him out of my mind.

I kept thinking about the way he laughed, how he'd dealt with things in Italy, his parents, the things he'd told me. His words about not needing to do everything. They were all moments that *felt* real.

He had gone through a lot. He knew what it was like to carry not only the weight of the world on your shoulders, but the added responsibility and protection of those around you.

In that way, he was remarkable, and as much as I hated to admit it, there was a part of me that felt inspired by him.

How would it feel to be at ease in my own skin? At ease with my own familia? To have their absolute trust?

"Just because you're capable of something doesn't mean you have to be the only one to do it."

I'd driven home purely on muscle memory, and I simply couldn't do that again. I couldn't let myself get lost in him, or my fantasies, hopes, or dreams, because I had no one who would try to find me if I did.

You're just tired. Yes, that's all. You just have a lot going on. It's okay. You're okay.

The excuse was hollow, but it didn't matter. Maybe I'd fallen slightly under the delusion of dinner, but it would fade by tomorrow. I may have had a good time with Marco, but that was where it ended.

I still didn't know what he wanted from me or what his favor entailed, but regardless of our contract, I assumed it had to have something to do with my familia.

He had money and power. My familia was the only thing I could offer him, the only thing of worth and value to my name.

I'll use him for what I can right now, but that's it. I can never trust him.

That reality kept me grounded—even as it crushed a piece of me. I was so tired, so, *so* tired of it all.

I had no one and nowhere to turn. I barely slept. I was always cautious, always waiting for the other shoe to drop, looking for danger around every corner. My entire being, my *soul,* was exhausted.

But even if I could rewind time, I'd still choose this life.

I kept my conviction, even as I thought of Marco, of his ease, and how nice it must have been to have a family who loved you, no matter what you did, no matter how deep and vicious your darkness might be. I kept that conviction as I took a shower, dressed, and slid into bed. But as I turned, my phone lit up.

MARCO

Goodnight, Catalina.

I bit my lip to stop the smile from forming.

Goodnight, Marco.

93

TEN

MARCO

I woke up to the blaring sound of my alarm, my neck aching from sleeping in my car again. Rotating my head, I tried to work out the crick as I waited for Catalina to leave her house.

This had been my routine for weeks now, and while I missed the comfort of my bed, getting these few extra minutes to watch my vicious little queen were worth it.

Like clockwork, she emerged from the garage. It was barely past dawn, but the sun's rays were visible enough, shining over her dark brown hair, which cascaded over her shoulder in a single braid. Her dark green silk blouse tucked into a black pencil skirt showed off the shape of her beautiful thighs and delicious ass.

Images of bending her over her desk, wrapping that perfect braid around my fist while I thrust into her flashed in my head. Her ass would provide the perfect cushion for my hips.

The sound of our bodies slamming together, the sounds of her moans...

Fuck. The vision sent a shiver down my spine and had my cock hard as a rock.

I'd wanted her before our dinner, but after last night I *craved* her. I couldn't get her out of my mind. The way she had a sarcastic comeback for everything I said.

She had a quick wit, was incredibly intelligent, and a fucking delight to be around.

And when she put her pasta and chicken in her mouth and let out a little moan, it drove me crazy. I wasn't even sure she knew she'd made the sound, but I'd heard it. The melody, tied with the explosion of pleasure on her face, stuck with me.

I would have done anything to experience that again. I nearly begged her to let me eat her out on the table right then and there.

I was addicted to her, and I never wanted to get clean. She was in my veins, *exactly* where she belonged.

Catalina was almost back in the garage when I picked up my phone and texted her.

> Good morning, Catalina.

She took out her phone without missing a step, read it, then rolled her eyes.

I grinned.

> Did you just roll your eyes at me?

Catalina glanced around, but she didn't appear panicked, simply watchful.

> Where are you?

> We just saw each other last night. Are you missing me already?

She scowled.

Not in your wildest dreams.

She huffed, making me laugh.

Then she got into her vehicle and pulled out of the driveway. I waited until she was completely out of sight, then left to head home, change my clothes, and prepare for the list of tasks I had to do today.

I stepped into the shower, the hot water cascading over my body, and sighed.

I'd just seen Catalina not even half an hour ago, yet I couldn't wait to be near her again.

I kept thinking about her laugh, her lips, how plump and round they were, how it would feel to run my thumb over them before I'd kiss her.

How long would it take for my fantasy to become a reality? How long would she fight against the inevitable? My cock grew hard at the thought of it.

I wanted her to fight me. I wanted her to challenge me. I wanted to prove I was worthy of her and her heart. That I could and *would* take care of her. I'd rather sacrifice my life for her than *ever* hurt her. There was nothing I wouldn't do for my vicious little queen.

Closing my eyes, I envisioned her before me, felt her skin against my own. I could smell her scent vividly, as if she was right there in front of me, too tempting to resist.

I could have slipped inside her house last night. Her intricate security system wouldn't have stopped me.

What did she sleep in? Did she prefer a baggy t-shirt or pajamas? Or nothing at all? I moaned at how delicious she would look, naked and vulnerable to me.

I'd trail my fingers over her skin, her breasts, and farther down her stomach to her sweet pussy. She'd roll over onto her back, thinking it was a dream, as I spread her legs and fingered her, tasted her until she came all over my face.

My cock throbbed, and I was so lost in my fantasy of her, I fisted it and stroked myself.

Her voice when she said my name rang in my ears, over and over as I squeezed my cock.

I braced my hand against the wall as I pictured her eyes wide, mouth parted, body sweaty and shaky as I made her come again. She'd welcome me between her legs, letting me slide balls deep inside her, fucking her exactly the way I *longed* to.

She'd be so hot, so wet, so *perfect*, and I'd make her come. Once. Twice. Three times. More. I wouldn't stop until I'd rung every ounce of pleasure from her.

And when she thought she couldn't come anymore, I'd make her. Her moans and pleas would be the perfect melody as I rammed inside her cunt.

My heartbeat thundered in my ears, mixing with the water from the shower. I thrusted into my hand like a madman, completely caught in the illusion of her.

It was too much.

Stream after stream of my come hit the tile wall and floor. It was so intense I had to rest my forehead against the wall and lock my knees to keep from falling over.

I hadn't jacked off since I was a teenager. Yet here I stood in my shower, reduced to nothing, after having the most realistic vision I'd ever had about a woman who could barely stand to be in the same room with me. And yet I still couldn't get her out of my mind.

I caught my breath and cleaned myself before getting dressed in a suit ready for work.

I had Samuel scour the dark web for anything they could find on trafficked victims out of New York or nearby surrounding areas. I put out calls to my famiglia in Italy, making sure they alerted me to any trafficking news, especially involving American women. I also instructed them to conduct their own investigations into any famiglias there who might be in the market to buy.

At noon, I sent another text to Catalina.

> Have you eaten lunch yet?

> No, and I'm not eating it with you.

> Hey, I'm doing you a favor by asking.

> And why would you think that?

I smirked.

> Based on our conversation this morning, you already missed me after we were only apart for a few hours. Who knows if you could handle a full day?

I chuckled, but I did actually have something to discuss with her.

I called, and she answered on the first ring. "Is it possible for you to actually leave me alone?"

"Of course not. I have information I'd like to go over with you on a few of the mafia families."

Her tone grew serious. "Do you think they're involved in trafficking?"

"I'm not sure yet. However, these are the families who have direct access to the port or border. Now, are you going to tell me what you want for lunch?"

She huffed, and I was almost certain she'd rolled her eyes again.

"I was planning on getting a chicken pesto sandwich from Jordan's Cafe."

"Got it. And what would you recommend for me?"

"Dog shit. Unfortunately, they don't have it on the menu."

I laughed, then heard her open what sounded like a drawer and flip through a piece of paper.

"Since you liked the steak last night, you might like their steak and mozzarella sandwich. They also have a mixed Italian meats sandwich."

Shock ran through me.

She remembered.

I'd honestly expected her to have hung up by now, but she'd actually thought about something I might like. *She'd actually thought of me.* I couldn't wipe the grin off my face.

"Thank you."

"You're welcome, and Marco, I let you get away with it last night, but this is not a lunch date."

"You're right, it's a working date."

"I hate you."

"If that's what helps you sleep at night," I said, smiling to myself. "I'll see you soon, Catalina."

When I arrived at Catalina's office, Olivia greeted me coolly, but didn't stop me from going back to see her.

Catalina looked up when I entered, then noticed the several bags and box I held and stood to help me. "What is all of this?"

I put everything down on a table, then pulled out a bouquet, a mixture of peonies, lilies, chrysanthemums, and dahlias. I knew nothing about flowers and had never seen Catalina buy any, so I didn't know what she might like. But the florist said these were her most popular ones this month.

Even if she doesn't like them, at least I'll know what not to buy her next time.

I cleared my throat, rubbing the back of my neck as I held the flowers out to her. "These are for you."

She froze, and when she finally took the flowers, her hands shook slightly. "Why?"

Because every time I see you, I feel honored to be in your presence and graced by your beauty, and I wanted to give you something beautiful in return.

"They reminded me of you."

She continued to stare at me, a dumbfounded look on her face. It would have been cute, but there was something else there. A panic she was trying to hold back, as if she was deathly afraid of what may happen if she released it.

"Do you not like flowers?"

"N-no." She cleared her throat. "I like them."

Yet she still didn't move, and the look of fear on her face didn't fall away. She trembled.

I wish you'd let me comfort you. But if I tried, she'd only push me further away.

I pulled out a glass vase to distract her. "Here. I got this in case you didn't have one."

She tried to nod, but it came out as a stiff jerk. "Thank you," she whispered, then she *ran*.

Dread filled my gut. What could have happened to her for this to be her reaction to flowers? What terrible memories had I just drudged up and how could I help her release them?

Doubting she was comfortable enough to speak with me about it, I began laying out the food, the sandwich she wanted, chips, a fruit salad, an assortment of bottles of juices, teas, and coffees I'd seen her order in the past, and a piece of chocolate cake, since she'd struggled to pick between that and crème brûlée last night. Then I laid out my food and threw away any bags I didn't think we'd need.

When Catalina walked back into the office, her eyes widened, looking from the food, to me, and back.

"I wasn't sure what you liked, so I bought a little bit of every-thing, and since you didn't pick the chocolate cake last night, I thought I'd bring you a slice today."

Catalina's hand flexed around the vase, her knuckles turning white. Her eyes narrowed, and she sneered at me. She'd never once looked at me with as much hatred as she was right now, like I was the *enemy* and she'd rip me apart if I said one wrong word.

"What do you want?" she bit out, rage radiating off of her in waves.

I rose to my full height and looked *deeper*, putting together the pieces of my vicious little queen that I'd learned so far.

Catalina had *never* run from anything. She always confronted her challenges head-on. She'd done so in the elevator when she thought I'd been working with her father. She'd done the same at dinner numerous times. Hell, the only reason she'd become the head of the Salazar Familia was because she'd constantly persevered.

She wasn't running *from* me. She wasn't being hostile *toward* me; it was to what I'd made her remember. She just didn't want me to recognize she was struggling, so she'd become defensive. That was the reason for her anger.

Right now, she was no different from a wounded bear or wolf desperate to survive another day. I had to show her I wasn't there to hurt her. But I wouldn't be able to fix this if she didn't give me a clue how.

Doing my best to keep my expression neutral, curious, I answered her question. "What do you mean?"

She waved a hand to the flowers, the table. "This is too much. No one would do all of this. Last night was one thing, but this? You want something from me. So tell me what it is and *get out*."

She was right, of course. I wouldn't have done all of this if my only aim was just to help her find the children. We wouldn't even need to communicate, much less meet, if it wasn't about them.

She knew I wanted something from her. She reminded me of it constantly. So why now? Why did it bother her so much when I'd only tried to do something special for her?

Then it donned on me. *She's never had anyone do something nice for her.*

She'd been surrounded by people, and yet no one attempted to relate or truly celebrate her. Not a single person ever asked her how she was doing, much less showed even an ounce of care for her on her birthday. They simply pushed their agenda on her, then dismissed her entirely when they were done.

And now that she ran her own familia, there were dozens of heads attempting to court or pressure her into an arranged marriage to seize control.

That was why she suspected me now.

Gifts, putting in thought for someone else, doing something as simple as picking up flowers—she didn't know how to deal with any of that because she'd never received it in the past.

But she would.

I'd make sure of it.

"Do you really want to know why I'm doing all of this?"

"Yes," she said in a bitter tone.

"Because I want to eat lunch with you and get to know you, so that when you look at me, you see someone you can rely on instead of someone you may have to kill." I took a deep breath. "I want to help you find the children. I want you to succeed in every endeavor you go through, and I want to be by your side while you do it."

Catalina stared into my eyes, her gaze intense, searching for something I hoped she'd find. After a moment, she looked away and placed the flowers on the windowsill. But when she stroked one flower delicately, her fingers shook.

"I'm sorry if I offended you," she said softly.

"You didn't. But should I not get you flowers in the future?"

She paused, then her shoulders slumped slightly, and she sighed. "No, thank you for getting them. They're beautiful."

Relief washed over me, but I needed to know more. I needed to push and find out how to avoid this in the future. But I couldn't ask her directly.

"Do you have a favorite flower?"

She shook her head, walking back to the table. "I've never actually received flowers before."

She sat down, and I joined her, but she wouldn't look at me. Then she bit her lip and continued, "Whenever we had flowers at home, it meant my father was going to demand something from me. I would need to play a part for him, and if I didn't, I would be... *punished*."

Her face darkened at the word, and my heart broke. I wanted to kill him, to dismember him. Take everything he treasured away from him.

He should have offered my Catalina the world. Instead, he was her worst nightmare.

Clasping her hands in her lap, she squeezed them tightly, then finally peered up at me. "When you gave me the flowers, it took me back there. I know you want something from me and I don't trust you... but you didn't deserve the way I treated you just now. I shouldn't have reacted so strongly. I'm sorry."

I wanted to reach across the table and hold her, to tell her it was all okay. That I'd never hold her past against her. That she was safe with me. But I couldn't say any of that yet.

That was the hardest thing about all of this. The yearning, desperate craving inside of me to be near her, to protect her, and knowing she wouldn't allow me to. If I pushed too hard, she'd only pull away.

Instead, I did what I always did when I was around her like this. I smiled at her. "There's nothing to be sorry about. Although I am happy that for once you acknowledge you misjudged me."

"Don't get used to it." A hint of a smile tugged at the side of her lips as she dipped her head before browsing the different cups of coffee. She stopped at one, and the smile fully blossomed before she took a sip.

"Is that your favorite?" I nodded to the cup in her hand.

"I like the others too and get this one sparingly because of all the sugar, but yes, it's my favorite. And since I snapped at you earlier, I'll act like it isn't incredibly suspicious that you somehow have all the different types of coffee I've ever ordered from Jordan's Cafe."

I grinned.

Mocha Frappuccino, but sparingly because of the sugar. Remember to write it down in her preferences document.

"Can I get it for you again?"

She tilted her head to the side. "Something tells me you don't just mean the drink."

I chuckled. "It excites me how quickly you're getting to know me."

She rolled her eyes.

I relaxed back into the couch with my own cup of black coffee. "What's it going to be, Catalina?"

She took another sip and side-eyed me. "Does it really matter what I say, when you're going to do whatever you want?"

"Humor me."

"I won't turn down free coffee." She gave me a small smile and my heart skipped a beat.

We spent the rest of the meal mostly in silence. I paid attention to the things she picked up, like the triple cheddar truffle chips, and noticed that when we were cleaning up, she put the mixed berry tea on her desk.

I handed her the paper files and a USB copy of the intel I'd collected.

"Thank you."

"You're welcome. I also have several searches going on regarding each family, port access, if there's anyone on the US Coast Guard that could have been paid off, or within one of the Italian famiglias. When I find something, I'll be sure to let you know."

I picked up my suit jacket, then paused at the door, turning back to her. "Think about what you want for lunch tomorrow."

She shook her head and laughed. "I should have known you couldn't last a day without bothering me."

"Of course not. I'd follow you to the end of the world just to do so."

ELEVEN

CATALINA

I rubbed my burning eyes and slumped back in my chair. I'd spent days combing through the files Marco handed over, but there was nothing here to implicate any of the families with direct ties to the port or Canadian border.

I felt like I was constantly sinking, being crushed under the weight of my life until I could barely keep my head above water.

I'd worked tirelessly, driving myself to the brink to find anything, to no avail. I'd even come to the club closest to the port tonight, in the hopes Fernando had stashed something away here, but there was nothing.

I'm so tired of coming up empty-handed.

According to the accounts I'd gotten from the few parents willing to speak to me, the trafficking started almost six years ago. Meaning, some of the children taken were now grown women and any photos their families had wouldn't help.

The only thing I could rely on were timelines and accounts. According to my investigations, Fernando had not integrated a new family in around two years, but that didn't mean he'd stopped trafficking. There were records of large deposits I couldn't reconcile until the day he died.

Still, I'd been running this familia for over half a year, and no one had approached me to continue any deals Fernando had previously put in place.

If his partner was still involved in trafficking, why hadn't they reached out to me or tried to establish some sort of relationship?

And if Fernando had been willing to traffic women for money, there was no telling what else he might have done. The deposits could have been from any number of things.

Fernando was incredibly good at covering his tracks. His personal guards were indoctrinated at a young age. Groomed, supported, and invested in to produce loyal soldiers that only he could control. But some of them had broken free.

Every few years, some of his men had died randomly, and I assumed it was to cover Fernando's trail. Perhaps they'd gotten tired of keeping his secrets, or he crossed a moral line they couldn't forgive.

But based on all the research I'd done, the last two men remaining were the ones I'd killed on my wedding night.

Fernando's entire system may have been a ticking time bomb, destined to cave in at any moment, but it was perfect for obedience and control.

There was a chance someone else in my familia might know something, but I was still winning over their trust, and this was a difficult thing to discuss.

When I'd approached some of the parents, several of them became so hysterical they couldn't even speak. Others just changed the subject. Only a few could share their story with me, and even less believed I'd be able to find their children.

They'd given up hope. They'd had to. If not, they wouldn't have been able to continue living their lives. They would have been stuck, feeling just as much of a failure as I did now. And that feeling could crush even the strongest spirit.

Between that, my day-to-day activities which were challenging enough, the gala party and award ceremony for Naya's non-profit, her clinic's completion, and my own issues, I was falling apart, drowning in a deep void with no end in sight.

And then there was Marco.

He was constantly around, throwing me off balance with his flirtatious banter and unexpected gestures. He texted, called, and emailed multiple times a day. He stopped by to eat with me daily, even when he had nothing new to report about the trafficking or mafia families.

He was always *there*. In fact, I half expected him to appear out of thin air in front of me right now.

Marco kept doing things I didn't expect, things no one had *ever* done for me. He brought me some random gift every day, always gauging my reaction to see what I liked and disliked. He brought flowers every week, always something new and different, like he was trying to figure out which ones I loved most.

He remembered my favorite coffee order, how much I loved chocolate, meals I preferred from specific restaurants we'd eaten from in the past. He'd gotten so good at observing what I'd liked that he could blindly pick something up for me, and it would fit with my tastes perfectly.

He spent so much time with me that I wondered how he got anything done in his own family.

I'd begun to grow used to him, finding his presence to be both unnerving and comforting—which made it that much worse. He was becoming something he shouldn't be—a constant fixture in my life.

I'd started watching for him, waiting for him, anticipating his text or phone call. At breakfast or lunchtime, I'd decide what I wanted then subconsciously browse the menu for something he'd like. I'd caught and chastised myself for doing so multiple times, yet it seemed to be a habit I couldn't break.

Not only that, I started to miss his banter, his laugh, his voice, and that wasn't good. He wasn't my boyfriend, colleague, or friend. He was my enemy, and I needed to treat him as such. But every time I tried, my stomach tied itself in knots and my heart ached.

I needed to get ahold of myself and let go of whatever disillusions I had of him, and fast. I couldn't trust him, for the sake of my familia. For *myself.*

He had to stay at an arm's length, no matter what. Because if I let him in, he'd ruin me.

Closing my eyes, I listened to the softened beat of the club music below, trying to focus on it. I needed to clear my mind, think of anything else but that damning man. But it wasn't working.

My emotions, thoughts, and body were a wreck, and I couldn't work this way. I got no rest at home, at work, or anywhere else. I barely slept and was running on fumes.

It had to stop or else I'd be no use to anyone. I needed to go to the only place I could to let out some steam—my gun range.

I never imagined a gun, something that could take or save a life, could bring me so much peace, but as I pulled into the shooting range, my tension eased a little.

The hustle and bustle of the city echoed on the wind, the city lights gleaming over the hill. It was remote, filled with trees, no houses, and barely any passing cars: my haven.

When I first picked up a gun again with my instructor, I'd been terrified. Images of Fernando's fat, lifeless body filled my head.

The sound, the smoke, the weight of it in my hand filled me with dread. The uncertainty of whether I'd live another day, if I'd *survive* was endless.

Without adrenaline coursing through my body, I became weak. The fear running through me was suffocating.

This was where I practiced my aim. Where I cried, screamed, and released every bit of anger that threatened to boil over. Where I let myself wonder how I could lead the mafia. Questioned how I could understand a world that I'd never been in. Doubted if I could really manage countless businesses, families, *people* who depended on me all on my own.

It was the one place I could be vulnerable and embrace the deepest parts of myself. And if it weren't for this plot of land, I might not even be here today.

I hauled my assortment of guns out of my trunk and set them on a wooden table. I started small, with my pistol, Glock, then Magnum.

With each shot, I relaxed a little more. The tension and focus, how I had to hold my breath as I fired each round, the loud *bang* as it went forth, ripping into the wood, and the satisfaction when I hit the bullseye was like a balm to my nerves.

But while it physically satisfied my body, mentally, my thoughts were chaotic.

I needed more.

Another kick, a louder bang. Something that was turbulent, *ferocious*. Something with so much force it knocked me out of my head.

Picking up my shotgun, I adjusted my posture, and put my

finger on the trigger, when a car pulled into the field. While my men could use the range if they wanted, they rarely ever did.

I turned to face the vehicle. It was too dark for me to fully make out who was in the driver's seat, but once the door opened, I lifted the shotgun over my shoulder and sighed. "I'm not even surprised anymore."

Marco's lips curled into his typical mischievous smile. "I have something for you."

His voice carried a note of excitement that only made my curiosity peak higher. How did he know about my gun range? What did he have for me? Why had the noise in my head quieted down the moment I'd seen his face?

"I'm too tired to play games right now," I warned.

"I know." His voice was muffled as he popped the trunk of his SUV, but he sounded almost sad.

Does he pity me?

Marco rolled his sleeves, revealing swirls of tattooed ink over his muscular arms. I stared at them a moment too long—based on the sudden dryness in my throat—as he pulled out several cases from his trunk.

Focus, and not on him.

I walked over to help, but he waved me away and brought the cases to where my guns were.

"What's in there?"

He opened the case, and my eyes bulged. Nestled inside was a black bazooka.

I had to close my mouth before I drooled. It was a thing of pure beauty.

Marco smirked. "Have you ever used one of these before?"

I shook my head. "I've always wanted to, though."

He held his hand out for my shotgun and I gave it to him.

"Stand in front of me."

Before I realized it, I did as he commanded. It was something about his voice, the smooth, rich, authority within it. For a moment, I wished I could simply surrender everything, give up control, leave everything in his hands.

That revelation shocked me to my core, but I didn't have time to fixate on it. Marco lifted the bazooka, then placed it on my shoulder.

"Is it too heavy for you?"

"No, I thought it would be heavier." I adjusted my arms around it, holding it in place.

"It's a Carl Gustaf M4. It comes in a variety of sizes, but since we don't need to blow up a tank, this one is big enough to be useful. Do you see that red dot?"

"Yes, is that the targeting system?"

"Yes. I'm going to load it, then stand to the side and keep you grounded."

How does he plan to do that?

He loaded the weapon first, then stood beside me. His hand came to my stomach and the middle of my back, holding me.

Heat raced along my body. Even though his hands never moved, it felt as if he was surrounding me. His scent enveloped me. Something like cedar, vanilla, sandalwood, and musk. It was *intoxicating.*

I licked my lips. "Why does it feel like you're doing this for an entirely other reason?"

He chuckled, low and deep, his breath soft against my ear, sending shivers down my spine. "I brought them because you're a vicious woman and I was certain you'd enjoy them. My intentions are as pure and innocent as you want them to be."

Goosebumps rose over my entire body, and I huffed. "There's not a single thing pure or innocent about you."

He laughed softly. "Look at how good you're doing. You're getting to know me so well."

His tone was warm, flirtatious, but something about his words, his *praise,* nearly made my eyes roll into the back of my head.

"Shoot on a count of three. Don't worry, I'll breathe with you."

His voice jarred me back to my senses. I wanted to tell him it was impossible to shoot this way. I could barely focus with him beside me like this. How were we going to synchronize our breathing for the shot?

But when I looked at him, not a shred of doubt clouded his eyes. He actually seemed... happy.

Get it together, Catalina.

I took a deep breath until I could feel the pounding of my heartbeat slow, then nodded to him. I was ready.

"One."

I fortified my stance.

"Two."

I grasped the trigger.

"Three."

I held my breath with him. We were completely tense, still, and then I fired. One moment everything was calm, the next, my target was completely engulfed in flames.

It wasn't large and unruly like the movies, but it was wild, unique, *beautiful.* Excitement coursed through my veins as Marco smiled softly, and if I weren't still holding the bazooka, I would have thrown my arms around him and kissed him.

The thought was absolutely ludicrous, ridiculous, *crazy,* and yet the want was still there.

Would it be so bad if I just—

I mentally shook my head. *Absolutely the fuck not.* That would never happen, *never.*

"Feel better?"

My voice came out as a whisper. "Yes, thank you."

Marco was still standing far too close to me, the heat of his body invading every bit of sense I had left, and yet I couldn't pull away.

He had given me the best gift I'd ever received, an experience of a lifetime that made me feel *alive.* I couldn't remember the last time I'd felt so much joy and it was tied to him, like an extension of him that lived within me.

Whether he knew it or not, Marco had just seen a part of me no one else had, one I didn't even know I was capable of. His thoughtfulness brought that out, and though I'd never tell him, I was grateful. He had not only offered me a light to guide me through the darkness surrounding me, he'd yanked me out of it.

He cupped the bazooka, and I slipped it into his arms carefully, then took a step away.

"What are you doing?" he asked, slipping it inside its case before pulling out a fire extinguisher. "We're not done."

"What?"

He put out the fire, then walked back to me and opened another case holding an RPG.

As he had with the bazooka, he walked me through how to hold it, and the targeting system. He warned me about the weight and checked twice to make sure I was comfortable with it. Then he stood behind, but to the side to support me.

And when he wrapped his arm around me, my stomach flipped. I had to swallow to soothe my scratchy throat, hoping he wouldn't somehow see my hard nipples beneath my clothes.

I was terrified he'd find out the truth—that no matter how much I fought it or what I said... I wanted him.

I thought it would go away as soon as I fired the RPG, that the pretty explosion would calm me down and distract me. But when I turned around and looked up at him, he looked so pleased with himself, with how happy he'd made me, that it only grew.

We went through a similar cycle with the next weapon—a machine gun. Every shot I fired had our bodies bumping, vibrating against one another.

I'd never been so turned on in my life.

I all but shoved the gun back into his hands. If this was some type of seduction, it was working *far* too well and no matter how much I wanted to resist, I couldn't.

After all I'd gone through, I thought I'd never want a physical relationship with anyone ever again. The idea of a kiss or sex being pleasurable seemed like a fantasy to me. I'd had sex. It hurt, it left me empty, and I didn't understand why people craved something so painful.

But if Marco touched or flirted with me again, no matter how much I knew I shouldn't, that *we* shouldn't, I'd let him do whatever he wanted to me. *Especially*, if he wanted to fuck me.

I wanted to know what it would be like to feel his warmth on every inch of my skin. I wanted him to kiss me, to hear him moan and grunt in my ear. Feel him thrusting inside of me. I *ached* for it. I was so fucking wet that I was dangerously close to begging for him to do something, *anything*.

Marco put away the machine gun while I took several deep breaths to center myself. I glanced his way, but he was looking at everything else but me.

Was he just as affected as I was? The thought pleased me far more than it should have and I bit my lip.

His eyes met mine, then slid down to my bottom lip as I released it from my teeth. A tic started in his jaw and I grinned.

Good. I hope you'll have to take a cold shower too.

Then I imagined him naked.

Fuck.

Marco took a step closer. His eyes were on fire, so deep and intense it felt like I was burning alive right with him.

I licked my lips, his gaze following my tongue, then slowly slid back to my eyes. If he bent down, just a little more, I could kiss him.

Something needed to cut the tension between us and *fast,* before I did something I'd regret. That was what gave me the strength to take a step back from him. I tucked a strand of hair behind my ear and cleared my throat. "Thank you for this. Even though I'm not sure how you knew I was here, and it concerns me you did, you helped me, and I appreciate it."

His fingertips grazed my chin as he gently tipped my head up. His grin was wide, his dimples on full display. "Of course, it's my job."

"Job?" His touch, his smile—damn it, *all* of him—left me breathless.

I should have told him to stop touching me.

I should have told him to continue.

Which do I want more?

"Yes," he hissed, running his fingertips along my jaw, to my hair, where he slid down the shaft of my braid all the way to my waist. "I told you, I'd follow you wherever you go, and I will always help you. I'm on your side, Catalina. No matter how much you push me away, I will always choose you."

Why did he have to say those words to me? Why now? When I can't ignore or doubt them?

All I'd ever wanted was to be someone's first choice. To be their priority, to have their attention, to be *wanted,* not needed.

Why? Why did he make everything so hard?

I wanted to hate him, to despise and be wary about him. I kept trying and trying, and trying, but I couldn't. Instead, I'd laughed, shared, and grown comfortable around him.

Somewhere along the line, I'd let Marco in. I started to believe him, believe *in* him, and I shouldn't have.

You stupid, stupid girl. How did you let this happen?

This was only going to hurt me in the end. I knew that, and the thought of that devastating pain helped me break whatever spell he'd so carefully woven around us.

Marco's hand fell away as if he could feel the sudden shift in the air between us. He clenched his fists, his knuckles turning pale from the force, then turned to carry the gun cases away.

I watched him retreat. And with every step he took, he stole something from me. I could feel it, like a tether I couldn't break. It was so strong that I wanted to call him back. Wanted to apologize, to change, explain, beg him, but I didn't know for what or why. I just didn't want him to leave like this.

But instead of going to his car, he walked to mine and said in a gruff voice, "Open your trunk."

I tilted my head, following him. "Why?"

He put the cases on the ground and held onto the latch for my trunk. "I didn't just bring these for you to use; they're yours."

My heartbeat sped up again. "Marco... you cannot keep doing this."

"As long as it keeps that look of joy on your face, I can and I will. Now open the trunk, Catalina."

Marco followed me in his car until we'd entered the city, making sure I'd gotten there safely. But even after he'd turned off, heading in his own direction, I still couldn't get him out of my mind.

I was stuck on the same question, the one I knew he wouldn't answer honestly. *What did he want from me?*

There was no tracker on my car. I'd checked multiple times, which could only mean he'd invested resources into watching me.

It wasn't that hard to find out what property I owned. If he could identify the name of my corporations, he could easily track a lot of the things he wanted, but there was nothing there that would benefit him enough to explain why he acted the way he did.

Yes, I had clubs, hotels, hospitals, and a slew of other revenue streams, but so did he. In fact, all of my research showed he had more money than I did. So why? Why go this far?

My past with men was simple. They always wanted something from me and they'd use their power to try to intimidate me into giving it to them. If that didn't work, they'd take it themselves. It was the same with my father, Fernando, even the other mafia heads who tried to get me to marry them.

But Marco wasn't like that with me. He was never aggressive. Never tried to bully or pressure me. He could have been trying to work a different angle, playing kind and adoring until I'd finally give him whatever it was he wanted, but I didn't think that was the case. At least, I *hoped* it wasn't.

If Marco wanted, he could have fucked me tonight. He had to have known that. I couldn't hide it, and there was no way he missed it.

He had plenty of opportunities to take advantage of me, and he never did. *Not once.*

When I got home, I took a cold shower, ate a flatbread pizza, and slid into bed. I checked my phone, but Marco hadn't contacted me.

Maybe that's for the best.

I turned off the light, then my phone buzzed.

MARCO

Goodnight, Catalina.

I had fun shooting with you. I hope
you'll invite me the next time you go.

I forced myself to ignore the warmth that ran through me when I read his messages.

Why would I bother when you always
invite yourself?

I'll be there either way, but I'd prefer it
if you asked me to come.

I smirked.

In your dreams.

TWELVE

MARCO

I sat back in my car and waited.

It normally took Catalina twenty to thirty minutes to fall asleep, which gave me more than enough time to think.

I hated seeing how drained she was and that I had done nothing to lighten her burden so far. It was my job to protect her, and I was failing at it.

That was the real reason I'd tracked where she'd gone and followed her to the gun range.

I planned to tease her a little and see how much she'd let me touch her. But I didn't expect how good it would feel to have her against me. How desperate I'd be for *more*.

Whether she meant to or not, tonight, she'd trusted me. She'd allowed me to support her body and shoot with her. Listened to me as I guided her through each weapon.

The way her small body felt along mine, how her heat seared into my skin was indescribable. Her scent was intoxicating, a mix of jasmine, violets, smoke, and leather. I wished I could wrap myself in it, in *her*, and never let go.

But it was the look in her eyes that shocked me the most. Catalina, my vicious little queen, *wanted* me.

Me.

She would have let me kiss her. It was written all over her face, from the way she couldn't catch her breath, to her dilated eyes.

And I wanted to kiss her. Throw all the guns to the ground, strip her slowly on that table, and fuck her senseless until she came all over my cock while I filled her to the brim.

Walking away from her was the hardest thing I'd ever done, and it had taken about an hour to finally convince myself I'd made the right choice.

Yes, Catalina wanted me then, but she wouldn't want me after.

Her desire was a momentary blip for her. If I'd fucked her tonight, she would have enjoyed it, then called it a mistake, and worked even harder to distance herself from me.

And I would *never* permit that.

When she finally allowed me inside of her, that would be it. There would be no going back, and if she tried to run away, I'd show her just how good of a hunter I really was.

I would chase her, tie her down to my bed, and fuck her senseless for days, weeks, *months* until she finally surrendered to what was between us. If that's what it took, I'd do it in a heartbeat.

But until then, I had a job to do.

Catalina deserved to relax, to ease the weight on her shoulders. Which meant she needed me as her devil, not her man right now.

I drove to my warehouse, where Anthony and Carlos were waiting for me.

I slipped on my leather gloves as I approached them. "The package?"

"Secure, boss," Carlos said.

I nodded and entered the building.

Paul Caprasi sat unconscious, bound to a chair, his hands cuffed behind his back. He had a single black eye, but otherwise seemed to be in good health. As long as he answered my questions, he'd stay that way—minus a few bruises.

I punched him in the gut.

His eyes flew open. Paul tried to bend forward to draw in air but couldn't.

Wheezing, his blue eyes darted from me to Anthony and Carlos, then back. Pure fear spread over his face.

I smirked. "Good. I would have been insulted if you didn't recognize who I was."

"Mr. Torrino. I swear I didn't do—"

"Paul, I haven't even asked you anything yet, and you're already trying to lie to me. That doesn't bode well for you."

"But Mr. Torrino—"

I delivered an uppercut to his jaw, sending Paul's head flying back. "Do not interrupt me when I'm speaking."

Paul's eyes watered, but he kept his mouth shut.

"Looks like we're on the same page now. How many families pay you to allow their shipments through?"

"Mr. Torrino, I-I can't say—"

I tsked. "Do you mean to tell me you're more scared of them than you are of me right now? I guess my reputation must have slipped while I was away."

He shook his head feverishly. "N-no, sir. I know what they call you, T-The Devil."

I grinned. "Would you like to know how I got that name?"

"N-no, sir. I swear. I meant no disrespect, I just—"

"Anthony, hand me the wrench."

Paul whimpered as I came closer. "No-no, please! *Please*! I'll tell you anything, please!"

"You're right, Paul. You will tell me everything I want to know."

Pulling off my gloves, I tossed them into the trash, then called Sam. "Did you get my email?"

"Yeah. I've already started working through it," Sam said.

"Good. I've highlighted the families we didn't know had their hands in the shipping business. I want everything you can find out about them by tomorrow."

"Got it."

I hung up and headed into the bathroom next to the interrogation room. Peeling off my blood-stained clothes and shoes, I shoved them into a plastic bag before turning on the shower.

Grabbing a bottle of soap, I washed away the last few remnants of Paul's body. While I'd at least found out something new, I wasn't sure it would give Catalina the answers she needed or bring her anywhere closer to her goal.

I slammed my fist against the tile. *Damn it!*

Running a hand through my hair, I tried to get my breathing under control.

It didn't matter if the information I'd beat out of Paul amounted to anything or not, because if it didn't, I'd just try a new angle.

I *would* get this resolved for Catalina. There was no room for any other alternative.

After a few minutes, I turned off the shower, stepped out, and donned fresh clothes—a crisp black shirt and trousers—before slipping into clean shoes.

When I emerged, Carlos had already placed Paul's phone, keys, and wallet aside, awaiting the cleaning crew.

"What would you like me to do with his body?"

"Put him in the cremation chamber. Then make sure the bones and metal go into the acid. Leave nothing behind."

Carlos nodded.

I exited the building, slid into my car, and called Anthony, who was watching over the cameras I'd installed in front of Catalina's house.

But when he answered, his voice sounded panicked, urgent. "Marco, Catalina's in trouble. A van just pulled up with eight men, maybe more. They're trying to break in."

No.

I floored the accelerator.

No.

The car shot forward, speeding down the road. I braked hard to turn, the tires screeching as I forced them through the movement.

No!

"Send my men to her address."

"Are you sure—"

"Just fucking do it!" I roared. I hung up, my vision turning red.

The buildings blurred together as I sped to her house.

Please. Let me make it on time. Please let her be okay. Please. Please!

I begged someone, anyone, whatever deity might be listening. Because if one hair on her head was out of place, I'd burn this city to the ground.

I parked behind the van, blocking it in Catalina's driveway.

Pulling out my gun, I slowly crept up the path. There was no movement outside, nor inside the van. Catalina's house was pitch black. Everything deathly silent.

My pulse thundered in my ears as I sprinted up the front steps. I popped open the keypad on her lock. They'd cut the wires, leaving the deadbolt as the only thing standing in between her and I. I pulled out my lock-picking set and got to work, my hands trembling with every movement.

I took a deep breath. *Steady.*

Picking a lock was an art form, something that required time. The complete opposite of what I wanted. I wanted to kick the door down, storm in, and get *my* woman. But I didn't know the situation inside.

What if she was in the middle of defending herself and the surprise gave someone else the upper hand? What if she was silently working her way through the house, about to shoot someone, and my noise alerted her away? Finding her hurt or worse would break me, but if I found out I'd been the cause? I'd take my life without a moment's hesitation.

I unlocked the door and opened it slowly.

Nothing.

I moved inside, my eyes adjusting to the darkness. A sliver of light flew toward me and I ducked at the last second, the knife embedding itself in the wall.

I never saw the person move until they were right in front of me.

They kicked at my head.

I ducked again and roared. "What the fuck did you do with *my* Catalina?"

The person stilled, long enough for me to pick them up and throw them against the wall.

The gasp at the impact was feminine, but I didn't fully register the sound.

"Where is she? Who are you?" I growled, shaking them. "If you touched one hair on her head, I swear it'll be the last—"

They elbowed me in the side of my arm, causing my grip to loosen.

"Marco, it's me."

My brain stopped, then skittered to life. My body responded before I even realized it had. I loosened my grip as the woman of my dreams, the owner of my heart, the master of my every desire, and the core of my being stood in front of me, confused with a glare on her gorgeous face.

"Catalina?"

She felt along a wall, then turned on the switch, bathing her house in light. Strands of her hair had escaped the bun on top of her head. Blood smeared her clothes, arms, neck, and face. She was beautiful, the perfect vision of a vengeful goddess that I'd pray to every day and night.

"Catalina." I brushed her hair back, checked her cheek, her neck. "Catalina, are you okay? Are you hurt? Where are you hurt? Did you get stabbed? Shot?"

Her voice was soft, but curious. "I'm fine, but what are you doing here?"

Fuck. She'd never told me where she lived. She'd never invited me to her house. Showing up at the shooting range was one thing, but this? She could see it as an invasion, as a line where I'd gone too far.

"I've been watching you for a long time," I murmured. It

scared me that this might be the moment she put more distance between us, and I couldn't blame her. In my rush to protect her, I'd made a mistake, but her safety was worth it.

I braced myself for her anger and fury as her dark brown eyes searched mine. Then her body relaxed slightly between me and the wall.

My eyes widened and for a moment I didn't move, barely even breathed. Was she really not going to go off? Curse at me? Nothing?

"Are you sure you're okay?"

She nodded, even as her body trembled slightly.

"Where are the men from the van?"

She motioned past her, and when I turned, I saw their lifeless bodies scattered around her home. I was proud and terrified. I admired her strength, but pure, unfiltered rage bubbled within me because she'd had to use it.

If I could, I'd resurrect the motherfuckers and kill them slowly. I'd torture them, pull their nails, their teeth, one by one. I'd take their eyeballs, slowly carve into their skin with a dull, rusted blade. I'd keep them that way for days until they told me everything they knew. By the time I was done, they would have regretted ever being born.

I clenched my teeth. "What happened?"

Catalina's gaze hardened. "They're my father's men. He sent them because I kept ignoring him. They were supposed to kidnap me and take me to a secure location where he'd pick me up."

She said the words flatly, like they were nothing, when they were *everything* to me.

I raised my head to the ceiling and took a deep breath, trying to keep my emotions in check.

I could have lost her. There's no telling what would have happened once her father had her in his clutches.

Did he know she was the head of the Salazar Familia? That if she disappeared, people would search for her? That *I* would search for her? Or had he thought she was simply a figurehead while someone else ran everything behind the scenes?

No, he probably thought she was disposable, that no one would miss her if she were gone, when that couldn't have been further from the truth.

I braced myself against the wall, then bowed my head to her. "I'm sorry. You shouldn't have had to deal with them alone."

She looked away but shrugged. "It's okay. I took care of it. I didn't need any help."

I grasped her chin. "No. It's not about whether or not you needed help. You shouldn't have *had* to go through this alone. I know what it's like to be alone, to have the weight of the world on your shoulders and feel like the only one you can rely on is yourself."

Her eyes met mine as she whispered, "You do?"

"Yes." My gaze softened as I rubbed her cheek.

"Is that why you came here? Because my situation reminds you of your own?"

"Maybe in a small way, but no. That's not why I broke about fifty traffic laws to get to you."

"Then why?"

"Would you believe me if I told you honestly?" I murmured.

Her eyes drifted to the side.

"That's what I thought." I pulled away, just a little, and for a second, she seemed to lean into me before righting herself, so I stepped close to her once more.

"Stay with me."

Her eyes widened. "What?"

"You can't stay here."

"N-no. My clean-up crew is on the way. Everything will be fine soon."

"That's not enough. How are you supposed to rest here comfortably? If your father did this once, he'll try it again."

"I can deal with him. There's nothing he can throw at me that I can't handle."

"No one's invincible, Catalina," I whispered softly.

She glared at me, but I knew she would have fought me if I'd spoken to her in any other way.

"I don't want you to get hurt. I don't want you to be in danger, Catalina." I clenched my fists. It was the only way I could stop myself from pulling her into my arms. "Please, stay with me. I have a spare room. I'll make sure you're comfortable there. I—"

She shook her head. "I have to stay here. For my familia."

"Then I'll stay with you," I growled.

"You can't. You have your own family to run."

"I can handle both."

Fire sparked in her eyes. "No."

"Catalina—"

"No!"

I threw my hands up in the air. "Why? Why do you want to stay in a house with literal pools of blood and bodies on the floor? Where someone's already broken in once and can do so again?"

"Because I can't stay with *you!* Marco, you are the leader of a mafia family. What will people think? What message would that send to the other heads?"

"I don't give a fuck, Catalina. I don't give a fuck about anything else but *you!*"

"Well, you should! You're already at my office every day. I've had to put up with a lot of trouble from other families, but if I stay with you, they're going to link us together. And that could disrupt the entire Underground." She flailed her hands around us.

"Both of our families are powerful and if people think we're going to combine, they will do anything they can to stop it. It won't just be us in danger, it'll be the people we're supposed to look out for too."

I ran my hand through my hair. I hated this. If she needed me to, I'd give up my family right now, without a second thought, but if I told her that, she wouldn't believe me.

She gently squeezed my arm, and the simple touch soothed me in a way nothing else would. "I really will be fine. There are plenty of other places I can stay if I need to."

That's not enough.

"Then I'm staying with you."

"Marco—"

I pressed my body against hers, trapping her between myself and the wall once more. Her eyes went wide. "I said, I'm staying," I growled.

She opened her mouth, but I grabbed her chin. "Stop fighting me on this, because you're not going to win. I will follow you to the lowest levels of hell, if that's where you want to go. But the one thing I will never do again is leave you to fend for yourself."

Her breath hitched.

I brushed the backs of my fingers against her cheek. "I know you've spent your life suffering and I know I can never make up for that. But you're not alone, not anymore."

I stepped closer, pinning her against the wall, leaving no space between us. *You're not going to push me away. Not this time.*

"Whatever battles you need to fight, I will fight them with you. If you want to celebrate, I will be there beside you, praising you. If you decide to burn the world down tomorrow, I will pour the gasoline and hand you the match."

"Marco, I-I—"

"I know you can't trust me or believe in what I'm telling you right now, so use me. Use me as a tool. Let me be a part of your arsenal. That will be enough for me. For *now*."

Her lips quivered, drawing my gaze, but then she nodded.

I stepped back before I lost the last of my control. Because if she tried to argue with me one more time about staying with her, I'd shut her up by kissing her pretty little mouth the way I'd been dying to.

She watched me, pensively, as if she were weighing her options. Then she swallowed and whispered, "Would you like to go to a gala with me?"

I'd barely heard the words, and if it weren't for the gentle expression on her face, I'd thought I'd imagined them.

She was letting me in, just a fraction.

"Tell me when and where, and I'll be there."

Catalina looked physically refreshed after her shower, but I could still see the exhaustion in her eyes.

The clean-up crew arrived and once they finished, we shared a meat lover's pizza on her couch.

Her eyelids grew heavy and, without meaning to, she leaned against me.

I didn't move, barely remembered how to breathe.

I loved the way she felt, how her softness melded into my body. Knowing I was of use to her, even being just a pillow, felt like a blessing.

I had a good life as a child. I'd been taught and felt love throughout my formative years. But I'd never been so at peace. It felt like I'd found my home, my purpose in life. I desperately wished I could be the person she always leaned on.

I'll just have to strive harder to make sure I am.

"Lina," I whispered, brushing a strand of hair from her face. "Let me take you to bed."

"Mmm," she mumbled, "...too tired."

She didn't say no.

I grinned. "I meant to sleep."

She chuckled, her eyes still closed. "Good, because I'd hate to have to kill you too."

I smiled, then picked her up, cradling her in my arms while she nestled her head in my chest.

Can you feel my heart racing, Catalina? If you can, I hope you know it's for you.

I turned down her hallway, knowing the layout of her house from all the nights I'd spent watching her, but this was the first time I'd seen her bedroom through anything but a window.

I wanted to look around, get a sense of the things she liked, what made her feel comfortable here, so if she ever stayed with me, I could make sure I had the same items in my home, but now wasn't the time.

Instead, I pulled her beige and brown sheets back, then laid her gently in bed. A single piece of long brown hair slid over her face, and I gently brushed it back over her ear.

"Should I braid your hair for you?"

"No, I'll take care of it in the morning," she said in a half-grumble, half-whispered voice.

I covered her, taking care to tuck her in snuggly. "Goodnight, Catalina."

As I turned to leave, she grabbed the cuff of my shirt. "Stay."

"What?" My eyes widened, but she'd fallen back to sleep.

What should I do?

Did she mean for me to stay, as in sleep in her bed or in her house? I glanced at her bed. It was large enough for both of us.

And the thought of holding her warm, soft body against mine sent a fierce surge of need through me. But how would she react if she saw me beside her in the morning?

I was certain that even if that was what she meant, she'd likely try to stab me first and ask questions later. I searched the room for a bench or chair I could sleep in instead, but then I saw some of the flowers I'd given her in a vase on her dresser.

I bought her new flowers every week. They were high quality and could last far longer than that, but I always wanted Catalina's office to be enveloped in a fresh floral scent. I didn't want to burden her with giving her something else she had to take care of, so I made sure they never wilted.

But I'd given her these flowers almost a month ago, and as I stepped closer, I noticed it was a hodgepodge of several of the bouquets I'd given her. She seemed to only get rid of them once they'd died, but the water was clear, and their stems were nicely trimmed.

She'd been meticulously caring for them, put them in her bedroom where she'd see them every time she entered or exited.

She's keeping the flowers I'd gotten her alive.

She cared about them. They mattered to her, and by extension, *I* mattered to her.

It may not be much, but it was *something*.

I walked out of her bedroom quietly, closing the door behind me, and took the couch, placing myself in the path between her front door and bedroom. I was a light sleeper, so I'd hear her and leave before she came out.

After all, even if she did remember that she asked me to stay, seeing me in her home would likely make her nervous.

It won't always be this way. One day, we would have a home together. One day, she wouldn't push me away.

One day I'd be able to call her mine.

Thirteen

Catalina

I woke to the sun streaming through my curtains. I blinked, clearing the sleep from my eyes, then reached for my phone and balked. It was after 10 AM. I'd never slept so deeply or so late in my entire life.

I swung my legs over my bed as memories of last night came back slowly, the men, Marco breaking into my house, how scared he was. How I'd asked him to stay.

I'd slipped up last night. I hadn't wanted to be alone. I was so tired—tired of fighting, living each day with my guard up, and pushing myself to survive.

I wanted to exist, to experience joy, happiness, *peace,* and I refused to let anyone take that chance away from me. But something in me broke last night. Something that simply couldn't be repaired in the same ways I'd gone about fixing myself before.

I desperately needed rest, to feel safe, just for a night. I couldn't remember the last time I'd been able to lay my head down on my pillow and not force myself to stay alert.

I always strained to listen for any out-of-place sound, peered around every corner waiting for a monster to jump out and attack me. Because in my experience, there was always one waiting for me somewhere.

They came in various forms—Simon, Fernando, my sense of failure and unworthiness—but if I wasn't careful, my demons would drag me under, deep into their depths, and I would never be the same.

But Marco was the light, *my* light. I should have asked him how he knew my address or about the attack, but I didn't. I was just happy to not be alone, to have someone that at least acted like they were on my side for *once.*

His presence made me *feel* protected. He beat away my monsters last night, helped me lock them behind bars, gave me the reprieve I needed. That was enough, that was *more* than enough. It was a blessing. But where was he?

He hadn't gone to bed beside me. The sheets were perfectly tucked in, and his scent wasn't in the room. I didn't hear any sounds in the house either. But I knew he'd stayed. I knew him well enough to know he'd never let an opportunity pass him by.

I closed my hand around the knob to open the door and investigate, but paused. What if he was asleep in the living room? And if he was, how were we going to talk about him staying the night? We had to, right?

It felt strangely good to be pinned between him and the wall last night. His warmth, his firm muscles. The strength in his body as he trembled from the fear of losing me gave me a rush. Had anyone ever reacted that way to me before? Had anyone ever begged me to stay with them and cared about my safety?

I felt so cared for, so *loved* when he cradled me as though I'd break, that my walls had fallen down and I'd bared a piece of myself to him. It wasn't just that I'd let him in this time. I wanted to stop pretending just for a night, to see what it would be like to be honest with him about what he was starting to mean to me...

I shook my head, clearing my thoughts. Even if he was here, nothing had technically happened between us. We could just talk about this like adults and go back to how we were before.

But did I want us to? Unfortunately, even though I knew it was stupid, I didn't.

I yanked the door open with a huff, then quietly crept to my living room. My senses told me he'd left, but I couldn't help the disappointment that came over me when I found out he truly was gone. The only clue that he'd spent the night was a small shift in the pillows and blanket he'd neatly arranged on the couch.

Running my fingertips over the blanket, I imagined him asleep underneath it. Then I pulled it up to my nose and inhaled. Cedar, vanilla, sandalwood, and musk, scents that were slowly beginning to feel a lot like comfort and home.

A small ping of jealousy zipped through me that this had been the last thing to touch him and not me.

I just got jealous over a blanket. Clearly, I've lost my fucking mind.

But I still couldn't help but smile. Marco could have taken advantage of me multiple times last night, but he didn't. Instead, he'd been caring, considerate, *protective.*

He truly liked me, at least a little bit. His flirting, gifts, and constant attention weren't just a game, there was at least *something* there. But I still didn't understand why. What did he see in me? What could he possibly gain from doing all of this? And why did those questions hurt my heart so badly?

I shook my head again and walked into the kitchen, where something smelled absolutely incredible. On the counter were two plates—salmon eggs benedict and a side of brioche-stuffed French toast—two of my favorites. It was even still warm.

A chuckle escaped me. I could see Marco buying the food with that smug smile of his, knowing I'd enjoy it, then slipping out of my house right before I'd woken up. It used to infuriate me that he was always right about me. But now, I was just grateful.

When had everything changed?

I ate breakfast, then called the office to let Olivia know I'd be in later, but she informed me Marco had already alerted her, but hadn't explained why. I filled her in, then hung up.

Why am I not upset at him for invading my space? He had no right to call Olivia or tell her anything, yet all I felt was a sense of appreciation. He'd taken care of it for me, and I was starting to realize that was something he did regularly.

I finished breakfast, got ready, and as I left the house, I checked for a message from Marco, but he hadn't sent one.

That isn't like him. I could text him first... no.

I never had before, and even if I'd had the courage to, I wasn't sure what I wanted to say. With a sigh, I shoved my phone into my purse and drove to work.

Stopping by the farmer's market, I picked up some coffee and muffins for Olivia. She deserved at least that, an extra-long lunch, and a bonus for how well she took care of things and kept my schedule on track.

A flower cart with a bouquet of yellow tulips caught my eye, reminding me of the one Marco had given me recently. A mixture of golden sunshine that reminded me of his smile. I couldn't stop myself from reaching out to grab them, but as I did, a hand wrapped around mine.

I recognized those long, strong fingers, the tattoos peaking at the cuffs of his sleeves, the scent. The firm body that pressed against my back.

"Hi."

I tilted my head up to look at him. He smiled, but it was different—jittery, nervous even.

"I was wondering when you'd show up." Even though my words were sarcastic, I couldn't muster up my normal snarky tone. Maybe it was because he was so close to me, or maybe it was because of the sudden relief that washed over me when I saw him. It shocked me, but I'd missed him.

The florist appeared and Marco grabbed a second bouquet of the tulips and paid for both. Then he took the muffins and coffee I'd been holding.

When we broke away from the crowd, he spoke to me in a soft tone. "I was nervous you might be mad at me."

"I'm not. Thank you for breakfast, and for calling Olivia."

"Did I overstep?"

He had, but I grinned at him. "Just don't make it a habit."

The tension left his shoulders and when he smiled at me again, it reminded me of the sun.

We walked to my office in comfortable silence, and when I got up to the top floor, I took the muffins and coffee and handed them to Olivia. "Thank you for taking care of everything today. Why don't you head to lunch and take an extra hour?"

Olivia beamed, but still asked, "Are you sure? Do you need anything?"

I smiled and waved her away. "No, not at all. Go enjoy yourself and we'll catch up when you're back."

She grabbed her purse and the coffee, and waved bye at us both, then Marco and I headed into my office.

Marco switched out the flowers for me while I put away my belongings. Then he plopped down into his usual chair. "Tell me about this gala we're attending tonight."

"I've donated a large amount of money to a non-profit for domestic violence and child abuse victims, the Center of Gentle

Love and Hope, and recently finished a clinic for them. I'll be presented with an award tonight, but the gala is mainly to collect donations for staff, additional centers, and re-homing their victims." I took a deep breath. "That will generate a lot of PR for me, which means my father will also attend."

Marco's eyes narrowed, and a tic started in his cheek. "And what are you planning on doing to him when you get him alone?"

His anger fed my own and when I spoke, it was in a low voice. "I need to talk to him, see what he wants."

Marco frowned. "It feels like he's getting off too easy. He tried to kidnap you, Catalina. You could've been hurt," he bit out.

I sighed. "It's the only move I have. Meeting him privately is too risky. He'd bring his guards, and since eight men weren't enough, I'm sure he'd double or triple it."

Fire raged in Marco's deep brown eyes, but I ignored it.

"I also can't bring along any of my men to support me while we meet. He likely wants access to my familia or to drag me back under his thumb. That's a risk I'm not willing to take," I said with more force than I meant to. But my familia could never know what I'd been through, that I was once weak and abused, or else they'd never look at me the same.

My gaze flickered to Marco's. There was a time when I feared the same with him. I never wanted him to see me as less than or incapable. But after last night, I knew he wouldn't. I couldn't explain how or exactly what he'd done to convince me, but the feeling was there with absolute certainty.

Clearing my throat, I continued, "That means this has to happen at a PR event where there's security and I'm in the spotlight. He won't do anything there until the event is over, and he wouldn't be able to bring a large group with him. I'll have the upper hand this way, no matter what he tries."

Marco clenched his fist, his knuckles whitening, before he slowly relaxed with a sigh. "What time should I pick you up?"

I gave him a small smile. "The gala starts at 7 PM, but I'd like to get there a little early."

"Okay."

I squeezed my hands in my lap, gathering my courage. "Do you want anything?"

He furrowed his brow. "What do you mean?"

"You're doing me a favor by coming with me and you're not getting anything out of this. Do you want something in return? For helping me?"

"You're wrong," he said with a soft smile, but his voice almost sounded sad. "I'm getting a night out with you, by your side. That's more than enough for me."

A dozen questions came to my mind, because that didn't make sense to me. But I was starting to understand that when it came to Marco, there wasn't much that did.

The venue buzzed with chatter and laughter as Marco checked our items at the door while I glanced around looking for Simon.

"Is he here?" he asked.

"Not that I can see."

Marco nodded, then placed his hand on my back. The warmth of his palm felt like a brand on my skin, causing me to shiver.

"Are you cold?" he whispered in my ear.

"Not at all." I kept my voice level, refusing to look back at him. I knew if I did, that stupid, infuriating smirk would be on his face.

Marco guided me to our table and pulled out my chair before

taking his own. The tables filled around us and finally, I spotted Simon.

At 7 PM, Naya took the stage. She gave her introduction and the speech she'd prepared for why she'd created the non-profit and how needed and important it was in our society.

Then her eyes found mine, and she nodded. "With that, I'd like to present this award to Catalina Salazar. She's helped more women and children than she'll ever know, and without her donations and support, we wouldn't be where we are today."

An applause roared around me, but I ignored it as I stood and stepped to the stage. Helping people who had been in a similar situation as I had was the least I could do. And I had more than enough money to do it.

I didn't think I deserved anything. It was one of the few things Naya and I fought over. She constantly told me I deserved to be praised for my efforts and the incredible impact I'd made on other people's lives.

"Thank you," Naya whispered softly, kissing my cheeks as she gave me the award. She smiled, and the kindness that shone in her eyes made me choke up, because it was all a lie.

Naya looked at me like I was a saint. But would she still feel that way if she knew where this money came from? That it was built on the blood, deaths, and stolen innocence of so many men, women, and children?

It left a bad taste in my mouth. Standing at the podium, I felt like a fraud. But when Marco's eyes met mine, the rest of the room faded away.

His lips spread into a soft smile, and each clap of his hand was purposeful, out of sync with everyone else's, and it slowed my heartbeat. He inhaled and exhaled. My body heard his silent command and followed his breathing. Then he tipped his head in a nod and it was over.

The exchange lasted all of a few seconds, but in that time he'd managed to yet again save me from the monsters clawing their way to the surface.

I gave my practiced speech while Marco scanned the crowd. His gaze touched on every entrance and exit, every security guard, and the location of Simon and the men around his table.

He's doing this to protect me. If anything happens, he'll know exactly where we should go.

I'd done the same; the platform was the perfect vantage point and excuse. But knowing how much attention he paid to me and how he valued my safety filled me with a warmth that refused to leave, even after I'd finished my speech and sat back down beside him.

The band resumed, and after dinner we left for the more communal area. Marco stayed by my side as several people approached us, more interested in my status as a senator's daughter than the event itself. But I made sure to always steer the conversation back to the non-profit.

I grew tired of it all. It was exactly why I hated events like this, but I needed to stay just a little longer.

Marco's fingertips danced along my spine, drawing my gaze from the dining hall where I was waiting for Simon to exit. "You look absolutely bored out of your mind," he whispered into my ear.

"Is it really that noticeable?" I'd need to adjust the look on my face and my attitude if that was the case. Even though I was using this event for my advantage, I didn't want to ruin anything Naya had built.

"Not to anyone else but me," he said in a low voice.

I side-eyed him, and his mouth tipped up into a smirk.

"Would a glass of champagne help?"

"Yes, please."

He squeezed my waist, then walked off to grab our drinks.

Simon entered, laughing with one of the attendees.

Finally.

I approached him, slipping into my old role with ease. The smile on my face was warm, welcoming, and entirely fake.

We exchanged kisses on our cheeks, then he held my hands. "I was just telling these gentlemen how proud I am of you."

Bullshitting as usual, I see.

"Thank you, Father."

He waved to a man beside him. "This is—"

"My apologies." I bowed my head. "I'm being called over there, but we'll catch up later."

"Of course we will," he said, his smile never reaching his eyes.

I returned to where Marco had left me, only to find him speaking to two women. His back was to me, but I could see the women's faces. They were interested in him, and it bothered me far more than I could have ever expected.

Marco was an attractive, charming man. He was funny, intelligent, and he carried a type of charisma that oozed confidence. He could have anyone he wanted. And for the first time, I realized that while he'd been showering me with attention, he could turn it to someone else at the drop of a dime.

I didn't like that thought at *all*.

Shooting her wouldn't be enough. I wanted to gouge her eyes out with the knife attached to my thigh.

It wouldn't take long. I'd be on her in five seconds. and it wasn't the first time I'd removed an eye from its socket.

It left a bloody mess, but it would be so satisfying. Just karma for her coveting something that belonged to *me*.

But he wasn't mine. He wasn't my anything. What even were we? Allies? Friends? Confidants? Co-workers? Every word disgusted me, because it wasn't what I wanted. None of them were enough.

What I wanted was him, deeply, completely, in a way where he could never be removed from me. I wanted him injected into my veins, into my soul. I wanted his infuriating smiles, flirtation, voice, *touch* to only be for *me*.

Freedom used to be my only dream. It was the goal I fought for, the reason I'd powered through and survived. Then, it became my familia, their protection and my duty to them. But somewhere, hidden in the darkest part of my heart, where my deepest fantasy and truest desires laid, was Marco. He'd infiltrated that space, and I couldn't get him out if I tried.

One of the women laughed a little too loudly, trying to put her hand on Marco's arm, but he turned, dismissing her attempt entirely.

I couldn't have that happen.

Another woman could *not* touch him, *ever*.

I walked up to him, and his eyes softened when he saw me. His lips, which were in a frown before, slowly curved into a blinding smile for *me*.

He completely left the woman there, her mouth open at how quickly he'd forgotten her. Then he handed me my flute of champagne and wrapped his arm around my waist, settling his hand on my hip. Only then did he seem to relax, and I couldn't help but grin behind the glass.

When the women left, he sighed. "You came at the perfect time. That woman was persistent, and I was only putting up with her so she wouldn't cause a scene."

"Are you sure you weren't just desperate for attention?" I meant to say it in a joking manner, but it came out hard and cold.

He leaned in, his breath warm against my ear. "The only woman I want paying me any attention or by my side is *you*."

Goosebumps danced along my skin and I cleared my throat. "We'll be meeting Simon later."

"Good," he said, rubbing my waist.

"You can remove your hand now, you know."

"I do, but I won't."

I tilted my head. "Why not?"

"Because the same jealousy you had when I was talking to those women is the same way I've been jealous of every man who gets to lay eyes on you tonight."

I opened my mouth to say something, but the intensity in his eyes stopped me. He wasn't joking. He looked deadly serious, like he was barely holding himself back from slaughtering everyone in the room.

The gala wound down, and Marco and I began to make our exit. As we approached the doors, two of Simon's men stopped us.

"Your father is waiting for you," one of them said, his voice gruff and emotionless.

I exchanged a glance with Marco, who tightened his grip on my waist. Everything was going according to plan.

We followed the men, our footsteps echoing against the marble as we turned into one of the previously locked rooms.

Simon stood there, a smug smile plastered on his face.

He stepped forward, and to my complete surprise, he ignored me.

He extended his hand towards Marco. "Mr. Torrino, it's nice to see you again."

Marco's jaw clenched. Tension radiated off him, filling the air with malice.

He stared at Simon's outstretched hand like it was something rotten and diseased.

"Why aren't you offering your hand to Catalina?" Marco said, his voice low, dangerous.

Simon chuckled. "Come now, we both know who holds the power here, and it isn't her."

Marco's body tensed, fury coiled around him, like a snake ready to strike. But before he could do anything, a bubble of laughter escaped my lips.

It started as a giggle, quickly growing into full-blown laughter. The dumbfounded look on Simon's face only made me laugh harder.

When I finally sobered up, I shook my head. "Some things never change, do they?"

I smirked, meeting Simon's gaze. "So, you tried to kidnap me to what? Get Marco's attention, thinking he'd taken Fernando's place?"

Simon's face darkened, while Marco's arm around my waist tightened.

I shrugged one shoulder. "Sorry, *Dad*, but *I'm* the leader of the Salazar Familia now. And I hope you understand that whatever deals you had with my late husband—whom I killed, by the way, similar to how I killed your men—are null and void."

"What?" Simon shouted. His face turned beet red, only adding to my delight. "You will re-establish those deals immediately!"

I raised an eyebrow. "And why should I?"

"Because I have access to the ports," he snarled. "I can get material across them unnoticed."

My humor left me completely, the air in the room growing heavy, like I was trying to breathe in cement. "What *material*?" I whispered.

Simon twirled his hand in the air. "Anything from stolen art to illegal substances."

A chill ran down my spine. "Did you ever traffic people?"

He shrugged, as if it wasn't inhumane, and he had every right to do whatever he wanted without suffering a fraction of the consequences. "I wouldn't know. It wasn't my job to know. I provided the containers, and I got them out to sea. That's it. Now—"

"You never checked?" I yelled at him. I wanted to claw his face, shred his skin until there was nothing left so he could feel even a *hint* at what those that had been trafficked had.

Marco's voice was cold as ice. "No, he didn't give a shit. I'm sure he was paid for his *discretion*."

"Handsomely so," Simon confirmed with a smirk. "Which is why I want to continue the arrangement. I waited for over six months for my last payment, and you owe me money." His eyes flashed dangerously, then he brushed his blazer, as though this entire conversation was nothing but a blight on his day. "I want my 10% cut plus interest."

Rage coursed through my veins. My father gave Fernando access. He was how Fernando got whatever, *whoever* he wanted, in and out of this city without anyone's notice. He benefited and had been doing so for years, and he didn't care who he hurt along the way.

I knew he was a greedy bastard who would do anything to get what he wanted, but seeing it, witnessing his nonchalant attitude when he could have contributed to the agony and torture of dozens, maybe even hundreds of people, was a new realm of evil.

My voice dropped low. "You can take your 10% plus interest and shove it up your vile, disgusting ass."

"How dare you!" Simon roared.

He raised his hand to hit me. But before I could strike him first, Marco did.

He punched him. The sound of knuckles hitting bone sent a satisfying crunching sound through the room. Simon's men moved to intervene, but I whipped out my gun.

"If you take one step, you'll end up just like the rest of your dead friends."

They looked at each other and froze in place as Marco beat Simon to a pulp.

"Did you really think I was going to let you put hands on *my* woman?" he snarled. "You hurt, mistreated, and abused Catalina all her life. You should have treated her like she was your world, your entire universe, but you didn't!"

He kicked Simon in the ribs who curled into a ball, trying to protect himself. But it was no use as Marco continued to kick and stomp on his head.

"Every day, Catalina has to fight through the trauma you inflicted on her, and instead of giving a damn, you're trying to hurt her again. You're worse than a fucking rat."

Marco bent down, grabbing Simon's collar, holding his limp torso off the ground. "If I had it my way, I'd drown your ass in the East River," he growled. "The sole reason you're alive today is due to the grace of your beautiful daughter." He pointed at me, his eyes never leaving Simon's bloodied face. "And if you want to stay that way, you'll learn to pay *her* some respect."

Marco let him go and Simon fell back onto the floor, hard. "Because if you don't, I will hunt you down, and I will take great pride in killing you."

As Marco stepped back, his eyes met mine. The fury and rage that had consumed him moments ago was replaced by a gentleness that made my heart skip a beat.

I tilted my head towards the door. "Let's go home."

He nodded, and as we turned to leave, I glanced back at Simon's men. "I assume I don't need to tell you not to try anything, right, boys?"

They nodded nervously, but I kept my gun trained on them as we left.

The drive back to my house was silent. I kept replaying Marco's words over and over in my head. The way he beat Simon was so satisfying, so incredibly attractive, but I was worried about the repercussions.

Simon could afford to be sloppy because he had the power of the law and government on his side. He also liked to make friends in high places. And I didn't want any of that to come down on Marco's head.

Simon wouldn't leave Marco be after the way he had beaten him, especially in front of his own men. Pride was everything to my father, and Marco had just shown how little of a man he really was.

But knowing Simon was likely involved in the trafficking and had benefited from it meant that when I was living with him, I had too. And that made me sick to my stomach.

Marco parked in my driveway and turned to me. "I'm sorry," he said softly. "Not for beating him. He deserved that, but for losing my temper when you needed me."

I shook my head. "Come inside. Let's get you cleaned up."

Taking his bloody hand, I led him into my house and had him sit on a kitchen stool. Then I grabbed the first aid kit from the bathroom. Soaking a makeup remover pad in alcohol, I gently cleaned the blood splatter from his face.

Marco remained tense, silent as I worked.

When I finished, I moved to his hands, brushing my fingers

over the lingering dried blood. "You didn't have to do all of that," I murmured.

His eyes met mine, intense and unwavering. "I did. I wasn't going to let your father hurt or insult you, not *ever* again."

A small smile tugged at my lips. "You're constantly surprising me."

His brow furrowed. "How?"

"You beat the absolute shit out of my father for me," I breathed, gripping the towel so I didn't lose my nerve. "And you also seem a little too comfortable calling me yours. Your woman, your Catalina."

He said nothing, and his silence made my heart rate quicken, but I still had to know, had to ask. "Do you mean it? Calling me yours?"

Marco's gaze softened as he looked into my eyes. He brushed his thumb against my cheek. "Yes."

The single word sent warmth through me, flooding my entire body. My heart felt impossibly light. That one word made me feel wanted and cherished.

But then I remembered my father's response and the single, terrible truth within it. "Would you still want me to be yours knowing that it's possible my father helped traffic innocent women, and I benefited from his misdeeds?" I whispered, trying to keep my voice steady.

He brushed my cheek before grabbing my chin and lifting my head, forcing me to look at him. "There's never a moment where I wouldn't want you to be mine."

There was no hesitation, no doubt, and he looked so sure that I found myself sinking into this fantasy. One where I was worthy of him, where I could be with someone like him.

"Does that mean you're mine as well?"

A dazzling smile spread across his face. "I'd be honored to be yours, if you'd take me."

Yes! Please. I want you to be mine, more than you know.

But I didn't answer him. Instead, I focused on cleaning his hands, because in the end, that dream could never become reality.

Fourteen

Catalina

I took a deep breath, rising from my desk. My fingers hovered over the door of my office, but I couldn't open it and step out. The weight of what I was about to do pressed down on my shoulders, threatening to crush me.

My capos were waiting for me in the conference room, where I would tell them what had been going on, about the trafficking, my father's potential involvement, everything. But I was terrified of what their reaction would be.

I'd worked so hard to earn their trust and respect. To be tough, but fair. To show them I could protect them. That they could rely on me, regardless of what anyone else said. Yet, my own flesh and blood might have been the cause for their pain.

Why wouldn't they blame me? Resent me? Wouldn't this undo all the work I'd done?

For over five minutes I'd been trying to make it past my door and I just... couldn't. But I had to, for *them*.

Suddenly, I thought of Marco. Maybe if I just called him, and heard his voice, it would be enough to get me through this.

No.

I couldn't do that. I'd relied on him more than enough.

My hands shook, and I clenched my fists.

Calm down. You can do this on your own. You don't need anyone else. You never have.

The words were empty. The overwhelming shame, disgust, fear, and sorrow blended into something so dark I couldn't see past it. My despair threatened to consume me.

I was spiraling, falling deeper and deeper into a dark hole. Every time I tried to grab onto something, it disintegrated in my hands. I was scared, so, so scared of losing everything. Of failing everyone.

I fell to my knees, my throat tight, like I was choking on something. I wanted to scream, but I couldn't. I bit into my palm, hard. The pain flashed through my body as tears clouded my vision and I rocked back and forth on the floor until I could breathe again.

These attacks rarely happened. I was more sensitive to them whenever the weight of the world felt like it was too much.

I'd thought it was location based, but this was the first time it had happened in my office—a place I normally felt safe.

The attack drained me until I no longer cared about seeming weak. My pride had left, and without a second thought, I called Marco.

He answered immediately.

"Hi," I said, my voice barely above a whisper.

"What's wrong?"

I rested my head back against my door. "How did you know something was wrong?"

"I can hear it in your voice."

I bit my lip. "Are you busy?"

"Never for you. But before you tell me what's going on, take a deep breath." His tone was so warm and gentle that I followed him without meaning to.

"One more time," he commanded.

I took another deep breath, sighing as I exhaled, just like he did.

"Good girl."

His praise sent a zip of electricity down my spine.

"Now tell me what's wrong."

"I... I'm about to meet with my capos to tell them about the trafficking and my father." My chest was hot, itchy, and I started to scratch at my skin.

"Are you still feeling guilty about it?"

"How could I not? I hated my life and my father. But now, knowing that he may have made so much money sacrificing the lives of innocent people—people I'm now responsible for—all while proclaiming to the world how he's a good, just man, and putting together laws to give support to women and children sickens me."

"You're not your father, Lina." Marco's voice was patient, but firm.

"I know I'm not. But I benefited from what he did."

"How? Through clothes, jewelry, parties? Catalina, I watched that man almost hit you last night in *my* presence. I can only guess what he would have done if I hadn't been there, and what he's likely done before."

I fell silent, because even though he was right, I couldn't find the courage to admit it.

"You see yourself as someone who benefited from the gain of other people's suffering, and that's warring with your conscience. But you suffered too."

His words made me freeze. It felt like a light bulb was slowly warming in my mind, dim but beginning to grow. "But I didn't suffer as much—"

"Didn't you? Your father abused and tortured you, Catalina. Then he sold you off to the highest bidder, knowing full well how that man treated women," he bit out. "He didn't care about you or your livelihood, and it scares me to think of what might have happened to you if you hadn't killed Fernando. Even if I would have come to your rescue, it still would have taken time, and the damage would have been incredibly difficult to repair."

"Even after knowing everything, would you still have come to save me?"

"Of course I would have," he said without a moment of hesitation. "I told you that after I came back from Italy, and as I told you last night, you're mine. *No one* hurts, or even *dares* to touch anything that belongs to me. Especially *you*."

My heart thundered so hard I was scared it might leave me and run away with him. I bit my lip and shut my eyes, trying to get myself together. But I was so vulnerable right now, especially to Marco, that I was starting to believe his words.

Would it be so dangerous to? To acknowledge the pain and agony I'd gone through, and not judge it against someone else's? To think of and see myself better than I typically did? As someone worth saving and protecting?

"Much like I would have saved you and still will whenever you need me to, you're working to save your people. That's all you can do," he said in a warm, soft tone.

"It's not enough," I whispered.

"No, it isn't enough to fix everything, but it is more than enough from *you*. Instead of holding yourself accountable for a crime you didn't commit, focus on ways to take down your father and right his wrongs. You're a good person, Catalina."

I scoffed. "I'm definitely not."

"You are." His voice was firm, absolute. "In your heart—in the deepest parts of you—you want to make the lives of those around you better, and you're willing to sacrifice whatever you need to do so. *That's* what makes you a good person. It's something I find admirable and inspiring about you, and anyone worth a damn can see that in you, too."

I blushed. "Th-thank you."

It sounded like he was smiling when he spoke again, and I could picture it vividly. "You're welcome. Your men will understand. You just need to not put the blame of a situation you had no control of on yourself. And if they don't, I'll just kill them."

I rolled my eyes. "You can't just kill everyone that disagrees with me."

"I can and I will."

I shook my head and chuckled, despite everything.

"Do you feel better?"

"Yes, thank you, really."

"Anytime. I promise to always be there when you need me. Now, when are you planning on being back in the office?"

"Around three." I picked at the helm of my blouse, trying not to take his promise to heart.

"Okay. I'll see you soon with your favorite sushi."

I still felt his presence and strength within me when we hung up the phone. Marco's words grounded me, reminded me of who I was and what I was fighting for.

With a deep breath, I stood, straightened out my clothes, and reached for the doorknob, ready to face my capos. Whatever came next, I could handle it. I wasn't alone, at least for now.

I walked back into the office, an extra spring in my step, feeling lighter than I had in weeks. The meeting with my capos had gone better than I could have ever imagined. Instead of blame or resentment, I was met with understanding and support.

They had all but applauded me when they learned about everything I was doing to take care of their families and rectify Fernando's wrongs, and they promised to help in any way they could.

For the first time since I'd taken over, it felt like we were all on the same page, fighting on the same side. A small part of me dared to hope that maybe, just maybe, I could finally trust them.

The thought thrilled and terrified me, but I stuffed the fear away, because I needed this. We needed a win, and this felt like the start of one.

I decided to throw a dinner over the weekend for everyone to commemorate our familia's solidarity. I'd already alerted Olivia, who had immediately started the preparations in our event hall and was looking into potential catering companies.

As I entered my office, I saw an enormous bouquet of red roses sitting on my desk and frowned. Marco had bought me flowers a couple of days ago, and these didn't feel like him at all. I wasn't a fan of roses, and Marco knew that.

Moreover, these were extremely over the top. There must have been at least a hundred roses, maybe more. It felt more like a showpiece than anything thoughtful.

I plucked the card from the bouquet.

"Beautiful flowers for an even more beautiful woman. From Felipe Alvarez."

I huffed. Yet another mafia leader trying to charm me to gain whatever he wanted. It was insulting that they thought I'd spread my legs and serve myself and my familia up on a silver platter for the smallest bit of attention.

Fucking men. So many of them think they're a gift to the female race, when they're not even good enough to lick shit off the bottom of my Louboutins.

I thought about throwing the entire bouquet in the trash, then sighed. They were just flowers. As long as he didn't hide anything in them, it was technically fine to keep them. I'd bring them down to the lobby later and if anyone wanted to take them, they'd be more than welcome to.

After checking to make sure there wasn't a hidden camera or something else in the arrangement, I put them in water.

An hour later, Olivia called, informing me Marco had arrived with lunch. A smile spread across my face the moment he entered the door. Even though I'd spoken with him only hours before, it wasn't the same as being around him.

Having him near me, sharing the same air, filled me with a sense of peace like nothing else. And no matter how many times it happened, it was a feeling I still couldn't get used to. But I was grateful for it, for him. I'd never admit it to him, but he made my day, no, my life, better.

I moved to take the bags and help him spread out our lunch, when he went completely still. In a split second, the joy on his face fell, replaced with complete and utter rage.

"Who sent you flowers?" he growled.

I didn't have to tell him, and if it were anyone else, I wouldn't have. A part of me even wanted to tease him. Seeing him so jealous made me feel important, cherished, even.

But I couldn't. Marco mattered too much to me, and I didn't enjoy seeing him so angry. In fact it made me want to beat the fuck out of Felipe, because he hadn't just insulted me, he'd upset someone I deeply cared for.

I approached Marco slowly taking the bags from his hands. "It was Felipe Alvarez."

His gaze snapped to me, and I could feel the weight of it—his anger, his care, his *possession*. "What did he want?" he bit out.

"Nothing remotely important. I threw away the card and only kept the flowers in case one of my employees wanted to take them home. But if you want, I'll happily toss them in the dumpster right now or even burn them to a crisp."

Marco's eyes widened. "What?"

"We can get rid of them," I said again, more firmly this time.

He still seemed a bit stunned, but I gently guided him to sit down while I took the sushi out of the bags.

He studied me for a while. "Why?"

I met his gaze. "Because I don't want you miserable, and the only person allowed to push your buttons or give you a hard time is me."

He opened his mouth to respond, but before he could, my phone rang. "Yes?"

"There's a man with six additional men heading up to this floor," Olivia said. "They were allowed past security as per our protocol, but the reception area informed me the man was extremely hostile."

My body tensed immediately, readying for a fight. "I'll be right out."

"Should I call security?"

"Have them on standby."

I got up, and Marco shot to his feet. "What's going on?"

I opened the drawer, grabbed my gun, then put on my holster, using my blazer to hide it before checking to ensure my knife was still fastened to my thigh. "Apparently, I have an uninvited guest who wants to have a dick measuring contest, even though my non-existent cock would be bigger than anything he could ever pull out of his pants."

Marco smothered a laugh as he checked his own gun and followed me out. We arrived in the reception area just as the men exited my elevator. It was Felipe.

"What the fuck do you think you're doing in my office?" I shouted.

Felipe's gaze switched from Olivia to me, then to Marco. "You!" He pointed, his hand shaking in barely controlled rage.

I glanced at Marco. "Do you know him?"

"Not well enough for him to be this pissed off at me."

Regardless of the situation, I couldn't help but grin at Marco's response.

Felipe stomped toward us. "You're always sniffing around like the piece of trash you are!"

Marco stepped forward, but I held out a hand in front of his chest, glaring at him. His eyes narrowed back at me as we communicated without words.

This was my property, my grounds, and Felipe was disrespecting me and my familia. Marco wasn't a part of that, so he couldn't interfere without undermining my authority. I could take care of it.

He huffed. The look on his face told me he'd stand down for now. But if anything happened, he would protect me regardless of my wishes or the consequences.

I nodded in thanks before turning my full attention and rage on Felipe. "I'm not going to ask you again, Felipe. Either state your business here or get the fuck off of my property."

"My business," he bit out, "is you. And I don't like stray dogs messing around with my possessions."

I pulled back. "Excuse me?"

"You heard me." He slammed a piece of paper down on Olivia's desk. "Read it."

"No." The demand irked me, and I bared my teeth at him, taking a step forward, invading his space. "You see, I don't give a fuck what's on that piece of paper. What I do give a fuck about is that you marched into my building, disrespected my employees, my assistant, my company, and me, not once, but multiple times. I don't know what power you think you have here and I don't care what delusional bullshit is on this piece of paper to make you think that your words hold any weight, but let me show you what you can do with it." I grabbed the piece of paper, and my eyes flashed at the words, "Marriage License."

Felipe had already signed it, and for some idiotic reason, he clearly assumed I would as well.

"You." *Rip.* "Can." *Rip.* "Shove it." *Rip.* "Up." *Rip.* "Your." *Rip.* "Ass." I threw the pieces of paper at him, and they rained down on the floor.

"You fucking bitch!" He moved to draw out his gun, but I was faster.

Grabbing the knife from under my skirt, I shoved it between his legs, pressing the tip hard at his balls. His eyes went wide, and he raised his hands in surrender.

"Do you know what they call me in The Underground, Felipe?"

"Señora de la Muerte," he choked out.

I pressed the blade harder, cutting through his pants and boxers with ease. "And do you know why?"

He gulped and shook his head.

"Because, every time someone tries to kill me, I send them to Death themselves." I smirked. "You see, I enjoy taking retribution on those who want to harm me. And this knife, right here." I jabbed it harder, digging the tip into his balls. "I like to keep it nice and sharp, for rude, disrespectful men, who are lower than the goddamn sewage that runs through this city."

I swirled the knife along his ball sac and his eyes grew bigger. I nearly laughed at the terror on his face. With a flick of my wrist, I'd castrate him, and the vision of him bleeding out on my office rug was *incredibly* appealing.

Guns were drawn around us and I felt Marco move behind me, but my focus had to stay on Felipe. I couldn't let him grab his weapon. As long as that didn't happen, his men wouldn't be able to shoot me without hitting Felipe first.

"Now, explain to me like your life is on the line—because it is —why did you think you have some claim to me or any of the things I own?"

"B-because your father—"

I chuckled. "Ah, I see what happened here. Did daddy dearest strike a deal with you and tell you that if you marched in here, you could drag me out?"

He grimaced but didn't say anything.

"Felipe, sweet, naïve, Felipe. Let me clear this up for you." I sliced the skin of his scrotum, not deep enough to remove his balls entirely but enough to make blood coat my knife as it trickled down his pants and legs.

Felipe shook, biting his lip to keep from howling in pain, and it only made my smile grow.

"Once upon a time, my father did have some control over my life. But those days have long ended. If—and this would never happen—but if there was ever a chance of us making a deal, you would be dealing with *me* directly. Not my father. Not any man, *me*." I sneered. "Now, tell your men to lower their weapons and get the fuck out of my office before I castrate you and slit the rest of their throats."

"Lower your weapons!"

His men did so, and I removed my knife, stepping away from him.

Felipe stepped back, refusing to turn around and face his men until he was a good distance away from me. "You're going to regret this. You and your familia. I'll drag you all to the ground," he hissed.

I smirked and watched them leave, waving goodbye with my knife coated in his blood. When the elevator doors closed, I turned to Olivia. "Call security and have them followed out. Make sure they leave the building and parking lot. Then I want you to head home for the day. Make sure someone from security goes with you, too."

"But—"

I gave her a warm smile. "It's okay. It's already late in the day. Plus, Marco's here." I turned to look at him, but his eyes were fixated ahead, like he was waiting for Felipe to come back. He was still, like a predator, his malice tangible in the air.

"Marco?"

He finally looked at me, and his gaze was strange, almost haunted yet full of rage. The threat was over. Everything was taken care of for now, so why was he still on guard?

I tilted my head back to my office. "Why don't we head back?"

He followed me silently. But the minute I closed the door, he was on me. He took my hand, checking my fingers, my palm, inspecting my skin.

"Marco?"

"Are you hurt?" he bit out in a low growl.

"I'm fine—"

"Where are you hurt?" He brushed my wrist, gently tilting in every direction.

"Marco?"

But he wasn't listening. He just kept repeating, "Are you hurt?

Where are you hurt?" like a broken record. He continued to check my body, his large, warm hands so gentle as they followed up my arm, then he switched to my other hand and did the same. Nothing I said got through to him, and I didn't understand why.

"Marco," I tried again, "I'm fine. I'm not hurt. No one hurt me. See—"

"Where are you hurt?"

I sighed and gently put my hand on his chest, trying once more. "Marco?"

His hands stilled, but he refused to meet my gaze. He stood hunched over, his head bowed.

I touched his cheek, gently stroking his skin, and tried to make him face me. He shuddered so hard I felt it through my palm. "Marco, I'm right here. I'm okay."

When his eyes met mine, he stared at me like I was an alien, or a ghost.

"Talk to me," I whispered as softly as I could. "Tell me what's going on."

"This is the second time, Catalina." He was breathless, like he was barely holding himself together. "This is the second time that you've had to fight on your own, and I couldn't help you."

"That's always going to happen, Marco. It can't be any other way. I've accepted that, and I can take care of whatever I have to," I said softly.

"I don't want you to! I want to take care of you!"

I pulled back as much as I could, but he refused to let my shoulders go.

He trembled around me, crowding me against the door. "I've never felt so weak, Catalina. I've never felt like less of a man than I do right now because you wouldn't let me help you. That because of our roles, I truly couldn't. And you didn't need me." His body shook harder. "The only thing I could do was make sure his men wouldn't try to shoot you, and you even had that covered."

I cupped his cheek with my other hand. "Marco, I wouldn't want you to help me, not because I don't trust you. I do." It was the first time I'd said those words out loud, and as scary as it was to admit, it was the truth. "I wouldn't want you to help me because it would endanger you and your familia. If some asshole wants to march in here and act like he owns the place, I can put him down, but I can't drag you into that fight. You don't deserve that and neither does your familia."

"I don't care."

"Marco—"

"I don't care, Catalina! I don't care what hell I have to walk through for you. I'll gladly take it, anything, everything. I'd rake myself over hot coals if it would make your life easier. If I had no feet, I would crawl to you. If my hands were tied, I'd break or chew them off for you. There is nothing I wouldn't do for *you*." He grabbed my arms, his gaze piercing. "If I had to give up everything I own, every possession, every bit of the power and money I've earned, I would for you, without a second thought."

I didn't know what to say or do. It felt like my heart was being shattered and rebuilt by his hands. All because I believed him.

It was in his eyes. He was *terrified* for me, something no one had ever been.

He'd been the same when Simon sent his men after me. And maybe I was a fool, maybe I was wrong or stupid and he was just too good at lying. But when he pulled me into his arms, I didn't pull away.

He asked for nothing, said nothing. Just held me.

At first, I didn't know what to do with my hands, but he squeezed me tighter until it felt too odd to leave them at my side.

Touching anyone was new for me, especially a man, but

touching Marco was a strangely beautiful feeling. Something where once I let myself do so—even if it was a small pat on the arm, or an accidental brush of our fingers—I craved more.

Gone was the strong, confident man I knew. In his place was someone who cared about my safety, *my* life. How could I resist him when he was like this?

I wrapped my arms around him, holding him just as tight. Instantly, the tremors in his body stopped, as if my touch was all he needed.

Gently, tentatively, I followed his lead. When he stroked my back, I stroked his. When he squeezed me, I squeezed him. I absorbed his warmth, let it soak into me, and buried my head in his neck where his scent was the strongest.

I inhaled and sighed, a type of wholeness wrapping itself around me, one I'd never felt before, and I wondered if it was the same for him.

I had no idea how long we stayed that way. But a thought kept circling in my head. Why did this feel so comfortable and yet so heartbreaking?

The longer our embrace lasted, the more I wanted to cry until the realization donned on me. No one had ever held me. Not once in my life. Not even as a child.

When I scratched my knee or bumped into a table, I was yelled at for not being careful enough. The love and attention that I should have gotten would go to that inanimate object. The smudge of my accident would be polished, the remnants of my mess cleaned. But me? I was forgotten. *Always* forgotten.

And yet this man—someone who I still didn't understand why he gave a damn about me—was holding me so tightly, like he couldn't bear the thought of ever letting me go.

I tried to hold back my tears, but they spilled from me, embarrassment flooding through me at crying in front of Marco.

But he simply took my face into his hands, and gently wiped them away. "Why are you crying, mi pequeña reina viciosa?"

I laughed. "What kind of nickname is that?"

"It's one of the many I have for you. You are my vicious little queen, after all. Now tell me why you're crying. Your tears make my heart ache."

His voice was so full of genuine sincerity that I couldn't take it. I looked away, but he drew my gaze back. "Tell me, Catalina."

"I've... I've never been held," I whispered.

"What?"

"N-no one has ever held me. This is the first time."

Marco's eyes widened. "Not even as a child?"

I shook my head. It scared me to look at him, to think he'd see me as something else—less than or weak—for my admission.

But he put on his best smile, even though it didn't quite replace the vengeance in his gaze. "I am always here for you. I'll hold you whenever, for as long as I can." He stroked my cheek. "I won't lie and tell you it's only for you. It's not. Having you in my arms feels like heaven, and I'm a greedy, selfish man when it comes to you. But I'm here, do you understand? Whatever you need, whatever you missed, I'll take care of it all, and I'd be honored to take all your firsts."

I bit my lip. How could I tell him that I wanted him to? That I wanted this, to stay in his arms? To feel like I had a safe place that I could come back to when the world was too heavy for my shoulders? How could I tell him he had become that for me, when caring for him left me both terrified and hopeful?

I wanted him. I wanted it all, even if it hurt, but I couldn't move. I couldn't take the next step. I couldn't let the words slip from my tongue.

But he waited. He didn't push. Didn't pressure me, just waited to make sure I understood.

Finally, I swallowed the large ball of emotions in my throat and forced myself to nod.

His smile was radiant, his dimples on full display, perfectly encased by his beard.

My heart fluttered. I couldn't stand it so I just hugged him, because at least then I could bury my head back in his neck, inhale his scent, and be with him even while I hid away.

But as my tears dried, and the minutes passed, something else took over. I knew the moment he felt it too.

His hands began to knead my tight muscles.

I squirmed from his touch, it felt so good. He chuckled. It was a deep, low, breathy sound against my ear and neck. The sensation made me shiver, sent goosebumps over my arms.

"Are you cold?" The mischievous tone in his voice told me he knew I wasn't.

"No," I whispered, burrowing more into his warmth.

I should have pulled away. This was heading into dangerous territory that I wasn't ready for—that I might never be ready for—but I stayed in his arms. And as he kept rubbing and massaging my back, eventually a soft moan slipped from my lips. I had my head buried as much as I could, but he heard it and shivered at the sound.

"You're so tense, my vicious little queen. How you even lift an arm with your muscles like this, I don't know."

I hummed, not in agreement, but because I couldn't put together a single thought when he was touching me.

He chuckled.

"Shut up," I said, but my voice was too breathless for my words to have any bite to them.

"Does it feel good?" He massaged my shoulders, kneading into a tender spot I didn't even know I had, bringing warmth while releasing the tension, without pressing too hard.

It was so perfect I moaned again and nodded.

"Use your words, my vicious little queen," he said in a deep, husky voice.

He touched the spot again, and I hissed. "Yes."

"Good girl."

I hummed again at his praise. It made me want to agree to anything, give him complete freedom to do whatever he wanted, no matter how sinful. I was under his spell now and there was no going back.

I couldn't seem to remember why I'd been so hesitant with him, why I hadn't just fallen at his feet and begged him to touch me before. But now that I knew how it felt, I would. I'd beg and plead anytime. Anyplace.

"Do you want me to stop?" he whispered.

"No!" I said too quickly, too loudly.

He chuckled again, his hands sliding down, lower, lower, until he brushed the top of my ass before he slid them back up, slipping his hands in my hair, sliding it to my opposite shoulder, leaving my neck bare to him. He growled in my ear, "Beg me for it."

I bit my lip, smothering the moan that almost escaped me from his words. "Please."

He groaned, and it sounded so good I wanted to hear it again.

"Please, don't stop," I whispered in his ear.

Another throaty moan of pleasure, then he grabbed my ass, pulling me tight against him. When he shifted, I felt his erection. He was so big, I gasped.

What would it look like to see it, see him, completely naked? How would it feel to have him inside me? Thrusting hard and fast? Taking me? *Owning* me?

If he told me to bend over right now, I'd ask him how far. I wanted to see him in ecstasy, hear his moans and grunts. Wanted to feel his come inside me, on top of me. I was so fucking wet, my pussy throbbing, and all he'd done was massage my back.

It wasn't fair that he was so controlled when I wasn't. But I didn't know what to do. If I rubbed him in the same way he was massaging me, would he sound like this? Would this be enough to affect him, when I knew he was far more experienced than me?

I sighed, and he shivered. Realizing I was right against his neck, I exhaled, blowing along his skin, and he shuddered.

His reaction delighted me.

I gently kissed his skin. At first he was still, barely breathing. I kissed him again, and again, following the path from his collarbone to his neck. I reached a little spot between his ear and neck, and he moaned for me. My heart felt light, elated, nearly danced out of my chest at the rough sound.

His fingers slipped to my shoulder, gathering the strap of my shirt and bra, sliding them down.

"Marco, what are you—"

"You wanted to play, so let's play." He kissed my shoulder, and at first all I felt was a slight tingle. Then he continued kissing my skin, and when he got halfway between the end of my shoulder and my neck, he bit me and a moan ripped out of my throat.

He licked the area gently, soothing the pain, and if he didn't have such a firm grasp on my ass, my knees would have buckled from the pleasure.

I'd never felt anything like it. Didn't even know I *could* feel like this.

He licked higher, then blew, drying his saliva on my skin, as if he longed to leave his brand on me, but once he got to my neck, he changed.

He kissed, licked, sucked, bit. Shifted from one to another, and all I could do was cling to him.

I buried my hand in his hair and tilted my head, giving him all the access he wanted.

It felt so good. So good to be touched, lavished. To feel such delicious pleasure.

Each moan made him bolder. His bites grew harder, as did the way he sucked my skin. Then he kneaded my ass.

He licked my neck, then smacked my ass, gripping it hard. I gasped at the dual sensation. He caressed my ass, then did it again, alternating between pain and pleasure.

Picking me up, he pinned me against the door. He slid his thigh in between my legs, pulled my hips, made me drag myself along it.

"Marco..." I whimpered.

He growled, dragging my hips more until *I* was rolling them myself. I leaned my head back against the glass door, my eyes closed, moans filling the room. Every time I said his name, he groaned as if he was reaching the same state of nirvana I was.

He cupped my face, his eyes dark, predatory, *hungry.* Filled with the most beautiful desire. And it was all for me. His gaze went to my lips, and I knew he wanted to kiss me and I *wanted* him to.

I'd never been kissed. That was the one thing I'd kept for me, the one thing I wanted to give someone I cared for, and I wanted to give that to him. But my inexperience made me worry, and he must have seen that fear in my eyes because he stopped immediately.

"N-no—"

"Shh," he stroked my cheek, "I want to make it clear that I'm not sorry for this. Kissing your skin, feeling your body against mine. Bringing you pleasure is a dream come true. But I shouldn't have rushed you."

"Y-you didn't, I just—" I tried to take a deep breath but I

couldn't. I was so scared he'd be disappointed in me, that he wouldn't want me if there was something I was simply not good at or didn't know. And I didn't know how to admit that to him or if I even could.

"It's okay." He grabbed my chin, forcing my eyes to his. "Hey, it's okay. I told you, I'm right here. I'm not going anywhere." He slipped his knee from between my thighs and held me, but I felt terrible and stupid for breaking apart a moment that I was so desperate for.

I clung to him and with each soft stroke of his hand against my spine, I started to settle.

"Can you tell me what happened now?"

I nodded, but I was still too embarrassed to face him, so I whispered my truth into his ear, bracing myself for his judgment. Because I was a twenty-one-year-old woman who was more comfortable killing someone than being intimate because violence was all I'd ever known. "I... I've never been kissed before."

"You haven't?" There was shock and something that sounded almost like devilish glee in his tone.

"Yes. I don't know how to be intimate with someone, except to lie there. I don't know what to do. I... I'm sorry."

He stiffened. It was quick, gone so fast that if I didn't have my arms wrapped around him, I would have thought I'd imagined it.

He pulled back and took my face in his hands. "There's absolutely nothing for you to be sorry about. It actually makes me so happy to hear that."

"It does?"

"Yes. I told you, I want all your firsts. I wasn't joking when I said I'm a selfish and greedy bastard when it comes to you, Catalina. I'll take anything you offer me, and then I'll demand even more until everything you are is *mine*."

I shivered at how possessive he was. It was so dirty, so seductive, and I wanted him badly. But I knew whatever had almost happened between us was over, and that hurt.

He leaned down, cupping the back of my neck. "I want you to understand the only reason I'm not kissing you right now is because I want to do this right. I want to teach you how fantastic all of this can be between us. I want to know everything that you crave. Every desire and fantasy you've ever thought of and never told anyone, and I want to show you all of mine, too." He took a deep breath. "But if I touch you right now, that'll go out of the window. I'm barely holding onto my control. And you could make a saint give up his resolve and fall to the deepest levels of hell with a smile."

I beamed as a zip of pleasure went through me, knowing that he felt the same needy, crazed desperation for our next touch as I did. And while I was happy to at least know it would happen in the future, I couldn't fully mask my disappointment that it wouldn't happen now.

But as always, Marco saw me. He kissed my palm, and the tender gesture filled the space where I still felt less than.

We fixed our clothing, and as I smoothed my hair, he gently tucked it behind my ear.

Without meaning to, I blurted, "Would you like to go home with me?"

Flames flickered in his eyes, dancing there, like I was the oxygen he needed. Then he closed his eyes and tilted his head back. His Adam's Apple bobbed, his neck corded, and he looked like he was fighting the hardest battle of his life.

"Marco?"

"Resolve of a saint, Catalina, resolve of a saint," he grumbled, and I realized the innuendo of my question.

I hiccupped a laugh, smothering it with my hand, and he peered down at me.

"And then you wonder why I call you my vicious little queen when you make me fight like this every day."

FIFTEEN

CATALINA

Marco opened my car door, and I slid inside, then he handed me the leftover food from our lunch.

"I'll follow you home."

I peered up at him and tilted my head. "You don't have to do that."

He grinned and bent over my car door. "I don't do anything I don't want to, Catalina. And I'm always looking for an excuse to spend more time with you."

Heat flushed from my chest to my cheeks. I reached for my seatbelt, but Marco pulled it out of my hands. "What are you—"

Slowly, he leaned over me, reached across my body, and buckled me into my car. Then—as if it was a completely normal reaction instead of something that made the blood rush through my veins faster—he pulled away.

"I've got to make sure my vicious little queen makes it home safe."

I was speechless.

He smirked. "Don't forget to start the car." Then he gently closed my door.

I sat there for a moment, completely frozen, before I finally pressed the start button. The air came on and I folded over the car seat, resting my head on it. "He's going to be the death of me."

By the time I settled, he was waiting for me, and we started the drive home.

He didn't need to follow me. But I liked being able to glance in the rear-view mirror and see his brown eyes staring back at me.

Maybe I liked it a little *too* much.

There was a spark of electricity every time our gazes met, and between that and the memory of his lips on my skin, I had to clench my legs together. But with each look, my desire grew until I became frustrated with myself.

I thought I was strong. I thought I could conquer anything, do anything I put my mind to. Yet, admitting I didn't know how to be intimate, how to please him—even though I wanted to— made me feel weak.

It wasn't normal, but nothing about this was. Nothing in my life had prepared me for this, and there was nowhere I could turn to get more information.

Sure, there was porn, but that was a fantasy. There wasn't anything I could practice on unless I did so with Marco. And while the thought sent another surge of heat down to my core, I wanted... I wanted to be good for him.

I wanted to make him feel *good* the same way he'd made me feel in my office. I wanted things to be perfect between us. I didn't want him to be disappointed with me.

But underneath all of that, there was something else, something deeper, darker. *I don't want to lose him.*

Marco saw through the mask I wore for everyone, through the walls I'd built, the distance I maintained, but he hadn't seen this version of me. The me who was scared of doing something wrong, of everything being my fault... of letting people down all the time.

I knew he liked me. But he didn't know that inside, I was broken.

I had moments where I'd get so wrapped up in my fears and past abuse that it spilled over. I'd erupt, shatter into pieces, and always had to pick them up by myself. I was damaged goods, and there was no fixing me.

There was no relying on someone to hold my hand and tell me it was all okay. I had too many people I had to be there for. I needed to be an impenetrable dam that could protect my familia from the dark waters of The Underground.

I couldn't show anyone who I was in the deepest parts of myself. Couldn't admit I didn't have all the answers, that some days I was barely holding it together. That I wanted so much to protect everyone while wishing, *begging*, someone would be there to protect me, too.

Marco may have felt that he couldn't have done anything to help me when Felipe showed up at my office, but that wasn't true. Knowing he was there gave me courage. Not being alone felt... good, like a dream come true.

But my courage was fleeting. At least, it was when it came to him. Because I still didn't know what he wanted.

I knew he wanted to fuck me, and some of the sweet words he'd whispered to me were his true feelings, but to what extent?

My subconscious said I was scared to trust him, because I was scared to trust myself. And that was true.

I'd been hurt so many times by those that should have loved me, and I didn't want to be hurt again. And if Marco left tomorrow, I would never be the same.

I would never let another man touch me, get close to me, integrate into *any* part of my life. My heart would forever be behind a cage. That was how much he meant to me.

If I took a chance and wasn't enough for Marco, I'd be devastated. My pride would be destroyed. And somehow, that was what I needed.

I couldn't keep going like this. At least if I tried now, opened up, let myself be vulnerable and he couldn't handle me, it would hurt less now than it would later.

I craved his presence, attention, time, affection, care, and devotion, but for right now, I could survive without him. I'd find a way. My familia could be my sole purpose again and that would be enough.

But if this continued? I'd reach a point where a life without him wouldn't be worth living. And every day I spent near him made me realize how dangerously close I was to that future.

I parked my car in the garage while Marco pulled in behind me. He helped me grab our leftovers and followed me into my house, then made his way to the kitchen to put everything away. Watching him do so, as though he'd been here multiple times and knew his way around, strengthened my resolve.

Marco walked back to the garage, then turned before he left. "I won't be able to see you for the next couple of days, but I'll be at the party."

I squeezed the doorknob as a burst of pain racked through me.

He's not leaving for good, it's okay. If he said he'll be back, he will.

"Is everything okay?"

He leaned against the door frame, which was far more attractive than it should have been. "Yes, just some *pests* I need to take care of, and I want to make sure it isn't tied to you."

He said the word like a curse, and I bit my lip. I wanted to ask who he was going after and what happened, but I truly didn't have any right to. A dark, heavy, nasty feeling settled in my gut.

This must have been how he felt when he couldn't get involved earlier.

"You don't have to protect me."

"I know, but I want to, always." He slid one finger under my chin, tilting my head up to his. "Now, aren't you going to tell me you'll miss me?"

I shifted my eyes from his penetrating gaze. Normally, I'd say no, that he was delusional for even asking. But I didn't want that to be our last interaction. Not after today. I wanted him to know the truth, just this once. "I will."

His eyes widened, and he drew back, his surprise making me smile. It felt like I'd found my balance again.

Slowly, his lips spread into a grin. "Don't worry, I'll text and call you so much it'll feel like I never left."

Good. "So you'll annoy me to no end, hmm?"

"Well, I can't have my queen thinking I forgot about her." He twirled the ends of my hair around his finger, then sighed. "I'll see you soon, Lina."

He turned to leave, and I almost let him go, my courage and fear in a fierce battle. But watching him walk away gave me the strength I needed to try. "Marco?"

He turned back at the sound of my voice, and I grabbed him by the collar of his shirt, stood on my tiptoes, pulled him down to me, and kissed him.

He didn't move, didn't blink, and when I realized what I'd done, I slammed the door in his face.

Marco

I jammed my foot between her door and its frame at the last minute. Catalina tried to push the door closed again, but I refused to budge.

She opened the door, confused, then looked down at my foot. Slowly, her eyes traveled back up my face and she shrank back.

I moved forward.

She stepped back.

Forward.

Back.

"Marco."

I stalked into her house and slammed the door shut behind me.

Our dance continued until she was pressed against a wall with nowhere to go. I braced my hand above her head, leaned down, and tilted her chin up. Her eyes were wide with a mixture of fear and desire.

"Did you really think I was going to let you get away after you kissed me?" I growled.

"I—"

I gripped her chin harder. "Let me tell you what's going to happen, Catalina. I'm going to kiss you. I'm going to be gentle with you, teach you what a kiss between us feels like. And then, when you've learned, I'm going to devour that sweet little mouth of yours like the starving man you've reduced me to."

She gulped, then, in the sweetest surrender, her eyes drifted closed. She *trusted* me, and it was the most beautiful gift she'd ever given me—until I kissed her.

Her lips were soft, perfect. The way her mouth felt against mine was a type of divinity I didn't deserve.

I struggled not to get lost in her, to take her how I wanted to.

But when I felt her gently, tentatively, move her lips against my own, it renewed my strength.

I pulled away and her eyes were half-lidded. I cupped her cheek and kissed her again and again.

I barely pressed my lips to hers, focusing on guiding her. She was killing me, but I'd happily sacrifice my life to something this glorious.

But I *needed* more, *wanted* more, and when she gripped my shirt, and her soft breaths grew faster, I knew she did too.

I traced her face with my hands, the only touch I allowed myself to have.

My body ached for her. My soul yearned for her, but I needed her to know that this wasn't just for today. Whether or not she meant it, this would be for the rest of our lives.

But then, she whispered, "Please."

The word went straight to my dick, and every noble thought I had went out the window.

I crushed my lips to hers and she gasped. I gave her a single second to breathe before I took her lips again.

Lifting her against the wall, I pinned her with my body, drinking her in.

I devoured her, nibbled her lips, bit, sucked, and she whimpered, crossing her legs behind my hips. I gathered her hair in my hand, fisting it at the back of her head, and her delectable moan made my cock throb.

Tilting my head, I deepened the kiss, pouring all of my want, my ache, my *desperation* for her into it. Her fingers went into my hair, nails biting into my scalp and neck, and I loved the pain. I hissed, and she made a soft noise of pleasure at the sound.

I kissed her again and again, slipped my tongue into her mouth and she was surprised, but she let me. I explored her, rubbed, teased, licked, and sucked her tongue all while she filled my ears with her delicious moans.

I kissed her until her lips were sensitive and swollen and even then I didn't want to stop. I wanted to rip her shirt off. Wanted her nipples in my mouth while I rammed my cock into her. I was damn near ready to come just from the thought of it.

This woman had me wrapped around her finger and she didn't even know it. I would fall to my knees at a single word, offer my life if it would bring a smile to her face. And that was exactly why I reined myself in.

I forced myself to stop, even as she whimpered, clinging to me, pressing her nails into my back, grinding her hips against my own. I softly, *regrettably*, broke the kiss.

I couldn't fuck her and leave, and I had to take care of Felipe Alvarez. He'd try to get revenge on Catalina the moment he could, instead of taking it out on her father, all because she bested him, had him *literally* by the balls.

I could protect her outside of her office or her familia's territory. But I had to act independently of her, because if I didn't, she'd try to take care of everything herself again. And I refused to let that happen.

I stared into her eyes, ran my fingers over her cheek, and whispered, "There's nothing I wouldn't do for you."

Her eyes softened, but not with joy. Instead, something close to heartache filled her eyes. "Why? What do you want from me, Marco?"

I knew what she was asking. Why did I form an alliance with her? What was the favor I'd ask for later? Why had I spent so much time with her?

But was she finally ready to hear the answer?

"I tell you every day, Catalina." I rubbed my thumb over her lips, mesmerized by them, by *her*. "Every single day. But you never listen."

Gently, she kissed my thumb, and I had to bite back a groan.

"And what if I was ready to listen now?"

Then you'd make me the happiest man alive.

I caressed the side of her neck. "After the party, save some time for me, and I'll tell you. I'll make sure that you know exactly what I want from you, without a shadow of a doubt. Can you do that for me?"

"Yes," she whispered.

I kissed her forehead and pulled myself away, because if I didn't, we wouldn't leave her house for weeks and there wouldn't be a single surface in her home I hadn't fucked her on.

Sixteen

Catalina

It had been three days. That was it, and yet I missed Marco so much I physically *ached*.

He'd been true to his word, had called, texted, or emailed me multiple times a day. He made sure I never skipped a meal, even sent me snacks and desserts he knew or thought I would like.

But none of it was enough.

I missed seeing him. I missed his dimples when he smiled, his scent, the hints of his tattoos at his collar and wrists that I was always so curious about. I missed his presence, the sound of his footsteps and breathing when we worked quietly in my office. The way he brought life to a room. And now that I knew what his lips tasted like, how his hands felt on my body, I missed that, too.

After he left, I wasn't sure how I'd feel—if there would be regret or if I'd feel ashamed and foolish. But I didn't.

Every time my mind spiraled, the memory of his lips, the brush of his tongue against mine, the sound of his soft groans, and firmness of his body came rushing back to me, leaving me wanting more.

I couldn't wait to see him. I *needed* to see him, and hopefully soon I would.

The party was in full swing, the room filled with laughter, music, and the clinking of glasses. It was everything I had ever wanted—a *real* family that I felt like I belonged in—but somehow, I still felt empty.

Until Marco walked in.

Dressed in a black button-down shirt and black pants, he looked like sin. His hair was perfectly messy, as if he'd raked his hands through it several times.

Our eyes locked, and when he smiled at me, I once again felt whole.

Several men followed him in, I assumed from his familia, but my eyes never left Marco's. When I took a deep breath, the air felt cleaner, fresher, like it had been tainted since the last day I saw him.

Marco ignored everyone as he approached me, and with each step, my heart beat faster. The surrounding people fell away. No one dared to enter his path, and when he was finally standing close enough to touch, he took my hand and brought it to his lips.

His devilish smirk grew into a full grin. "I've missed you, my vicious little queen," he whispered, bringing my hand to his cheek, nuzzling it, sending warmth through my body.

"I've missed you too, my devil."

He raised an eyebrow, and I giggled.

"It turns out your nickname matches you perfectly."

He chuckled, spinning me into his arms, swaying with me in time to the music. "How so?"

I wrapped my arms around him, intertwining my fingers at the back of his neck. "You show up everywhere you shouldn't. You're entirely too smooth, and you're constantly trying to tempt and seduce me."

He leaned down, the timber of his voice low and deep. "Is it working?"

"A little too well," I murmured.

Marco laughed and spun me out, then pulled me back in. "Well, let me try a little more." He ran his hand down my back, holding me possessively at my hip. "I missed you so much. It felt like I couldn't breathe without you next to me." His eyes burned as they met mine. "You look so beautiful, and I'm jealous of everyone who got to see you before me."

I laughed. "Everyone?"

"Yes, man, women, child, anything and anyone." He squeezed my back. "But at least I'm the only one who gets to have you in their arms right now, and for that I'm tremendously honored."

Heat rose to my cheeks, and I blushed, biting my bottom lip.

He groaned. "I'm dying to kiss you, and I swear I'm trying to be respectful, but if you keep looking at me like that, I won't be able to."

"Like what?"

"Like you want me to."

A shiver ran up my spine. I opened my mouth to respond, but then a loud popping noise started outside.

Gunshots.

I broke out of Marco's arms, my heart racing, adrenaline surging through my veins. My phone rang, and I answered it immediately.

"Doña, they're shooting at us!" Another round of shots went off in the background. It sounded like he was in a war zone. "Thirteen SUVs are approaching the event, heavily armed. We can't get them all!"

"Just hold out as long as you can. We're coming!"

I quickly rounded up my capos and Olivia. Marco called over

his men, and I slid back into my façade, using it to hide the rage boiling in my blood.

This event, something that was supposed to bring peace and happiness to everyone, would soon be ruined. My men were out there fighting for their lives, and I would kill each and every single person who dared to hurt any of the people in my familia. Then I'd hunt down the orchestrator and show them a hell they could have never imagined.

"Listen up. We have thirteen SUVs incoming. They're armed and currently shooting at the main entrance. We need to act fast and decisively. Olivia, take four men with you and usher everyone to the back door and into the parking lot. The rest of you, we hold the line here. Do your best to keep one of them alive so we can find out who's behind this."

My capos nodded and instructed their soldiers.

"Two of you, go with them," Marco said to his men.

We exchanged a glance and I nodded. I couldn't afford to stop him this time. He and his men were in just as much danger as my own, and every second counted.

I unholstered my gun as nine blacked-out, unregistered SUVs drove up to the entrance. We fired immediately.

We shot out one of the SUVs' tires, making it run into the signage at the building. I got one more, but the rest braked. Almost thirty men poured out of the cars, and all hell broke loose.

The sound of gunfire was deafening. I tried to shoot them around their car doors, but the damn things were bulletproof. Switching tactics, I aimed for their legs, taking out three of them. Marco got another four, while the rest of our men worked to annihilate the enemy in front of us.

Some men jumped back in their cars, planning to drive off. But one of Marco's men had a high-powered rifle. He shot out the windows and a minute later they were dead.

Movement from the side drew my eye. Someone had crawled close to the building. They were flat on their stomach, their shot lined up to the window—exactly where Marco was.

My heart froze. Gripping my gun tight, I fired. The man's head snapped back, his lifeless body crumbling to the ground. Shots rained around me, the air thick with the smell of gunpowder and the metallic tang of blood, but there was only one thought echoing in my mind. *Marco could have died.*

I stood there, my breath coming in short gasps, my hands steady despite the tremors running through my body. I fought to keep my composure, to hide the fear clawing at my soul.

I couldn't let it show. Not even when the shots stopped.

Later, I would feel. I'd let it all in, the anxiety, the panic, the absolute terror, but for now... My familia needed me.

I straightened my back, forcing myself to appear calm and in control, even as my heart pounded in my ears. I checked our surroundings for anyone we'd missed, anyone who could hurt Marco, and even though I couldn't find anyone, I stayed vigilant.

Slowly, we approached the vehicles, searching for any survivors or information we could get.

One of my capos flagged me down. The driver of one of the SUVs was unconscious, slumped over the steering wheel, but still alive.

My capo pulled the bastard back. "Fuck! These are Alvarez's men," he snarled.

I glared at the bodies decorating my event center lawn. *Felipe Alvarez has no idea what is coming for him.* But he would. I'd make sure he felt every ounce of my wrath before I choked the life out of him with my own two hands.

"Take him to interrogation. If you find anyone else, kill them on sight."

I squeezed my dress, using it to wipe away the dampness from my palms. My men at the entrance had stopped four of the vehicles, but we'd lost three men, and two were in the hospital.

I'd finally finished dealing with the police, all of them on my payroll. They would do the best they could, but the whole situation was a mess.

My movements would be restricted for the next couple of weeks, which meant I couldn't take my revenge on Felipe *yet,* but his days were numbered.

I glanced at Marco, and his eyes immediately met mine. He'd been assisting me, using his own contacts, but every time he came near me, I turned away.

I found someone else to talk to, another person to check on, anything to keep me away from him.

He'd noticed, but he never stopped staring at me. His eyes bore into the back of my skull, a constant reminder that he was there, waiting.

But now that everything was settled, I couldn't hide from him or the truth any longer.

Marco could have been hurt or killed all because he was beside me, and I would never accept the possibility of waking up to a world without him.

Felipe had torn open Pandora's box, and I'd have to retaliate for my familia. If Marco stayed by my side, he'd be dragged into a war that had nothing to do with him.

The only way to protect him was to break our contract, stop our alliance, and end whatever our relationship had been morphing into. After today, we'd be nothing more than strangers.

That reality broke my heart, and I would have begged and pleaded to whomever or *whatever* for another solution, but there wasn't one.

I'd sacrifice anything for Marco, do anything to keep him safe, no matter how much it destroyed me.

I approached him, and he crossed the distance between us.

"Can we talk?"

His expression grew grim and dark. "I've been waiting for us to."

I led us up to my office.

He shut the door behind us. "What's going on? You've been off since the shooting. Did something happen? Are you scared, hurt, or worried about your familia?" He reached for me, but I stepped away.

"Lina—"

"Stop. Just stop." The way he called for me, reached for me, made me want to run to him. I wanted to be in his arms, to feel his warmth—but I couldn't.

"Lina... why are you crying? Talk to me, please." His voice was soft, tender, filled with the same misery I felt.

He stepped closer, but I couldn't let him pull me in. I *couldn't.* "Please, just stop," I begged.

"How can I? Lina, if you don't want me to touch you, I won't, but I'm *not* leaving you like this."

I swung my head, panicked. A coldness seeped into my bones, and I wrapped my arms around myself to stave it away. "Yes, you are."

"Lina—"

"You're leaving! You have to!" My voice broke. "I... we can't do this anymore."

"What are you talking about?"

My hands fell to my sides, and my lips tilted into a small, sad smile as I gazed up at him. "You've won."

"What?" He looked so confused. His eyebrows were in a frown, arms out at his sides. It was so disarming I couldn't stop myself from telling him the truth.

"You've won," I repeated. "I tried. I tried so hard to keep you out. But you're here—" I tapped my arms "—under my skin, and you can't be."

"Catalina," he called, reaching for me again, but I stepped away.

"You're charming, charismatic, seductive. You're incredibly attractive, a smooth talker who could sell the Golden Gate Bridge without the deed." I laughed, but it came out bitter and hollow. "And I tried so hard not to feel anything for you, but I do. And I can't. I *can't*."

He opened his mouth to say something but I continued on.

"I have a duty—a responsibility to my familia and so do you— but as it stands right now, if I had to choose between them and you, I'd pick you, and I can't. I can't do that, not for the sake of the people who depend on me. Felipe wants a war," I breathed. "And if you stay around me, you and your familia will be at risk."

"I don't care," he hissed.

"But I do! I care! Earlier today, one of those men almost shot you, and my entire world flashed before my eyes. The thought of you lying dead in a pool of your own blood is all I can see when I look at you right now! That can't become a reality!" My shoulders dropped. "But if you continue to stay close to me, it will, not just for you, but for your familia—the people you're supposed to protect."

He stepped closer, holding out his hands. "Just take a deep breath, talk this out with me, and everything will be okay."

I nodded. "It will be when you *leave*. If I need something, I'll make another alliance with someone else, someone I can be objective towards. But this, all of this, your help, how you're always around me—it ends today. I'd rather live in a world where I never speak to you again, then one where you're no longer breathing."

He stepped forward, and this time, when I backed away from him, he didn't stop. I scrambled back, hitting a wall.

He stalked toward me.

"Stop," I said weakly.

He didn't listen, just kept coming, until he stood in front of me. Marco tried to grab me, but I slapped his hands away.

He pinned me against the wall, but I pushed at his chest. Grabbing my hands, he slammed them against the wall, holding my wrists above my head.

I struggled and yelled at him, but he didn't move, didn't even speak. I tried to stomp on his foot with my heel, but he pulled his leg back. I went to knee him in the balls, but he blocked my thigh. Readjusting his grip on my wrists, he grabbed my thigh from the back of my knee, pulling my leg around his waist, making my dress bunch up at my hip.

"Marco—"

"Be a good girl and keep your leg wrapped around me. Because if you try to get away from me again, I will hunt you down and tie you up." His voice was deep, dark, *dangerous.*

"Marco—"

"No. You said enough. Now it's time you listen."

Seventeen

Marco

Red filled my vision. Knowing that Catalina cared so much about me was all I'd ever wanted, but not like this. I didn't want to see her crying over the thought of losing me, and I never, *ever* wanted her to think about working with someone else.

"I tried to be patient," I growled.

Catalina's eyes widened. "What?"

"I tried to be patient with you. I tried to give you time, to not pressure you, or ask you for more than you were willing to give. Clearly, I must have gone wrong somewhere if you really thought I'd ever let you go."

She sank against the wall. "Marco, please."

"The only time I want to hear those words come out of your pretty mouth is when you're moaning them for me. Now, we're going to settle this, and then, I'm going to make you come three times before I fuck you so hard you won't be able to move without feeling me inside you."

She gasped, opening her beautiful mouth to say something,

but I grasped her chin, squeezing her jaw to silence her. I pushed against her, pinning her to the wall, and the softness of her body gave way to mine.

Her warmth and scent enveloped me, and every cell in my body came to life. I was lost to her, and when she squeezed her leg around my waist, pulling my hips harder against hers, I knew she felt the same.

I smirked grinding my cock against her. She tried to fight it, to hold back on the sound I wanted to hear from her, but she couldn't—she moaned.

"See? Your body knows exactly who you belong to, no matter how much you try to fight it." I slipped my hand to her throat, trailing my fingers over her neck, squeezing the sides hard, and she moaned once more.

"You see this? What's between us? It's never going to be over," I whispered huskily into her ear, and when she shivered, it filled me with delight.

"Marco—" she tried, but I flexed my hand around her neck.

"The moment I laid eyes on you, this was always going to be the outcome. It didn't matter how long it took, what you needed or wanted. Whatever it was, whatever you demanded of me, I'd give it to you immediately. Because having you is worth any cost."

She bit her lip, her gaze sliding away from mine. I dragged my fingers along her neck, and her pulse raced as her skin flushed from her chest up to her face.

"Do you want to know what I get out of this alliance, Catalina? What I want so badly?" I growled.

Her eyes darted back to mine, burning with a dark, insatiable hunger that made my cock twitch.

She looked so beautiful like this, desperate and greedy for me.

I slid my fingers lower, following the curve of her breasts, grazing her hard nipple, looping around to the other, before slipping down her stomach, over her hip to her thigh.

She bit her lip and whimpered, nodding quickly.

"You," I hissed. "You were going to give me three weeks. No interruptions, no hesitations, just us. So I could show you how good we are together."

I stroked her clit through her underwear. She jumped at the first caress, but I kept going. "See? Your body wants me. You're so wet for me that I can feel it through your panties, and I've barely touched you."

She tried to close her legs, but I slid my finger under the tiny scrap of lace and circled her clit.

"I—" she moaned. "Marco—"

"Yes, my vicious little queen? Tell me what you want."

"What about"—another sweet moan—"my familia?" She panted. "D-don't you want that too?"

I pinched her clit, and she gasped.

"I'm a businessman, Catalina. Combining our families would be good for both of us. But no, I don't want you for your familia. If you had no power, no money, nothing to your name, even if you were homeless, I'd still want *you*."

Her eyes glistened from unshed tears as she pursed her lips.

"There will never be anyone else for me. Nor for you. It was always meant to be and will always be me. And you can't tell me you want me, show me you care about me this much—which has been my only dream for over a year—then try to throw me away."

Her shoulders sank. "Marco, I just don't want you to get hurt. I want to protect you—"

"So your answer was to leave me, and get in an alliance with another man, knowing damn well he's going to screw you over every chance he gets? No."

"Marco—"

"No. If you tell me one more time that you'll side with any man that isn't me, I will kill every mafia leader in a thousand-mile radius and personally deliver their heads to you in a box."

I touched her again, using the pad of my thumb to rub and caress her clit.

Her breaths became short and fast. She shook, tightening her leg around my hip to keep me close, and it was the most glorious thing I'd ever seen. Every moan from her felt like a blessing.

I wanted her lost in pleasure for me, obeying my every command, giving me her complete submission. I yearned for it, not just from her body, but her mind. I never wanted her to ever say she'd leave me again. I needed her to know, to accept me *entirely*.

"Y-you can't..." she panted, couldn't even finish her sentence. Her moans were more frequent, higher in pitch. She was getting close.

"I can, and I will. I'll personally see it as a challenge." I pinched her clit once more. "You like when I'm violent, don't you?"

She moaned, grinding herself against my finger.

"You like knowing I'll fight for you, bleed for you. *Kill* for you. Don't you, my vicious little queen?"

She moaned louder, tried to close her eyes, to hide from me, but I slapped her pussy.

She gasped and jerked, pushing her breasts against my chest. I couldn't wait to see them, touch them, pull them into my mouth.

"Tell me you like it," I whispered against her lips. "Tell me you're mine."

"Yes." She struggled against my hold on her wrists, trying to pull her hands free, but I wouldn't let her. Not until she came for me.

"Say. The. Words. Catalina," I bit out, rubbing her faster.

"I do, f-fuck I do." She trembled.

I smirked. "And?" I matched the rhythm of her hips, keeping in sync with her. I tested the pressure on her clit, rubbing harder, until she backed her hips away just slightly, showing me what she liked, what was going to get her there, but I held back.

I wanted to hear the truth, to know that she couldn't deny me any longer.

"I'm yours. I'm yours, Marco! *I'm yours!*"

"Good girl," I growled. "That's my good girl." Applying the pressure she wanted, I watched her completely shatter apart.

She gasped. A mixture of pure, unfiltered pleasure and surprise lit her face. *She's never come before...*

I continued to rub her clit, as she bucked her hips against my hand.

She was confused, unfocused, but her body knew what it wanted. It was so beautiful to see her lost in her pleasure, completely at my mercy. The sounds of her whimpers and moans were music to my ears.

When she came for me again, she cried out my name. Arching her back, she pressed her breasts against my chest. Her eyes fell shut, and I gave her just a second to catch her breath before I crashed my lips to hers.

She moaned into the kiss, tugged at her hands, and I finally let them go.

If she tried to fight me now, I'd hunt her down. She was my prey and as her predator, I'd never let her get away from me.

But she didn't. She wrapped her arms around my shoulders like I was her lifeline, the only thing keeping her grounded on this earth. She held me as if she lived for me in the same way I did for her, breathed for me, just as I breathed for her.

The feeling of her acceptance was intoxicating. But the way her body melted into mine was a type of euphoria I simply couldn't define. Like a poor man who found a chest full of gold, or a homeless man that had tasted a five-star meal for the first time.

She'd told me I'd won. But it wasn't until this moment that I tasted victory. I'd found my purpose, fulfilled my soul's mission, every time she brushed her lips against mine.

Catalina tangled her hands in my hair, keeping me close. I tilted her head, kissing her deeper, more passionately, licking the seam of her lips and she opened for me.

I explored her, tasted her sweetness, rubbed and swirled my tongue against hers, before sucking it into my mouth.

She moaned as I gathered her dress in my hands, sliding my hands along her skin, lifting it above her ass. She stiffened, just slightly, and I pulled back to look down at her. Her eyes were half closed, but I could see the nervousness there.

"I remember," I whispered to her softly. "I remember what you said, that you didn't know how to do this. It's my job to teach you, and right now, I just want you to feel. Can you do that for me?"

She bit the inside of her lip, then slowly nodded.

I tipped her chin, forcing her to meet my gaze fully. "I need your words, your consent. Your acceptance of me gets me so fucking hard, Catalina. Won't you give that to me?"

"Yes," she whispered. "Yes," she said again, more firmly.

Fuck. If I wasn't careful, I'd have a permanent imprint of my zipper on my dick. Knowing her, she'd find it hilarious and laugh at me until I was balls deep inside her.

I stared into her eyes, raising her dress over her ass. "Don't look away from me. I want to make sure you're here, experiencing every second of this with me."

"Okay." She said the word so quietly I barely heard it. I knew I was pushing her, but she needed to know that this was where I wanted to be, wrapped in her arms, with her body against mine.

I didn't want any more barriers between us or unspoken

words. I refused to allow them, and shedding her clothes was like breaking through the last wall she could use to push me away.

I raised her dress slowly, wanting to kiss and lick every freckle, mole, or mark, but I knew if I looked away, even for a second, she would shy away from me. So I resisted the urge, no matter how hard it was. But I couldn't stop myself from touching her.

Sliding my palms up her soft skin to her sides, I followed each rib until I'd gotten to her chest. For a moment, neither of us moved. It was my silent request to continue. And when she lifted her arms, I had my answer.

The moment the dress hit the floor, I scanned her body. I memorized every bump, even the smallest scar. I took them all in, all the things that made up the woman I loved. They were a map of her, the owner of my heart, my perfect vicious little queen.

Gathering her into my arms, I kissed her again. Kissed her with every bit of my elation and the deepest depths of my desires. I poured everything that I had, that I *was*, into that kiss.

She moaned, my blood rejoicing at the sound. I slid my hands down her back to her bra and undid the closure. Then I slipped it off, groaning when her bare breasts pressed against my chest.

I closed my hand around her throat, choking her, her loud moan music to my ears.

I stroked her skin, then coasted down, plucking her hard nipple. She gasped, and I shared my air with her, kissing her once more while I kneaded her breast in my hand. She writhed against me, shifting her hips, and I smiled into our kiss.

"Tell me what you want, Catalina."

"Keep doing that."

"This?" I pinched her nipple, and she moaned.

"Yes, please."

I trailed kisses down her neck, biting the junction at her throat, and she tilted her head back and to the side, giving me as much access as I wanted. The softness of her skin on my lips and her moans were the sweetest form of sin.

"What else do you want, my vicious little queen?"

Catalina whimpered, and I grabbed her breast, squeezing it hard. She arched her back, pressing her hips against mine. "Make me come again... please."

I would have done it regardless, but my queen knew I liked it when she begged. I pulled her panties down and she kicked them and her heels off. Then I lifted her in my arms, and she wrapped her arms and legs around me.

Cupping her pussy, I rubbed her clit with my thumb. "I want you to be vocal with me, Catalina. I want to know every little thing you like, and you will tell me, with your mouth." I kissed down her chest to her breasts, her breathing growing more rushed. "With your moans." I licked her nipple, and she gasped. "And with your body." I rubbed her clit harder, faster, as she convulsed against me. "That's it, just like that. You're such a good girl. So perfect for me."

She shuddered at the praise and I took her nipple into my mouth, biting it. She jerked, moaning for me. Then I licked the bite, and she whimpered. Again and again I alternated, giving her both pain and pleasure. She responded to them so beautifully. She trusted me to appreciate and worship her body the way she deserved, and it was the greatest honor I'd ever received.

I moved to her other breast, sucking her nipple into my mouth. Her head fell back against the wall, her eyes half closed, mouth parted as I tore every moan I could from her. They were mine—all that she was, every breath, every inch, every heartbeat— and I reveled in them.

I slid my finger down to her core, slipping just the tip inside, testing her. I searched her face for any sense of discomfort, but found nothing but pure pleasure, so I pushed deeper, rubbing her clit while I sucked on her nipple, and her moans grew louder.

She fisted my hair, clung to my shoulders as I slid my finger out, then back in. Out. In. I fucked her with it. And when I slid another finger inside of her; she cried out.

Slowly, I moved them within her, thrusting all the way to my palm, preparing her to take my cock. "You're soaking my hand, Catalina. Does it feel that good to you?"

"Y-yes," she moaned.

Her body trembled, and I fucked her faster, harder with my fingers. I wanted her to come all over them. I wanted to taste it. I wouldn't survive the night without burying my face between her silky thighs.

I curled them, and knew exactly when I hit the right spot because her mouth formed a perfect "O".

She shattered.

She bucked against my hand as I fucked her with my fingers. I refused to stop. Her orgasm was so glorious I simply needed to see it again.

She clung to me, moaning my name over and over, and then she came so hard a guttural growl tore from within her.

Pride filled my chest.

Catalina pushed against me, panting. "N-no m-more—"

"You can say no to a lot of things, but orgasms aren't one of them, and I'm not done with giving them to you."

I pulled her back from the wall just slightly, grabbed her ass, and lifted her until her legs were spread over my shoulders.

She gasped. "W-what—"

I licked her pussy.

She shuddered so hard her tremors vibrated on my tongue. She tried to push my head away, but I pushed her back against the wall, keeping her pinned between it and my mouth. Then I licked her again.

She moaned, squirmed, and I kept licking her. I growled at her taste. She was decadent, divine, and I was enslaved to her. She was my mistress, my queen, my goddess, and I worshipped her.

I ate her like a starving man. Thrust my tongue inside her, felt her walls contract as more of her wetness gushed into my mouth. The moment she lost her shyness and ground against my face nearly made me come.

I gripped her ass, kneading her cheeks as I fucked her with my tongue. I rolled it, slid it in and out of her, until she cried out. Then I licked from her pussy to her clit and bit it.

She jerked her hips, and I bit her clit once more, before sucking it into my mouth. I swirled my tongue over it, and she went wild, fisting my hair, trying to bury my face into her pussy.

Shifting her weight to one of my arms, I used my other hand to slide two fingers into her cunt while I sucked and licked her.

She'd completely surrendered to her pleasure, but I wanted more. I wanted to own her every sense, every thought. I wanted her to be enraptured in this, in *me.*

I pulled my head back. "Cross your ankles behind my head."

"W-why?"

"Because I want you to use me."

"B-but you won't be able to b-breathe that way."

"If suffocation by your pussy is how I'm going to go, it'll be a damn good death."

"Marco!"

I kissed her thigh, and she shivered against me. "Just trust me, Lina."

She finally did as I asked, and I smirked.

"Good girl. Now, whatever you need, I want you to take it."

"What—"

I licked her pussy again, folded my tongue, and slid it in and out of her wildly. She arched her back, and now that her ankles were crossed behind my head, and I had her pinned against the wall, I could grab her breasts.

She cried out, bucking against my face as I squeezed her breasts, rolling her nipples between my fingers.

Her hips jerked as she moved faster, riding my tongue. The way she showed me what she liked, took control of her own pleasure, had pre-cum leaking from the tip of my cock. It was pure perfection.

I kept fucking her with my tongue, over and over, faster, as I used my nose to rub her clit. Her body trembled, legs shook, and then she came, screaming for me.

It was the sweetest sound, and I growled as her taste flooded my face, covering my lips. Her wetness leaked down her thighs and under my chin as she squirted for me, and I couldn't wait anymore.

I shifted her in my arms, and she adjusted immediately, wrapping her arms and legs around me as I lowered her, then kissed her.

She didn't care that I was covered in her come. If anything, it only seemed to drive her wilder.

I walked to her desk and shoved everything off. Something crashed and broke, but I didn't care. I'd buy her a new one.

I laid her back, and she watched me undo each button of my shirt, tearing it off my body. She looked me up and down from my chest, to my stomach, then back up and over each arm.

I unbuckled my pants. "See something you like?"

Her eyes were glazed over with lust. "Your tattoos. I always wondered what they looked like," she breathed. Catalina traced from the wing of the phoenix at the base of my throat, down its body over my arm.

I shuddered at her touch. "Just my tattoos?"

Her lips tilted up at the edge, slowly, seductively, and my cock swelled. "No, all of you."

I held still as her fingers danced over my skin. Her touch was so light, as if she were in awe of me. She slid her fingers back up, over my chest, to the claw of my wolf tattoo. Then she gently brushed the back of her hand on my nipple.

Electricity shot to my dick.

I wanted to tease her, to hear more of what she'd imagined, to know if she fantasized about me in the same way I did about her. But each stroke of her fingers and nails, as she slowly scratched down my chest to my stomach, was a heavenly type of torture. And when she reached my pants and looked up at me with a shy, yet desperate expression, I was done.

I pulled my zipper down, kicked off my shoes, then shoved my pants and boxers off. When I stood up, her eyes zeroed in on my cock and went wide. Her jaw dropped open, and I smirked.

"Marco," she panted.

"Yes, Catalina?" I grabbed her by her ankles, pulled her to the edge of the desk, then spread her legs.

"I don't think that's going to fit."

I chuckled, angling my hips with hers. "It will. You were made to be mine."

I paused, scanning her face, wanting to make sure she wasn't scared or uncomfortable. My Catalina had been through so much already, and I didn't want to accidentally trigger a horrible memory for her by not paying attention.

There was something there, mixed with the same nervousness I'd seen when I first tried to kiss her. It wasn't just inexperience or timidity, but a question she wasn't sure if she should ask.

That wouldn't work for me. I wanted her to bare her soul to me.

I kissed her palm and her eyes softened. "I'm right here. Whatever you need or want. Your every desire. You can say it to me. It's not going to drive me away."

She licked her lips. "I-I've only..." She swallowed hard. "Should we use a condom?"

My eyebrows nearly shot off my head. Then a slow smile spread across my face. I took her hands and pinned them over her head. "Are you telling me no one has ever come in that sweet pussy of yours, Catalina?"

She bit her lip, then shook her head. "No, and today was my first time..." her gaze flickered down, then slowly back up to my eyes, "coming. I've never done that before. Only with you."

Fuck!

I squeezed the head of my cock hard. I'd need every inch of patience for this.

"After I fuck you, tell me the name of the man who touched you. If he's still alive, he won't be by the time I'm done with him."

She whimpered softly, squirming under me.

"I love how much my brutality turns you on." I stroked my dick between her slit, coating it in her wetness. Then I slowly slid the tip inside.

We both gasped. The feeling of her pussy was incredible. She was so hot and wet. Nothing could be better than this. *Nothing.*

I waited for her to relax, grow used to the intrusion. Then I moved deeper, so achingly slow, giving her inch by inch. She tried to pull her hips back, but I grabbed onto them, holding her in place, pushing in while listening to her whimpering moans.

"There are only two reasons a man uses a condom," I bit out, then moaned loudly as I finally slid balls deep inside of her. "If his woman asks him for one, or if he's nothing more than a little boy with no intentions for the woman he's fucking."

Slowly, I pulled out. Catalina wiggled beneath me, trying to make me move faster, but I refused. She huffed, her eyes blazing into mine.

I smirked, leaned over her, and thrust back inside. "I'm a man, Catalina, and I have serious." *Thrust.* "Permanent." *Thrust.* "Intentions." *Thrust.* "For you." *Thrust.*

I grasped the desk with one hand while I rammed inside of her. "Do you want me to use a condom, Lina?"

She shook her head rapidly, wrapping her arms and legs around me as if she could burrow into my skin. "No... please... Just like this."

I grabbed onto her thigh, slamming inside of her again. "Regardless of the consequences?"

"Yes. *Yes!*"

My eyes nearly rolled back into my head.

Good. I'm dying to fucking breed you.

Her acknowledgment, her *permission* to come inside of her drove me crazy.

I fucked her. *Hard.*

Rammed into her over and over, driven by her moans, her body, the way her pussy gripped me like a sleeve. The way she whimpered every time I left it, and moaned every time I thrust back in. She welcomed me inside of her, *wanted* me inside of her.

She'd surrendered to me fully, and I was going to take everything that she was, everything she had to give and more until I'd claimed the deepest corners of her soul.

"Fuck, look at how good you take me," I growled.

I thrust into her so hard her heavy wooden desk scraped against the floor. I didn't care; I kept ramming into her like a madman. The desk moved. I stepped closer, rammed harder, and it moved again like a game, until it hit the wall.

Then I braced my hands around her head, laid down, and pounded inside of her. I kissed her neck, bit it, wanting to leave my mark. Wanted to brand her so everyone would know she was taken. That she was *mine*.

I wrapped my hand around her throat and she cried out, digging her nails into my skin so hard she might have drawn blood, and then she came. Her pussy spasmed around me. Her toes curled against my ass. She coated my cock in her wet come and I kept going.

I wanted to feel it one more time. Wanted to drive her to ecstasy the way she deserved.

I knelt on the desk, tilted her hips, and barreled into her. She cried out from each thrust, her eyes filling with tears, and I smiled as she called out my name.

"That's it, baby. Let everyone know who's fucking you." I ground into her, rubbing her clit, and she bucked beneath me.

The room filled with the scent of our sweat and sex. Our moans, the wet sound of me slipping in and out of her pussy, echoed around us. I sucked her nipple, worked my thumb over her clit and she grabbed my hair, twisting, gripping it in her fist as she silently pleaded for me not to stop.

I couldn't. I *wouldn't*.

I was so lost, so enraptured by her, that the entire world fell away until there was only us wrapped in our carnal pleasure. She came once more and I couldn't hold back anymore.

My balls tightened, my hips jerked, and I came. I pulled her hips hard against mine, pushed into her as deep as I could, filling her with every ounce of my come. Stream after stream left me as I shuddered above her.

I fell on my hands to keep my weight off of her, and she mewed in disappointment.

"I'm too heavy for you," I panted.

She shook her head and reached up for me.

How could I ever say no to her like this?

I kissed her stomach, in between her breasts, then laid on her, while she kissed my damp head.

My cock twitched inside her, shivers wracking my body as I tried to catch my breath. But when I did, I kissed her, softly.

I brushed her damp hair away from her forehead. Her eyes were half-closed, a small, relaxed smile playing on her lips, even while she was trying to catch her breath.

Her fingertips gently worked through my hair, over my neck, her legs trembling from her orgasm, but otherwise she was completely limp, glowing. *Sated*.

Tilting her chin, I kissed her again. There were so many things I wanted to tell her. That I loved her, that everything I was, was hers. I wanted to ask her to marry me, to chain her to me, and knew in this state, she might just say yes.

But that wasn't how I wanted her. She was agreeable now, but part of what I loved about her was the way she challenged me, kept me on my toes.

I loved her sarcasm, her humor, and when I got down on one knee, I wanted her to say yes when she was fully cognizant and felt the same way I did. When she no longer wanted to hide it. Couldn't if she even tried.

She was almost there. Her entire reasoning behind pushing me away told me that much, but it wasn't enough.

I wanted her to not be able to live without me, because that's how deeply I loved her. Nothing in this world would matter without her, and I'd throw it all away just for her to smile at me the way she was right now.

That was what I poured into our kiss. My affection. My loyalty, devotion, care. Love, desire, *everything*. I sucked her bottom lip, licked softly in her mouth, then kissed her once more tenderly before pulling back.

She stared into my eyes, searching for something, like she was trying to understand, but couldn't quite grasp what I was telling her.

I expected that. Catalina had never been loved by anyone, much less someone like me. It would take her time to realize she was worth that and so much more. And I'd give her as much time as she needed. But at least she knew there was something there, something more and that it was *real*.

I finally slipped out of her, lifted her up by her ass, and carried her to the couch as she kissed me softly. We didn't speak, simply shared gentle kisses and held one another.

It still felt like a dream, having her in my arms, feeling her body against mine.

She was so incredibly affectionate. For once, she didn't withhold any part of herself from me.

There was no doubt or suspicion. She was connected and present in this space with me. It felt as though she'd closed out the rest of the universe like I had, and I was honored to be allowed into her own world. To see and experience who she was when she felt free.

Minutes passed, and our kisses grew longer, deeper, more passionate. I gathered her hair in my fist and held onto her hip as she ground her wet pussy against my cock.

It was already hard, aching for her. It never took much from her, a single look, a breath, just the smallest bit of her attention.

She moaned as I rubbed the head against her clit, before sliding it down. She lifted her hips, and I aligned myself with her entrance. "That's it, baby, take my cock into its home."

She sunk down as I pushed up, thrusting into her. She groaned, and I pushed her down harder, impaling her on my cock.

Then she rode me. Bounced so beautifully on my dick.

I stared into her eyes, thrusting into her as she gasped and moaned, pressing her nails into my chest.

I took her ass in my hands, smacked and kneaded it, and she moaned louder, her head falling back.

"Eyes on me, Catalina. I want to make sure you know who's fucking you," I growled.

She looked at me, as if she could stare into my soul. "I know," she moaned. "It's you, Marco. Just you. *Only* you."

I lost my fucking mind.

Tilting her hips, I bent forward, and when she wrapped her arms around my neck, I pounded into her. Her head fell back again, and this time I didn't care.

I rammed into her hard, like the feral beast she'd reduced me to. Then I rubbed her clit. She shook, writhed, ground her hips against mine, then bucked and came crying out my name.

I turned, throwing her back onto the couch, slamming back into her. She cried out, bracing her hands against the arm of the couch to keep from hitting her head from the force of my thrusts.

I wrapped my hand around her throat, keeping her right where I wanted her while I fucked her hard and fast. I kept thrusting, her words repeating in my head.

"Just you. Only you."

Yes!

I was the only one who had ever seen her like this, the only one who *ever* would. If someone else tried, I'd kill them and fuck her while the blood oozed out of their body.

I ground against her, rubbing her clit. Then I stopped, shoved a pillow under her hips, put her legs on my shoulders, and started fucking her all over again.

"That's it, Catalina. Take it all."

She cried out my name, moaning it over and over, then her spine went straight and she came once more, dragging me with her. I roared out my release, pulled her hips tight around me, and pushed into her, making sure she got every drop.

Even after I came, I couldn't stop thrusting into her. But this time, it was deep and slow.

I leaned down as she tried to catch her breath and kissed her. I kissed each tear rolling down her face, swiped them away from her eyes. Trailed kisses along her jaw, her neck.

I breathed her in, basking in the scent of her mixed with me, the saltiness of her sweat, and how she shook in my arms.

"Was I too rough with you?"

"No, but why did you get like that?" she whispered, running her fingers over my spine.

I kissed her neck, slipping my fingers into her hair, rubbing her scalp. "Because I'm territorial and possessive over you. You can't tell me I'm the only man who can fuck you and not expect me to lose control."

"Oh."

I chuckled and kissed up to her ear. "You're mine, Catalina, and I will not share you with anyone."

She nuzzled my neck, panting softly against my skin as I moved within her. "I don't want you to. I just want to be yours."

My cock hardened immediately.

She gasped. "Marco—"

"Don't blame me. I told you I'm territorial and possessive."

The loud chime of her phone went off, breaking our serenity. And I watched as the weight of our world rushed back into her, and every relaxed muscle in her body tensed. Our moment of peace was gone.

I got off of her, and she turned, sitting up on the couch.

"Don't move."

I found her phone in her skirt and brought it to her.

She gave me a nod in thanks, then took the call while I went to the bathroom and cleaned up.

I wasn't mad at the intrusion. Eventually it would happen, but I was worried.

How would Catalina look at me now?

If she tried to put distance between us again, I wouldn't let her. Yes, we had other priorities, but she was my main one and I would not let her get away.

I grabbed a towel and dampened it, then went back to find her off the phone, trying to find her clothes while attempting to not let my come leak down her legs.

I sighed and picked her up.

"What are you doing?" she squealed.

"I told you not to move." I placed her down on the desk. "Spread your legs."

"Marco, we can't—"

"As tempting as it is to fuck you again, and it really is." I took her chin, forcing her to meet my eyes. "I know your familia needs you. But you also need aftercare. This is the least I can do for you before you leave. Now spread your legs before I take it as a challenge and clean you up with my tongue."

She flushed, finally doing as I'd ordered, looking away from me while I couldn't take my eyes off of her.

I slowly scanned her body, mapping out every place I'd bitten her, where I'd kissed and nibbled her skin. Her nipples were still hard, and I had to force myself not to suck them again.

My gaze slid lower, over her flat stomach, in between her luscious thighs. Her pussy was still wet, so filled with my cum that it had leaked and started to dry on her thighs and ass.

Fuck.

My cock twitched, and I took a deep breath. *Later.* It didn't matter when or where, I'd get back into her pussy if it killed me.

Gently, I touched the towel to her core. She jerked immediately, but I held her still by her hips and cleaned her. "Good girl."

She melted a little at the praise, then I gathered her clothes in one hand, and picked her up, bridal style.

She didn't object, even though she refused to look at me. I stepped into the bathroom and lowered her onto the toilet seat. "Don't rush to get up. Your body is going to need time. I know you have business to attend to, but you can't do so if you can't walk. I'm going to get dressed, and I'll bring you back some water and something to eat, okay?"

"Okay."

A zip of satisfaction flew through me, and I grinned. She was so agreeable and shy. *Utterly adorable.*

I cupped her head, drawing her eyes to me, then I kissed her.

She kissed me so sweetly, and when I pulled away, she whispered, "Thank you."

I kissed her forehead. "You're welcome."

When I returned with her sandwich and two bottles of water, she was fully dressed, with her back to the door. She shoved her phone into her purse, hard, and I sighed.

I placed the items on the table in front of her, then pulled her into my arms, and while her shoulders and spine relaxed slightly, she was far too tense for my liking.

I caressed her stomach. "I know you have a job to do, things which need to be handled, and people relying on you. I told you once before that I admired you and one of those reasons is your dedication." I kissed her shoulder. "You give one-hundred percent to anything you put your mind to, but I also know to do that you have to keep your guard up. It keeps you safe, and for that I'm thankful. You matter to me," I whispered.

"For the last two hours, you had your guard down, which is one of the greatest honors you could ever give me. And all that I ask is that when you're in my arms, you let it slip. Talk to me. Tell me what's on your mind, honestly, without fear or worry. Keep your guard up for everyone else, but please, let me in Catalina, I won't hurt you." I breathed. "I'd take my life before I ever hurt you."

Catalina shuddered, but said nothing.

I nuzzled her neck. "Do I need to get on my knees and beg?"

She leaned back against me, allowing me to be her strength. "I should have known you'd be more cocky after we had sex."

"Of course. Nothing strokes a man's ego more than pleasing his woman and hearing her call out his name."

She huffed.

"Talk to me," I whispered.

"I need to figure out what I'm going to do about Felipe. The office was one thing, but this? He just declared war."

I nodded. "Especially after I explicitly warned him what the consequences would be if he so much as *thought* your name."

She whirled around in my arms. "What the fuck were you thinking, Marco? This is exactly why—"

"I know. I know. You didn't want me involved. But I was going to be, regardless. He wasn't going to leave you alone. You know that as well as I do."

The fury left her eyes, and she closed them as if she was praying for patience.

"I'm in this. I was always going to be," I whispered, stroking her cheek.

She placed her hand over my heart, rubbing the spot with her thumb. "But that puts you in danger. I could have lost you, Marco."

"The man at the window?"

She nodded. "And that's not something I'd ever let slide. No one touches *you*."

Pride filled me at the possessive and protectiveness in her tone.

She sighed. "What did you threaten Felipe with?"

"The locations of every single one of his businesses, which I promised to blow up along with him."

She hummed, her expression turning thoughtful.

"You don't just want him to die, do you?"

When she met my gaze, her eyes were the hottest of flames, yet beautifully chilling. "No, I want him to suffer. I want to take everything from him like he tried to do to me. I want him, his mind, heart, spirit, *everything*, until all that he can do is beg for death."

I grinned. "Your wish is my command, my vicious little queen. Once your rage is satisfied, Felipe Alvarez will die at your feet."

I walked up the steps to Catalina's house. It was quiet, dark, and she was probably asleep, but I had promised her I'd see her again later tonight.

I'd meant to stop by earlier, but things had taken longer than I planned.

That's what happens when you go to war.

I had to make sure our weapon inventories were stocked and buildings were secure. Then I briefed my men on our next moves, and now, finally, I was ready to sleep with my woman.

She'd repaired her keypad, but that wouldn't stop me. I'd watched and stalked her for over a year. I knew the codes she used and how frequently she changed them.

I entered her home, then locked the door quietly behind me. Kicking off my shoes, I placed them neatly on her rack, then made my way to her bedroom.

As I opened the door, I listened to her breathing. I knew what she sounded like when she was asleep, how soft and slow her breathing was, and right now she was wide awake and ready to fight if needed.

"It's me."

She sighed. "I almost stabbed you."

"I wouldn't have minded as long as you didn't hit a vital organ. You're cute when you play doctor."

She mumbled something under her breath, and I chuckled.

I folded my blazer on her chair, then undressed. "I can feel you watching me, you know."

"I'm trying to figure out what you're doing."

"Isn't it obvious?" I slid into bed next to her, then put my arm around her waist. "It's called cuddling."

"Is it called cuddling when you break into someone's house?" Despite her words, she snuggled back into my body and I held her tighter.

"Absolutely," I whispered in her ear, before kissing her neck softly. "I missed you, and I did promise I'd see you later tonight."

"I wasn't exactly imagining this when you said that."

"Oh?" I bit her earlobe, trailing my hand down her stomach. "And what were you imagining?"

A chill ran through her body. "That it would be when I was awake."

I chuckled again, and when she wiggled her body against mine, I slid my arm under her head for her to use as a pillow. "There is always the morning."

She hummed. "We'll see."

We fell silent, and I basked in this, her presence, her closeness. The way her body felt against mine, how she smelled and breathed.

"Marco?" she called in a sleepy voice.

My lips curled into her neck. "Yes, my vicious little queen?"

"I'm happy you came."

"Me too, Lina, me too."

Eighteen

Catalina

The drive-by had been a wake-up call. Felipe's brazen attack meant I needed to take precautions with my familia.

I canceled any unnecessary events, worked from home, promoted Joseph as my right-hand man, and took my guards with me wherever I went.

It irritated the fuck out of me to play it safe, but I had to. I needed Felipe to believe I was scared, that he'd gotten to me. It was the only way he'd let his guard down while I put my plans in place—one of which was scheduled to come in any second now.

My email pinged just as my phone buzzed and I smirked. The group of hackers I'd hired off the dark web had finally come through with the data I needed.

Marco could find out a lot of information on his own, but this was something *I* needed to do. Felipe wasn't the only one I was hunting.

I'd left my father alone because of all the legalities that came with attacking him when he was a senator. I'd had bigger issues to resolve, and handling him needed tact. But now? He seemed to be at the center of everything, which meant he was involved in far more than I knew.

I was tired of operating blindly, and I knew Simon best. I knew his weaknesses, how and where he liked to hide, and if I could follow his money, I'd find all the answers I was looking for.

The encrypted file was a treasure trove. Everything from Simon and Felipe's schedules, travel plans, bank account information, the works.

I opened their banking information to see if there were any transactions between them. As far as I was aware, Felipe wasn't a known member of a mafia family outside of The Underground. He wasn't on any watchlists, so any transactions between the two wouldn't have been flagged.

My eyes widened, and I drew back into my chair. Simon had sent more than $200,000 to Felipe. Some was sent the day before Felipe had shown up at my office. But what was the rest for?

As I reviewed the information, several of the transactions began to look familiar. I'd seen similar, odd amounts withdrawn from Fernando's accounts.

I pulled up Fernando's accounts. The withdraws were for the same amounts, on the same days.

But I thought these were the transactions that coincided with human trafficking.

No.

Please no.

I opened the files I'd put together for my investigation into the trafficking and checked. Six of the transactions coincided with accounts of Fernando's kidnappings and were far too large to just be a shipping fee.

That was it.

That was the proof I needed.

My father, the man who had built his entire career off of protecting children and their families, had willingly taken part in human trafficking, and I held the evidence of his cut in my hands.

It hit me like a ton of bricks, and I collapsed into my chair. Beads of sweat covered my forehead, making my palms clammy, and I trembled.

This isn't enough.

Proof wouldn't do anything to my father. He could laugh it off, pay someone to doctor the transactions from his banking institutions. This wouldn't get him investigated by the FBI. And it wasn't even enough to blackmail him.

He could easily say he didn't know what or who was in the shipping containers, and I had nothing to prove the contrary.

While there were some checks deposited and large withdrawals, those were also around his campaign dates. Sorting through them would take forever.

Without evidence of a bribe, or some sort of inventory record, at most my father would lose the support of a couple of his followers and with a few months of apologetic behavior, it would all get swept under the rug. *Like it always does.*

I searched through the emails I'd gotten access to, his texts, everything, but there was nothing that jumped out at me. And even if I combed through each of them for days or *weeks*, I likely wouldn't find any damning evidence.

Simon Herrera had always been a monster, and a monster knew how to not get caught.

My head pounded. Spots danced behind my eyes, refusing to clear no matter how many times I blinked or shifted my gaze. But I couldn't stop. I needed more.

Maybe, just maybe, Felipe would have something I could use against my father.

I opened Felipe's text messages and my throat went dry.

The name was different, the number untraceable, but I knew from the text pattern it was my father. He had funded the drive-by.

Simon and Felipe planned to take my familia hostage at the event and force me to marry Felipe, giving him total control of my empire.

But when I read the rest of their messages, my body went cold. My bones froze and my blood turned to ice. *Simon paid Felipe to kill Marco.*

I began gasping for air. The shootout played through my mind, the man crawling toward the window.

I thought he'd simply been there to kill whoever he could. If he shot Marco, then me, it would cause complete pandemonium, giving Felipe's men the advantage.

But it never occurred to me his sole purpose was killing Marco.

If I hadn't seen him, if I'd missed, *Marco would be dead right now. My* Marco would be completely *gone.*

My heartbeat thundered in my ears as I stood slowly, my legs shaking. I didn't know where I was going, but I needed to leave. Needed to do something, get everything out, release it all. I needed to kill. I needed to kill Simon, Felipe, anyone. *Everyone* involved.

The doorbell rang, and I rushed toward it.

What if it was Marco?

I had to tell him. Had to warn him he had to go, run, *hide,* so he could *live.*

I pulled the door open to a courier.

"Catalina Salazar?"

I gripped the door frame, trying to stop the way my body trembled. "Y-yes?"

"This is for you. Sign here."

I squeezed the frame harder. "What is it?"

"We're not allowed to open packages, ma'am." He tried to hand it to me, but I backed away.

It could be anything. Hadn't I sent packages like this to bosses before with the leftover remains of their men?

It had been three hours since I'd heard from Marco. He was going into a meeting and promised to call me right after.

What if that's him? What if they've gotten to him already?

I locked my knees to keep from falling to the ground.

"Open it."

"I'm not allowed to do that, ma'am—"

"Open it!"

He jumped at my shout, rolled his eyes, then sighed and opened the box.

In it were two red boxes, each wrapped with their own sparkling white bow.

"See—"

"Those too."

"Ma'am—"

"Those. Too," I bit out.

He sighed again and mumbled, "Crazy broad," under his breath. Then he opened the boxes.

In one was a long gown, while the other held a diamond necklace. They may have been beautiful, but that beauty was empty.

My father used to dress me, give me jewelry, just to parade me around. He enjoyed showing off his hold on me, allowing people a taste at what it would feel like to lead me around on a tight leash while they stomped the life out of me.

He made a mockery of me. He couldn't leave me alone, let me have a single piece of the freedom I craved, or let me live what was supposed to be *my* life.

No. He wanted control of every minute of every day, and the

moment he found it slipping, he decided to take the one thing, the one person who mattered to me.

"I don't care what you do with the packages, but I'm not accepting them," I said in a low voice.

"But ma'am—"

I slammed the door in his face and made it two steps before my legs gave out, then I slid down the nearest wall.

My heart pounded so hard my chest rattled with each beat. The world seemed both too close and too far, like a thousand eyes were staring at me, while I could do nothing but cower under their scrutiny.

Then my phone rang.

The sound seemed almost out of reach, but it kept ringing and ringing, until it finally pierced through the noise in my mind.

I accepted the call without looking at the ID.

"What's wrong, Lina? Did you really hate my gifts that much?"

Marco?

My heart skipped a beat. He was alive, safe, for *now*.

But then my panic came back in full force.

Every bit of fear I felt and care I had for him melded together. I choked in a breath, trying to keep quiet so he couldn't hear how afraid I was.

"Lina? What's wrong?"

"What's wrong? What's wrong?" I shouted. Words poured out of me, a mixture of fury and rage that wasn't even meant for him, but I gave it to him, regardless. "What's wrong is that you think I'm some sort of whore you can run around and dress up however you want."

Stop. Stop, it isn't his fault.

But another voice, something deeper, stronger, *sharper,* was louder. *Push him away to keep him safe or else his death will be on your hands.*

"Lina, I didn't mean—"

I choked back a sob and forced myself to bite out. "No. Don't call me again. Don't come near me. I don't want to see you. I don't want to be *with* you."

Lies, all of it was *lies*.

Tears rolled down my face, and I covered my mouth, bit my tongue to stop myself from taking it all back. From apologizing, explaining, *begging* for his forgiveness.

It's better this way. It's better. He'll be okay.

But it hurts. It hurts so much to hurt him.

It hurts. It hurts. It hurts.

But I'm doing this for him.

I'm doing this for him!

"You know I'm not going to let that happen," Marco growled.

"If I find you on my doorstep, Marco Torrino, I'll shoot you myself."

I hung up and threw the phone away, and then I screamed. I screamed out my pain, my fury, my *ache*. I squeezed my ears and screamed over and over again.

My legs jerked from under me and I fell to the side, kicking at nothing, wishing I could hit someone, hurt them in the same way I'd just hurt him. And the same way I just destroyed myself.

But it was too much, and no matter what I did, I couldn't release it. Dots appeared in my vision again. Pain like I'd never experienced exploded in my skull, and the whole world went black.

When I opened my eyes again, it took me a second to remember where I was. This wasn't the first time I'd blacked out when the pressure got to be too much, but it was the first time I'd felt so numb, like the life had been sucked out of me.

I slowly stood, leaning on the wall to make it to my bathroom. Once I washed my face and felt more balanced, I set forth with making a plan.

I needed to pack a bag and leave because Marco would come after me.

The thought of him showing up at my door thrilled me, filled my heart with joy, but I shut the emotion down quickly.

That couldn't happen.

If he caught me, he wouldn't let me go, and he *had* to.

My phone kept ringing—it was Marco. I hovered over the accept button, just for a second, but then shook my head and put it on airplane mode.

I was only unconscious for ten minutes, and it would take Marco an hour to get here if he left his office immediately after our call. That meant I had fifty minutes, likely closer to thirty if he was speeding.

I dashed to my room, grabbed my go bag hidden in a secret compartment in the back of my closet, and checked the contents. Cash, two guns, knives, clothes, a toothbrush, an emergency medical kit, snack bars, some bottles of water, and a duplicate copy of all of my identification.

I changed my clothes, popped the trunk and tossed everything inside.

It was ironic to me I first ran from a mafia man to save my life, and now I was running from one to save Marco's.

Hopefully one day, I can stop.

I wiped the few tears that clouded my vision, then opened the garage door and backed out.

A black SUV pulled in behind me, blocking me, and the man that got out set my blood on fire and chills up my spine—Marco.

He shouldn't be here.

He couldn't *be here.*

But he was, and he was *pissed*.

Every cell in my body wanted to open the door and throw myself at him—but I fought against it.

My hands shook as I put the car in park and forced myself to pull my bag over my shoulder.

I couldn't face him, couldn't let him touch me. Because if I did, I'd crumble.

I got out of the car and ran to the garage door, but as I crossed in front of my car, he blocked my way.

His eyes were ablaze, the tendons in his neck so strained that with every beat of his heart, they pulsed.

I gulped.

He wouldn't listen to me now, wouldn't see reason, and I couldn't bear to fight him. So I did the only other thing I could do —run.

I dashed out of the garage. He almost caught me as I crossed the entrance, but I ducked out of his arms and took a hard right.

I was off, speeding through my side yard, into the back where the woods were. His steps were as thunderous as my heartbeat pounding in my ears, but I picked up the pace.

If I could just disappear into the woods, I'd get away. I had enough food to last me for a week and knew this area better than anyone.

The trees became denser a mile from my house, and from my estimate, I'd be there in five minutes. Marco was larger than I was, and as the trees and brush morphed together, he'd lose me.

But it was almost like he knew it too, and he ran *faster*.

Suddenly, I was in the air. He picked me up, grabbing me by my neck and waist.

I tried to pull myself back down, to flip him, but he didn't let me.

I tried to pry his arm from me, but he choked me, and even though it shouldn't have, it sent heat straight to my core.

My adrenaline quickly shifted, my body recognizing him instantly.

He ripped my go bag away from me, then tore my shirt in half.

I tried to knock his arm off of me, but he pulled me back hard against his body. His hand tightened around my neck, his other grabbing my breast, squeezing it hard. His aggression fed my pleasure, and I moaned.

"Interesting reaction for someone who told me not to come near her," he growled into my ear, his hand working on my breast, pulling my nipple.

I wiggled against him, his erection pressing between my ass cheeks.

"Marco—"

"I warned you what would happen if you tried to get away from me again," he hissed.

He unbuckled his belt and ripped it from the loops.

Is he going to fuck me here as punishment? Will he take me roughly to get back at me? Make it hurt, the same way I hurt him?

I'd let him. I wouldn't even try to fight him off.

With an odd array of skill, he looped his belt around one arm, spun me around to face him, then wrapped my other wrist in the belt, tying them together.

"What—"

The world turned upside down as he lifted me over his shoulder like a damn potato sack and carried me back to my house.

"Marco, put me down!"

He laughed, but it was dark, admonishing.

"Put me down!" I shouted again.

He spanked my ass. Hard.

I gasped. He'd smacked my ass before, but not like this. He didn't soothe me immediately, or check to see if it hurt, because he wanted it to. And it made me so fucking wet.

"Do you know how many of my calls you ignored?"

"I—"

His hand collided with my ass again. "Thirty. And I'm going to spank you for every single one of those missed calls. For every second you made me worry. For every second you actually thought you could get away from me."

"Marco—"

Spank. I clenched my thighs tight as another surge of heat went straight to my core.

"How many times do I need to tell you I would follow you to hell and back? How many times do I need to make you understand that you're not leaving me?"

"Marco, Felipe is trying to kill you!"

"And?"

My blood chilled. "What do you mean 'and?'"

"Do you think this is the first person who's tried to kill me, Catalina? There's been so many I've lost count!"

My eyes widened and my body grew slack. I never thought, never could have even imagined that was the life he'd lived.

I'd been so stupid.

My life had value because everyone thought I was weak. They thought they could easily take from me because I was a woman. They didn't view me as a threat. Believed they could simply force me to do whatever they wanted.

But Marco? He was respected. He was *strong*. No one could take anything from him, which meant his life had no value.

A beast that couldn't be controlled was put down. And that's how everyone saw Marco.

"But that doesn't mean you should continue to risk it. Marco, I don't want you hurt and if you stay with me—"

"I'd rather die than live a second without you. If you run away from me, that's the life you're sentencing me to." His voice dipped, growing darker, more dangerous. "Is that it? Do you hate me so much that you want me to die? Because I'll do it. Say the word and I'll take myself out right now for you with a smile on my face."

"No!" I roared. "No. No. No. No!" I slammed my fists into his back. "How could you say that? How could you ever ask me that?"

"Because that's what you did, Catalina! When you told me to leave you alone, when you tried to run away from me, that's what you almost made me do. You constantly say that you have a duty to your *familia*, but you keep forgetting that you have one to me too!"

"I-I do?"

"Yes." He put me down, and the blood rushed back to my head, making me dizzy. He steadied me, and when the room stopped spinning, I realized we were in my house.

Gently, with so much tenderness that my breath stopped for a moment, he took my chin and whispered, "You own my heart, my soul. My *life*. My future is in *your* hands. I will have no one else. There will never be anyone else for me but you. So take care of me, as my teammate, my partner. As the woman I plan to share the rest of my life with."

His eyes searched mine as if begging, *pleading* for me to understand.

"I don't care if you agree with it. I don't care if you want me or not. You have me. So *accept* me."

I couldn't speak, couldn't move. His declaration was too much, his gaze too steady, too sure. He really would take his life if it pleased me. He'd kill for me, die for me, live for me. He'd given everything that he was to *me*.

His hand slid into my hair, pulling at my scalp, forcing my head back. "Accept me." His lips brushed over mine.

I wanted to. *I already have.*

I didn't know when it happened, but I knew that was the answer deep in my heart. It rose to the surface, but my fear shoved it down.

Did he truly understand what he was getting here, what awaited him if he shared his life with me? He wasn't the one who needed acceptance. He was perfect in every way. But, me? *I'm no one, nothing. A flaw, a failure, entirely imperfect for him.*

"I'm broken," I whispered.

"No, you're not." He cupped my face. "You have the strongest spirit I've ever seen someone possess. The things you've done, the obstacles you've conquered, would be impossible for anyone else to do. They would have given up by now, but not you."

He chuckled, and each soft puff of air against my lips felt like the only breath I needed. "You're not broken; you don't need to be fixed. But even if you were, a single shard of you is worth more than all the money in this world. You are like the sun, Catalina. Beautiful, blinding, the reason I wake up every day. You are *priceless*. I will always want you. Always *choose* you, my vicious little queen."

The monsters in me quieted, my every negative thought and fear crumbling away. I could no longer say no. I wanted him too much, even if it was wrong, even if I was selfish.

He told me once he was a greedy bastard when it came to me, and I supposed I was the same.

I wouldn't, *couldn't* risk him, and if the greatest danger to his life was me leaving him, then I would stay by his side for as long as he'd have me.

I was his, just as much as he was mine. And while I didn't know how many days we'd have together, I was too tired to keep running from him.

I wanted it all, every smile, every laugh, every fight. I wanted a life with him.

I balled my hands in his shirt and kissed him. And if I believed in heaven, this would be it. The taste of his lips on mine, the way his body pressed into me. He was my sanctuary, the one and only person I'd ever give everything I was to.

When he broke the kiss, he was smiling, but there was something devious in his eyes. A plan there I wouldn't be able to escape from.

He ran his thumb across my lips, and I parted them immediately.

His eyes darkened. "Get on your knees, Catalina."

Without a second thought, my knees buckled. I gazed up at him and basked in the joy my obedience gave him.

He took hold of my chin. "I'm still going to punish you for what you did, Catalina. You were a very bad girl."

"I'm sorry," I whispered, sincerity flowing through every fiber of my being.

"I know." He leaned down, towering over me. "While you receive your punishment, you will only answer to me with 'yes sir' or 'no sir.' Do you understand?"

His tone was firm, and a part of me wanted to rebel against it. I wanted to know what would happen if I broke his rule. But not this time. Today he deserved my compliance, and I'd give it to him willingly. I'd give him whatever he wanted, always.

"Yes... sir."

"Good girl, now wait here."

He left, leaving me kneeling on the floor, with my breasts exposed, my shirt in tatters, and my pussy sopping wet for him.

When he came back, he had a black duffle bag. Curiosity burned within me, but one look from him warned me that if I uttered a word, I'd be in more trouble than I already was.

I gulped, wetting my parched throat as anticipation built within me.

He pulled out a long black rope and I raised my eyebrows, but he revealed nothing.

Kneeling in front of me, he retrieved a knife from his back pocket.

I stayed completely still, barely breathing.

Then, he slashed away my pants and underwear until I was entirely naked.

Standing once more, his gaze swept over me like a physical caress.

He circled me, stopping behind me, and draped the rope over my skin.

Slowly, he looped it around my neck, my chest, replacing the belt around my wrists with the rope. He continued until he reached my ankles and removed my shoes and socks. The rope was soft and thick, and combined with his hot, rough hands, it sent shivers across my body.

The rope's patterns made no sense to me. They crisscrossed all over, yet were slack around my wrists and ankles.

Marco circled me once more, surveying his work. Somehow, I felt more exposed to him like this, as if he unlocked something in my soul I wasn't aware of.

The hunger in his eyes made me feel like his prey, and I welcomed it. I was desperate for him.

He could do whatever he wished, take me however he wanted.

He unbuttoned his shirt slowly, as though we had all the time in the world.

I watched him, taking him in. With each button he released, he revealed more of his beautiful golden skin.

His tattoos swirled over his chest, circling each nipple, extending down his abs past his waist, stopping low at his hips. The full sleeves of tattoos he had ending at his wrists turned his glorious body into a full work of art.

Even though I'd seen them countless times, spent the past week with him breaking into my house, sleeping in my bed, fucking me in the morning, preparing and eating breakfast with me before he went off to whatever meeting he had for the day, I couldn't stop staring. I'd never grow tired of seeing him this way.

"Catalina," he called, and my eyes snapped to his. "I will take your anger, your sadness, every emotion you have. They're a part of you, and I want them all. However," his voice hardened, "the fact that you ever questioned what I think about you, that you said I'm treating you like a whore is not something I can accept."

"I—"

His eyes narrowed. "Thirty-one."

I bit my lip to keep from speaking.

"Since you clearly don't know the difference between me treating you like a whore or a queen, I'll show you." He sank to his knees and claimed my mouth forcefully.

His kiss was demanding, like a brand on my lips, and I craved it. I loved the harshness, his anger, his possessiveness. Loved how he bit my lip, invaded my mouth, took control of me.

When he pulled back, I was panting and ready for him.

He ran his thumb over my lip. "I wouldn't kiss a whore." He moved behind me. "Spread your legs."

I obeyed him immediately, finally understanding why he used the rope. The slack at my wrists and ankles allowed me to balance on all fours, but that was it. I couldn't crawl, stand, or move away from him.

He made a noise, an appreciative hum. "You look so beautiful like this. Tied up, naked, and dripping for me," he murmured. "I definitely wouldn't do this for a whore."

Pleasure fluttered through my body.

In a way, I didn't know the difference. I knew he wanted me, and I believed in his words, yet I also thought I was worthless.

At least a whore sold her body for a reason: to survive. There was honor in that. But me? My worth had always been determined by someone else and what they could gain.

I'd survived out of spite, but in the end, I believed I was insignificant, just like everyone else did—except Marco.

Suddenly, he spanked me.

I gasped, and he spanked me again.

"I will not let you escape your punishment physically or mentally, Catalina. Your every thought belongs to me, and I'm going to ensure you stay right here, focused." Spank. "Present." Spank. "Do you understand?"

He smacked my ass once more, and my body responded. "Y-yes, sir."

"Good. Now count them."

"Wha—"

Smack.

"O-one!"

Smack.

"T-two!"

Smack.

"Three."

"You're soaking wet, Catalina. Maybe I need to be rougher with you since you're enjoying your punishment so much," he purred, then spanked me again, harder this time.

I gasped. "Four."

Smack.

"Five," I moaned.

He continued to spank me until I was delirious. He alternated between each cheek, squeezed my ass, caressed the stinging skin, and then spanked me again.

It was always different. Sometimes he caressed me longer, other times, he spanked me twice before soothing the pain away.

I was lost to the pain and pleasure, my mind a jumble of wants and needs. His touch set me on fire, and I was desperate for it, craving more.

He smacked my ass again.

"Fifteen," I moaned, panting, my body trembling.

"I wonder if you could come, just like this, with me barely touching you."

"Yes sir, please," I begged without a moment of hesitation.

He smacked my ass, one cheek after the other, then leaned over me. "Do you think I'd do this for a whore? Hmm?" he purred, slipping his hand to my clit, rubbing it in circles.

His touch was light, a tease, and I tried to move my hips, to grind against his hand, but he tightened the rope, and I whimpered.

"I asked you a question," he growled.

"N-no, sir." I tried again to push back, but couldn't. "Please," I begged again.

"You're so beautiful, especially when you beg." He rubbed my clit, applying the pressure I needed, and my eyes drifted closed.

I was so close, almost there. He pulled my hair, forcing me to arch my back. The rope tightened, and I wanted more. I wanted the bite, the pain. I *needed* it.

"I wouldn't do this for a whore, Catalina. If I wasn't so addicted to the way you look when you come, I'd leave you like this." He circled my clit, and I whimpered. "Wet, aching, begging for my touch. But you know what? I think I've discovered something about you, something you don't want anyone to see."

He pinched my clit, grabbed my breast, squeezing it hard, then whispered in my ear, "You like being my bad girl, just as much as you like the praise. I think you want me to treat you like a whore. *My* whore."

I came immediately. I felt like I was floating above the clouds, detached from my mind and heart—a being existing solely in my skin and the sensations he created. My arms gave out, and I collapsed chest first onto the floor.

Marco rammed inside me, his cock stretching me, filling me completely. He was so deep, too deep, and I tried to move my hips away, but the rope tightened around my thighs and breasts.

He spanked my ass and fucked me hard. My knees and breasts rubbed against the carpet, the fibers teasing my nipples.

He thrust into me like a madman, and maybe he was. Maybe we both were insane, because I loved it. I gripped the rug, the only thing I could hang onto while he took me.

That's what this was. He took me, *claimed* me, *controlled* me, and it was pure perfection.

He fisted my long hair, yanking my head back. "You like this, don't you?"

"Y-yes! Yes, sir!"

His other hand reached around, grabbing my breast, pinching the nipple. The pain combined with his thrusts made me cry out, pleasure flooding every cell of my body.

"You love me using you, don't you, my little whore?"

"Yes! Yes, sir." He pushed down on my spine, forcing me to angle my hips, and when he thrust in again, I nearly lost my mind. "Fuck!"

"Say it. Say you're my whore, Catalina," he growled, spanking my ass once, twice.

"I'm your whore! Yours! Yours!" He fucked me harder after every word. Then he slipped his hand down to my pussy and pinched my clit. I bucked beneath him, and when he rubbed it again, I came, screaming.

But he didn't stop. He kept going, working through my orgasm, building me to another one so fast it felt like my heart was going to explode.

"You're such a good little whore for your king." He circled my clit, then bit my shoulder hard, marking me, branding me, and I relished in the thought.

I could do nothing else but groan, moving my hips back, crying out every time he entered me, touched me, the ropes binding and restricting me. The room filled with our moans, my cries, the sound of his hips slapping against mine as he fucked my dripping wet pussy.

He slid his hand up to my chest, and with his other hand on my hip, pulled me back until I was sitting on his lap, the position allowing him to ram harder into me.

My breasts bounced with each thrust, rubbing against the rope. I moved, ground, pushed my hips back against his, desperate for him.

I didn't want him to stop, couldn't bear the thought of it, and even when he made me see stars, I couldn't stop moving, and neither did he.

He fucked me harder, faster, rougher, and I wanted it all. I needed to touch him, feel him come inside me.

"Pl-Please, sir."

"Tell me what you want, my little whore."

"I want to touch you."

"I don't know. Do you think you've done enough to deserve that?"

"I'll do whatever you want. Just please, come inside me."

He stopped immediately.

The rope was suddenly gone, and I didn't even register it before I was on my back, Marco between my legs.

"You need it, my little cum slut? Need me to fill you up? *Breed* you?"

"Yes, sir," I hissed.

He thrust inside me, filling me to the brim. My body sang as I wrapped my arms and legs around him.

"You take me so perfectly, Catalina," he growled into my ear.

I clung to him as he pounded inside me, the scent of our sweat and sex fusing in the air.

He bit my nipples, sucked them, and I arched my back, giving him everything. I'd give him every piece of me, whatever he desired, anytime he asked.

The world faded away, leaving only us. He kissed me, and I gripped his hair as he fucked me harder and harder. His tongue twined around mine, and I moaned into his mouth.

Pulling back, his hand wrapped around my throat, and I cried out in pleasure.

"You're my whore, my slut, my vicious little queen. You're everything to me." He leaned down, biting my lip. "Understand?"

The warning in his tone nearly brought me to the edge. "Yes, sir."

"Good girl." He pulled my hips close, fucking me deeper.

Each stroke hit a spot near my cervix. I lost all track of time, crying out for him, moaning his name as I got closer and closer to another explosive orgasm.

I clawed his back, dragging my nails down to his ass, and it was like he loved the pain just as much as I did, because he thrust into me faster.

I couldn't take it. The ground fell away, and I came, screaming his name.

He jerked, then roared, his hot come shooting into my pussy. Each stream was like the greatest reward, and when he was finally done, I couldn't wipe the smile off my face.

We stayed like that, our arms wrapped around each other, his cock half-hard inside me, while I was so full of his come it leaked out of me.

He kissed my forehead, but there was a note in his breath, a type of hesitation that made me meet his eyes.

"We need to talk about what happened earlier." He brushed strands of hair away from my damp forehead. "Did me buying that dress and jewelry for you really make you feel like a whore?"

I gulped hard. He deserved the truth, no matter how hard it might be to say. I was wrong for what I did and how I treated him, but it was his tenderness that drove the final nail into the coffin that held the last of my ego.

I held him tighter, using his warmth as a reminder that I was safe here. He wouldn't judge me or let me go. He was asking because he cared, just as I was answering because he was everything to me.

"I'd just found out about my father calling a hit out on you, and it caused me to have one of my... attacks."

He squeezed me in his arms, but said nothing. I was grateful for his silence, his patience, his willingness to listen.

"I don't know what they are, but they always seem to happen when I get overwhelmed. They make me feel like I can't breathe." I shuddered. "The walls start to close in, and it feels like my heart is about to explode. I was trying to fight through one when the courier came."

He kissed my forehead. "I'm sorry, mi pequeña reina viciosa."

That he still saw me that way, that I was still vicious to him, someone with so much power that he thought I should be respected as a queen, allowed me to keep going.

"When I was younger, my father used to dress me up in whatever fancy clothes and expensive jewelry he wanted. He'd parade me around as entertainment for his benefactors." I swallowed against the ball in my throat. "He used to tell me to make myself 'look pretty' because I had a job to do." I took a deep breath. "It always made me feel cheap. I knew I was worthless—"

Marco snarled, and I quickly added, "To him. And it made me feel like a whore. So when I saw the items—"

"It triggered you."

"Yes." I hugged him tighter. "I didn't know if he sent it or you did. I didn't really see the items themselves, but my mind was already stuck in the past and anticipating the worst."

"And then I called you."

I nodded. "I knew it was you, but it was like everything came together, and all I could think about was using my pain to push you away." I met his eyes, and his gaze was so tender it brought me to tears. "I'm so sorry. I'm so, so sorry, you didn't deserve that, and—"

He shushed me, pulled me so close there wasn't a speck of air between us, and I cried into his chest. I didn't even understand why I was crying or where it was coming from. But I couldn't stop.

Marco didn't ask me to explain further. He didn't ask for more or beg me to give him answers. He just let me cry, and it was the greatest comfort anyone had ever given me.

When my tears finally slowed, he gently wiped my eyes. "I'm so sorry, Lina. I'm so sorry that you went through something like that and that I triggered you like this. But I'm worried about you,

Lina. I don't like that you have these attacks, or that you had one while I wasn't here. That's dangerous."

"It is. I..." I paused, scared to tell him how bad this one was, but I needed him to know. "I didn't just ignore all of your calls. After I got off the phone with you, I blacked out."

"What?" he shouted.

"It's... it's okay. It doesn't happen often—"

"That's *not* okay, Lina. What if that happens while you're driving or when something else is going on?"

I wanted to argue with him, to tell him I was in control. But I wasn't. In fact, the attacks seemed to happen most often when I felt like I wasn't in control, and it could very well hurt me or those around me one day.

"I want to ask you something." He tugged my chin, staring into my eyes. "But I need you to know I'm asking for you, not me. I want you just as you are. You're more than enough for me, okay?"

I nodded, realizing how much I trusted him in that moment, because the voice that normally told me I wasn't enough for anyone had never been so quiet.

"Have you ever thought about going to get therapy?"

"I... No. I've never thought about it. There's too much that's gone on in my life to share with someone like that. And it's not like I could explain to someone that part of my stress is because I'm a mafia boss."

He kissed my temple. "Maybe you could. Therapists have certain legal responsibilities, but I'm certain we could find someone for you if you wanted."

"I don't have the time." The words spilled out of my mouth before I could stop them.

"You do, Lina. We can't do anything to Felipe or Simon right now without bringing down half the police department and governmental agencies upon our heads. If we could have, then we would have already. Now is actually the perfect time."

He had a point, and I hated that he did. Opening up to him was hard enough, but to a complete stranger who I'd pay to tell me what was wrong with me? Someone who would judge me, take notes on my past? See me as weak and pitiful?

I didn't want that. I couldn't even stand the thought of it.

Marco rubbed my cheek, and I looked at him once more. That was what made my decision for me, what quieted the scared little girl inside of me—him.

I never wanted to use my past against him like I did today. If we were going to argue or fight, fine, but I wanted to keep him in my life, and that meant I needed to be fair to him.

"If we can find someone, I'll... I'll go."

He rained kisses over my head, then kissed me so sweetly I thought I was going to melt.

We held each other until my arms went numb, and even then, I didn't want to let him go.

He'd done so much for me, become so much to me. Marco was my entire world. Life had been dull, colorless without him, but with him, everything was shockingly vivid. There was joy, laughter, happiness. And a feeling that I didn't know—one that filled my heart so entirely it removed every doubt I had when he was in my arms.

I kissed him. It was all I could do because there was no other way for me to convey my emotions.

I couldn't fathom how someone so wonderful had become a part of my life. But the one thing I did know was Marco Torrino belonged to me. And I would not let him go.

Ever.

Nineteen

Catalina

I stared at the office building where my new therapist worked, fear running through my veins.

I never thought I'd be here.

I'd gone through so much in my life, so much that I didn't know how to speak of or approach, so I'd just buried it as much as I could. But I couldn't do that anymore.

I wanted my relationship with Marco to last for as long as it could. I'd become accustomed to waking up with him in my bed, cooking beside him, eating and working together in my house. The smell and feel of him, listening to him breathe as I rested my head on his chest. He was my safe place, my home, and I never wanted to hurt him ever again.

Facing my fears was a small price to pay if it meant I could ensure his happiness.

But deep inside of me, there was another reason I'd agreed to come here, a hope I'd drowned out that came roaring back to life.

I didn't want to feel broken anymore.

There were so many things I had forced myself to work through that I often felt dysfunctional.

I had a responsibility to a lot of people. And for them, I wanted to be more aligned and balanced, but I also wanted to know what that version of me would look like.

I'd always thought I could do it later, when I'd escaped from my father, when I'd killed Fernando, when I'd found the trafficked victims.

But Simon and Fernando—even from his grave—were still causing chaos in my life, and it might never end. I might never find the young girls and women. And even if I did, who knew what other secrets Fernando and Simon had? Who knew how long it would take to beat Felipe and win the war he'd started?

I couldn't keep shoving my mental and emotional health to the back-burner, no matter how scared I was. Yes, this therapist might judge me, not believe me, or worse, but I'd handle it, just like I always did.

I made my way inside, took the intake forms from the receptionist, and sat down while I waited for Estelle—my new therapist —to see me.

I tried to detach myself as I answered each question, tried to ignore the shame I felt for coming here. It grew as I selected each symptom, because until now I'd never realized just how bad I was.

I'd thought my headaches were normal, even my heart palpitations, and shortness of breath. It never occurred to me that regular people didn't experience those things daily like I did.

It made me feel like a failure.

"I remember when I had to fill one of those out. It sucked."

I jumped at the voice next to me. I never heard her come in or a door open or close. The woman was beautiful, tall with long flowing blonde hair and crystal-clear blue eyes.

I should have noticed her, but I guessed I was too focused on the intake chart and my overwhelming thoughts to pay attention.

I couldn't afford to let myself get carried away with my thoughts like that again. I needed to stay alert for Marco and I, for our families. Felipe might try something again at any time.

"I didn't mean to scare you. I'm sorry." Her smile was warm, kind, and disarming.

I sat back in my chair trying to calm my nerves. "No, it's all right."

"Do you mind if I sit beside you?"

The entire lobby was empty with more than enough chairs for her to sit somewhere else. But maybe she was just chatty and needed someone to talk to.

I didn't really want to hold a conversation with anyone, but I shook my head. "No, go ahead."

"Thanks." She sat down, then turned to me. "I have a little bit of an agenda for coming over here."

I didn't expect her to be blunt.

"You remind me of myself when I first came in here."

"I do?"

"Yes, nervous, not wanting to be here, like you're ready to bolt at any second."

My eyes widened, and she laughed.

"You're good at hiding it but... I think when you've gone through certain things and responded to them in a similar way, it makes it easy to spot those same behaviors in other people."

I wasn't sure what to say to that. Knowing a stranger could see through me so easily felt... invasive. Not in a way that was uncomfortable; more like someone revealing their mask to me and asking me to reveal my own.

The thought of doing so made me vulnerable, pathetic, something I hated feeling.

I didn't like to wallow in my pity. I didn't want to share my story. And I didn't think anyone else could relate to me—especially not a woman like her.

She was glowing, had a beautiful wedding ring on her finger, and seemed like she had her life together.

That wasn't me.

I could never be that, no matter how much I acted otherwise, something that would be far too apparent to her if I accepted the olive branch it felt like she was extending.

She rested her head back against the wall. "I've been seeing Estelle now for about six years. There was a time when I thought I'd always be that person. That I'd always be weak, allow others to walk over me for the sake of upholding peace. That I'd always be willing to sacrifice myself for others. I thought that was the single good quality I had, the only thing I was good for. I'd happily be a punching bag if it meant taking care of those I loved. It didn't matter if I lived in fear, even if I didn't survive, as long as they were all right." She looked around the office. "When I first came here, I thought it was a waste of time. How could anyone relate to the way I was feeling?" Her eyes moved to mine. "Then Estelle asked me if I always felt like I needed to be the hero for everyone else, and I broke down crying."

I tightened my grip around the pen in my hand. "I don't feel like I need to be the hero," I whispered.

One of her eyebrows rose. "Really? You don't feel like you have a responsibility to everyone else? That you can't ever actually be the person you want to be? That you can't let your walls down or let people inside because if you do, they'll see you for who you think you are—which is probably the names of all the absolute worst things anyone has ever called you?"

Each of her questions flayed me open and showed my deepest, darkest fears—and I trembled from the accuracy of her words.

Her voice grew softer. "Do you believe you deserve to be loved, wanted? Cherished? That you have worth exactly as you are, not for everything you think you have to do or who you have to be for everyone else?"

I bit the inside of my lip hard. It was the only way to distract myself from the turbulent, overwhelming feelings choking me. If I didn't, if I let them out now, I'd sob like a little baby.

This woman could only be a few years older than me, and yet, the amount of wisdom she had was insurmountable. I couldn't imagine ever being like her. "Are you... do you believe those things now?"

Her smile turned slightly sad. "Most days. Some days, like today, the world still feels like it's falling apart, but it's not as severe as it once was." She interlaced her fingers. "It can be something small, like my children crying, and no matter what I do, I can't get them to stop or cheer them up. But the nightmares of what I've gone through have stopped. And I know that I'm not only a good wife, a good mother. A daughter, sister, and friend, but I'm also a good person to myself." Her eyes warmed. "I *believe* in myself, I *know* I have worth, and that I deserve at least better than I've been through, and that's *enough*."

I nodded. I'd never thought or tried to grasp any of that for myself. To me, living just meant being free. I'd never thought about love to others or to myself. I wasn't even sure I knew what that looked like.

I believed in myself to overcome anything I needed to, but that was simply because I wouldn't quit. And that wasn't what it sounded like for her, like having trust and faith in myself.

"How did you get there?"

"Estelle, a loving man that I get to call my husband, my children, and friends who have become my family."

Could I ever have that?

Yes, I was here to meet with Estelle, and I knew I cared about Marco just as he cared about me. But could he be my husband one day? Could we have children and dedicate ourselves to one another in such a permanent way?

That future scared me, knowing how much it would hurt if it never happened. If Marco disappeared from my life, he'd take my heart and happiness with him. I'd never be whole again.

I'd given him so much of me, far more than I'd realized, and I trusted him to hold those parts of me in his hands. But marriage, a family? Was that life really in the cards for me? Could that really happen one day? Could I even be a good mother when I'd never had an example of one?

"I don't know if I could ever have that. I'm scared to even fantasize about it. I don't even have any friends." I hung my head and whispered, "I'm not even sure what friendship looks like."

"You do now."

My gaze snapped to hers, and she smiled.

"My name is Johanna, but my friends call me Jo, and if you'd like, I'd love to be friends with you."

"I-I don't think... I'm not sure I'd be a good friend. I don't know how to be one."

Her smile grew, and her face softened. "You don't *need* to be anything else than who you *are*. Let me have the honor of getting to know that person. That's more than enough for me."

I wanted to tell her no, that it would be better if she stayed far away from me.

But then she pulled a card from her purse. "My husband's here to get me. Think it over, and if you decide you'd like to try, this has my personal cell number and email on it."

She got up, waved goodbye, and left. And even though there were a million reasons I shouldn't have, I added her as a contact in my phone.

It had been three weeks since I started therapy, and I'd never had such a volatile hate-love relationship with anything in my life.

I cried more than I ever thought possible and felt as though I was constantly coming apart at the seams, which was exactly what Estelle thought I needed.

She had a lot of concerns regarding the frequency of what I had now learned were anxiety and panic attacks, especially since they had reached the stage of blacking out. She thought it was best for me to learn how to actually feel my emotions safely. So we met in her office once a week and I checked in with her over the phone twice a week.

Estelle didn't go easy on me. She asked questions and listened, probed when I was quiet, but gave me time to sort my thoughts. The woman was brilliant and a bit terrifying. It made me respect her.

Though difficult, her therapy sessions gave me a lot of answers. She explained I had PTSD, which gave me something to research. And what I found made me feel like there were others like me, like I wasn't so alienated from the rest of society.

It was one of the very reasons I'd succumbed and called Johanna. Because if Johanna had seen herself in me, and had grown into someone who could allow love, family, and relationships into her life, that meant one day I might be able to do the same.

We talked almost every day, from texts to phone calls. She had even introduced me to some of her friends and family members, Daniella and Mya. It had been good for me, really good.

But now, I needed to shift my focus.

The police had closed the investigation into the shooting, which meant it was finally time to get revenge against Felipe.

Everything was set and ready to go. Tomorrow Marco and I would wage our war.

While we'd covered all the bases we could, Felipe was likely to run. And it was entirely possible we might miss someone in his familia or an alliance with someone else who would retaliate against us.

For that reason, I'd need to keep my distance from Jo, at least until all of this was over, and the thought of that made me oddly sad.

I hadn't known Jo for long. There were plenty of things I didn't know about her, and things she didn't know about me. I hadn't told her my real occupation or the reasons why I saw Estelle so frequently.

The voice inside of me, the one that spoke with so much doubt and negativity said that if I ever came clean to Jo, she'd leave. And I wouldn't blame her.

Even if I hadn't been raised to think so negatively about myself, my life was dangerous. At any time, someone could hire someone to kill me, or threaten the people I cared about.

But when I'd told Estelle about that, she said, "You cannot control the future, and no matter how much you want to, you cannot protect those you love from hurt, pain, or even death. That's part of life. What you can do is believe in yourself to handle life as it comes, and you can trust in those around you to do the same. If someone wants to leave you, that's their decision, but by trying to make it for them, you're doing the both of you a huge disservice. Wouldn't it be better to enjoy the time you have with them? Make memories and allow them to enter your life and fill it with joy? Let people have a positive impact on you, Catalina. You deserve it."

Her words stuck with me. They were what I used to get me through every time I thought I should run, every time I thought I wasn't worth the trouble.

I deserved to have good people in my life, people I could let in and show how much they meant to me—like Marco, my familia, and Jo.

After my therapy session today, Estelle had given me homework to tell at least one positive person in my life that I cared for them. And in all honesty, it was the perfect time to do so. After all, while I wanted to believe in the best possible outcome, we were about to step into a war. There was no telling how things might go.

The problem was, I didn't quite know how to. But I knew someone who did.

I called Jo, and she answered on the second ring.

"Hey! I was hoping I would hear from you today." Her voice, as always, was warm, happy, and peaceful. I let it wash over me and calm my nerves.

"Really? You're not too busy?"

"No, never for you. Plus, you sound off."

"Things are a little... tense. There's a lot happening all at once, and I'm not sure how it's going to pan out."

Jo hummed in agreement. "You said you were facing off against a competitor, right?"

That was the lie I'd gone with, the closest thing I could say to the truth. "Yes, and he's a piece of work."

"Just be careful, and if you need anything, I'm here."

"Jo, I could never involve you in anything dangerous." The thought of her being hurt broke my heart. I'd be devastated if it was because of me.

"Just remember what I said. I can handle a lot more than you think I can."

Her voice had a firmness to it that I didn't understand. She was always saying things like that, as if she'd experienced more violence and danger than I could ever imagine.

I wanted to ask, but I didn't. I didn't want to pry, and sometimes I wondered if she felt the same about me. But I hoped one day we'd be able to share those pieces of ourselves with one another.

"How did therapy go?" she asked, snapping me out of my thoughts.

"Estelle whooped my ass as usual," I huffed.

Jo barked out a laugh. "Is it too sore for you to sit down?"

"Almost. I don't know how you've survived so many years with her. She gave me homework, Jo. *Homework*! I thought I'd get a reprieve since we'd be out of touch for the week, but she just doubled down. She's worse than any professor I had in college."

"That's Estelle, all right. Her brand of therapy is gentle and blunt. It works though."

"Unfortunately, it does." I bit my lip. "That's actually why I'm calling."

"Oh?"

I fiddled with the hem of my skirt, then forced myself to stop and took a deep breath. "My homework assignment is to tell at least one person how I feel about them. Would you mind if I tried with you?"

"Oh Catalina... of course you can!" The smile in her voice warmed my heart.

I squeezed my wrists. A part of me felt silly for being so nervous. I wanted to chastise myself for it, tell myself to grow up, but that wouldn't fix anything.

Remember what Estelle said. It's okay to do things while you're afraid.

"Our friendship surprised me." I drew in a deep breath. "I

keep people at an arm's length and for most of my life, I've thought that's what I had to do to survive. I never thought I'd have a friend, especially not one so fast. It's hard for me to trust others like that."

Another deep breath. "But you make it easy. You've been nothing but nice... no, kind to me. You've involved me in your world and shared so much with me. You inspire me and I admire your strength to constantly fight against the trauma you've faced."

I swallowed hard. *Remember, it doesn't matter how long she's in your life or what happens tomorrow. This is about joy, experiencing and sharing joy, allowing someone in. You can do it.*

"I only hope to be half the woman you are and to leave as much of an impact on people as you do. Thank you for being my friend."

"I..." Jo choked, then sniffled. "Thank you. Thank you for sharing all of that with me, but can I tell you a secret?"

"What is it?"

"I feel the same way about you."

I gasped. "What? But—"

"You don't see it because you don't know how to yet, but you leave an impact on everyone you touch. You've left one on me, even on Daniella and Mya, and they've only met you twice."

She cleared her throat. "I know you haven't had a good life, that you haven't been treated in the way you deserve, but it's the truth. You are an absolutely incredible woman. Your courage is astounding. You're a leader, one that is so wise, patient, and determined to do the best for all of those around you, not realizing that you already do. You give your all, Catalina. I see that and anyone around you that doesn't is blind."

I opened and closed my mouth multiple times, unsure of what to say.

"I think that's why Estelle gave you this homework assignment."

"What do you mean?"

"I think she wanted you to share your feelings for someone close to you, but also hoped that you'd realize how much you meant to those around you, too."

"Oh," I muttered.

What Jo was saying made sense, but I didn't know how to wrap my mind around it and accept it.

It wasn't the first time someone had looked at me favorably. My familia did now, but I was doing something for them. That didn't diminish my efforts, but I thought it only made sense. Eventually, if you worked hard and helped others, they'd learn to lean on you. Even if that wasn't why I pushed myself so hard for them, it still had that outcome.

Marco was the first person who ever saw me differently. In the beginning, I thought everything he said, all his compliments and flirtations, were just to get something from me. But Marco didn't need me, not in the way others did. He simply wanted me in his life.

And now, there was Jo, one more person who didn't need me for anything but was still so kind and loving to me.

The monstrous voice laying within me awoke. Doubt crept into my mind. *I wasn't worth all of that. I didn't deserve love or affection.* No one could simply want me. They always had an underlying agenda.

I took a deep breath and practiced what Estelle had taught me. I didn't need to write down the worry or doubt. I'd always put my emotions in a jar, so the exercise felt familiar.

But this time, I took the negative self-talk, that I was worthless, broken, not deserving of anything or anyone, and gently placed it in a box. Then I visualized myself putting the lid on top, effectively sealing it out.

I took a breath, breathing in for four seconds, holding for seven, then exhaling for eight. I did it again and again, visualized myself being grounded. In my mind's eye, roots connected me to the Earth. We were one, a shared heartbeat that could never be destroyed.

Sunlight streamed across my desk, I held a pen in my hand, I heard the hum of my computer. Tasted the saliva in my mouth, smelled the scent of peonies and lavender, then lifted Marco's shirt which I'd begun wearing whenever he'd left my house, and inhaled the lingering scent of him too.

It brought me down from my anxiety, pulled me back to the present where I was safe and allowed to express myself freely.

It hadn't taken long, but Jo had given me space, staying silent as she waited for me to find my footing once more. "Thank you, not just for waiting, but for what you said. I never thought about it from that perspective."

"What happens when you think about it that way?"

"It scares me," I said quietly.

"It won't always." Her voice was gentle, yet firm.

Her reassurance felt like a warm blanket of energy that wrapped around me and settled into my bones. If I could have, I would have buried myself in it. But I wasn't out of the woods yet.

"I want to tell Marco how I feel. But if this is going to be my reaction..."

"How will you know if you don't try, though?"

I bit my lip. I wanted to try. I didn't want to have any regrets and not confess my feelings to him, but I also didn't want to make a mistake.

I tapped my pen against my desk, hitting it harder, faster, until finally I stopped and whispered, "How did you know you loved Luke?"

Jo shifted, and it sounded like she was getting more comfortable. "Our relationship was... complicated. I knew he was the one for me immediately. But, unfortunately, there were a lot of things going on that prevented us from being together. I could have, *should* have, asked him for help, but instead I decided to push him away, thinking that would be better for the both of us."

That's almost like what I tried to do with Marco.

"As you can guess, that didn't really work out." A soft smile crept into her voice. "As things settled down, and I got to know Luke, I grew to love him even more. He's wild. He makes me laugh. He's so kind and generous. He teaches me how to be a better person, how to live life in a way where every day is fun and enjoyable. I want to know more about him, learn more, grow more with him. My life wouldn't be the same without him in it."

I fiddled with the pen again. Her words made so much sense to me. They were exactly how I felt about Marco, but I was scared of being wrong, of leading him on somehow, or getting his hopes up and letting him down in the future.

I'd never known two people who were so deeply in love before, not until I'd met Jo and Luke. Anyone who sat down in a room with them for all of five seconds could see just how much they loved one another. It was written all over them. But was that how Marco and I appeared to other people? Was I too closed off to show that to him? Did that side of me even truly exist?

When I was a little girl, I dreamed of falling in love with my fairytale prince. When my father beat me, I hoped that prince would save me one day, make me feel loved and wanted. But I wasn't a child anymore, and those dreams had long since disappeared, taking the belief that I could be loved or give love with them.

"Did you ask me how I knew I loved Luke, because you think you might love Marco?"

"I-I want to, I hope I do, I'm just not sure. I never imagined myself trusting anyone, especially not a man, for the rest of my life. But he came and he just... never left.

"He was so persistent." I chuckled. "He pushed me to let him in, consider more, want more for myself and my life. And even though I tried not to, eventually I just couldn't imagine a second without him. But is that enough? Is that love?"

"I think love has certain similarities, but that every relationship has its own facets. But when it comes to you and Marco, I can say without a fraction of a doubt that you love him."

My eyes widened. "Really?"

Jo giggled. "Yes. When you talk about him, your tone softens. You laugh and smile more. You're warmer, serene even. There's a fire in you and he's the only one who ignites it."

I love him? Really? Truly?

My heart beat faster, but not in fear. I was overwhelmed with joy, with the possibility that I'd finally found something I thought I'd lost. That maybe, just maybe, the life I'd always longed for was right at my fingertips.

"I know it's scary. It's terrifying to let someone in your heart, to love someone, especially when you've gone through unimaginable suffering. But don't let that fear block what could be the best thing that has ever happened in your life."

I clutched my chest, felt the excitement and happiness flooding my veins. It was exhilarating. Marco was my person, *mine.* And if I believed that to be true, if I meant it when I promised him I'd never let him go again, then I could find a way to tell and show him I loved him today.

"I won't," I whispered, my voice full of fierce determination. "I won't let anything get in my way, not even myself."

TWENTY
Catalina

I pressed the button for the elevator. This was the first time I'd ever been to Marco's house, any of them. We'd decided it was best I come stay with him, as he'd been basically living at my house for multiple weeks now.

He slept over every night. We ate breakfast together. He even had a toothbrush and a drawer with clothes there.

It had been a smart decision for multiple reasons.

Marco had finally admitted to months of surveying and stalking me, which meant he knew every access and vantage point for my house and the roads around my property. He could point out security improvements that I couldn't, which made my home the perfect place to protect ourselves while we'd been forced to wait for our revenge.

However, now that we were ready, it made the most sense to come here. If Felipe had been tailing either of us or investigating our movements, he would have known where I lived, what our routines were, and exactly how to hunt us down. But me coming here would take him time to react—time we could use in our favor.

Even though I understood the logic of it, I couldn't help but be a little nervous.

Marco always seemed fine in my home, careful yet confident—as if he belonged there. But I didn't know how to be that way with him. This was his space, and I was invading it. Would my presence make him feel uncomfortable in his own home?

I mentally shook my head. *No.*

I knew and trusted Marco. If he didn't want me in his home, he wouldn't have offered. I refused to let my nerves get to me. Instead, I shoved them into my worry box.

I pushed my shoulders back, straightened my spine, and when the elevator doors slid open, I saw him standing there.

Marco reached for me, and I made it halfway before he kissed me like he hadn't seen me earlier that morning, and it had been days, weeks, *years* since we'd been together.

He kissed me like I was the air he needed, the water he craved and thirsted for.

I bunched his shirt in my hands as he fisted my hair, angling my head, deepening the kiss. The elevator chimed, warning us we hadn't pressed a button, and we laughed against each other's lips.

"I missed you, mi pequeña reina viciosa."

I giggled and kissed him again. "I missed you too."

He pressed the button for the penthouse floor, while I straightened my hair.

"I need to come up with another nickname for you one of these days, other than my devil."

He wrapped his arm around my waist. "You already have one for me."

I looked up at him. "No, I don't."

"You do. Sir, King, and after I kill your sorry excuse of a father, feel free to try out Daddy."

I laughed, even as my skin flushed. "I cannot call you Daddy in public."

"Oh, you can. I might even reward you for it," he whispered in my ear.

I smacked his chest playfully. "Do you ever not think with your dick?"

"Absolutely, but not when I haven't seen you in hours."

I chuckled at him, but even I couldn't deny the huskiness in my voice or the way my pussy clenched in need.

Stepping off the elevator, Marco opened the door to his penthouse, and we stepped inside.

His home surprised me. It was masculine, yet cozy. A mixture of browns, blues, grays, and blacks. The lighting was warm, and his foyer, living room, kitchen, and dining room all faced a wall full of borderless windows. It was the perfect view to watch the sunset.

I never knew a house could look like this.

My own was slightly haphazard because I hadn't known what I liked. It was the first time I'd been able to furnish and decorate a space all on my own. I didn't even know my favorite color, or which ones would have gone well with it. Eventually, I found I preferred deeper colors, dark reds, crimsons, teals, deep forest greens, and dark blues, and had settled on beige to tie them all together.

But my house, even with all the furniture, never truly felt lived in to me. Everything was clean, sharp lines. I didn't have a lot of art on the walls or décor anywhere. But Marco did.

It wasn't overwhelming or for show. Like Marco, it felt authentic, as if he'd truly wanted to make this space his own, his sanctuary.

"What do you think?"

I turned my head up to his. "It's beautiful."

His smile lit up the room. "I'm happy to hear you like it." He brushed my hair back behind my ear. "I was worried because you seemed nervous."

No matter how hard I try, he always knows.

"I was a little, but I'm fine now." I squeezed his hand. "Are you going to show me to my bedroom?" I teased.

His eyebrow raised. "You mean our bedroom?"

I smirked. "Who says I'm sleeping with you?"

He pulled me into his arms. "Mi pequeña reina viciosa, please don't make me break all the beds in the guest rooms. I really don't want to go out and buy more."

I stood out on the balcony, the wind blowing through my hair. I still hadn't told him.

I could have after we'd had sex in his bed, or after we'd eaten dinner, but I hadn't. I kept telling myself I had more time, knowing that couldn't be further from the truth.

The hacking group had already taken all of Felipe's money and transferred it to an offshore account that only Marco and I had access to. They'd also looped Felipe's camera feeds so he wouldn't be able to see when we captured his men, interrogated and slaughtered them, gathered whatever information and paperwork we could from his warehouses, then burned them to the ground.

After that, all that would be left would be Felipe's mansion. He had a small army there, but once we made it through them, there would be nothing stopping us from getting to Felipe. And it would all start in one short hour.

I have to say it now. I have to tell him how I feel while I still have the chance.

I turned around as Marco stepped onto the balcony and walked toward me.

"What's going on with you, Lina? You've been off all day. Is it being here? Is it too much for you? Do you feel uncomfortable?"

"No. No," I said again more firmly. "It's not that at all, it's just... I'm scared."

He wrapped his arms around me, and I burrowed into the familiarity of his warmth and smell, then sighed.

"Talk to me, Lina. Are you worried something will go wrong?"

"Yes, but that's not the only thing I'm afraid of." I slipped my hand into my pocket, squeezing the key there.

Once I give him this, I can't go back.

Then something, a strength I never knew I had, rose inside of me. It wasn't that I couldn't go back from this. I didn't want to. I swore I wouldn't let my fear get in the way, and that was a promise I was going to keep.

I took his hand, then gently placed the key inside it, and he cocked his head to the side.

"This is a key to my house. You're welcome to use it whenever you want. I can clear out more drawers, get another desk in the office, whatever you need, but I... I want you there."

"Lina..." he said slowly, carefully, as if I was a deer who might run away if he frightened me. "Are you asking me to move in with you?"

"I..." Taking a deep breath, I squeezed my hands into fists, then released them. "Yes. Or, if you prefer, I could move in here with you. Whichever you'd be more comfortable with but—"

He slammed his lips against mine. His kiss was hard, rough,

leaving me breathless and panting. Then he slipped the sash from my robe, pulling it open.

"Marco—"

He kissed my neck, sending shivers down my spine.

"Marco, someone could see us here."

"Then the last thing they'll see before I slit their throats is how a king worships his queen."

He took my breasts into his hands, then sucked my nipple into his mouth.

My head fell back, and I arched my back, giving him all of me.

He nibbled, bit my breasts, down my stomach. He was moving so quickly, rushing like he couldn't wait a minute longer for me. Then he got down on his knees and looked up at me. "Put your legs over my shoulders and feed me your pussy, Catalina."

His voice was so husky, his eyes so dark and dilated that I moaned at the command.

I shifted one leg over his shoulder.

He grinned. "That's my good girl. Come sit on my face."

Grabbing my hips, he lifted me, then settled me down on his face and ate me out like a crazed man.

I gripped onto the railing behind me as his tongue slid in and out of my pussy. He smacked my ass, urging my hips to move, and I obeyed immediately.

I ground myself on his face, and when I looked down at him, he was staring back at me, watching my every move.

I moaned loudly, sliding one hand into his hair, fisting it. I pulled his head harder against my pussy, felt the way his lips curled briefly before he gave me exactly what I wanted. His tongue thrust deeper, faster. Then he rubbed my clit.

I jerked, liquid pooling in my pussy.

The wind blew against my skin, eliciting goosebumps from the chill. His hands were warm and firm on my hips, his breath hot on my pussy as he drove his rolled tongue in and out of me and rubbed me faster. Not once did his eyes leave my body.

He was completely focused on me, worshipping me with his attention and devotion.

I tightened my legs around his head, silently begging him not to stop, not that he would.

Marco loved to make me come, to make me lose my mind for him, and with one more thrust of his tongue, I did.

I cried out, my hips grinding wildly on his face as he licked me. He bit my thigh, sucked my clit, then went back to feast on my pussy.

I caught my breath just a moment before he lifted my hips. Then he was standing, pulling me against him.

I wrapped my legs and arms around him, kissing him as he thrust into me.

I tasted myself on his tongue and reveled in it. It was primal, possessive, like I'd left my mark on him, *claimed* him.

He fucked me hard, one hand wrapped around my waist, the other bracing us against the railing. My breasts were pressed against his chest, our stomachs constantly rubbing together as he kept ramming in and out of me.

His tongue wrapped around my own, sucking it into his mouth, then nibbled and bit my lips before kissing me again.

He carried me from the railing to a corner of his balcony, pinned me against the wall, and drove into me even harder.

I tilted my head back and met his gaze with half-closed eyes.

He was wild, feral, as though his sole purpose, the reason he was put on this earth, was to take me. And I'd give him every inch of me, every part of my being, every ounce of my heart. Every space in my soul, anything, *everything* that I was.

My feelings for him bubbled up and spilled out of me and I couldn't stop myself, didn't even want to. "I love you," I moaned.

He froze. His eyes widened, jaw dropped, and a shiver went through his entire body while his cock twitched inside of me. "Wh-What did you just say?"

It felt like time had stopped. I couldn't hear the birds chirping or the sounds of the street from below, and the sky couldn't replace the absolute brilliance of his eyes.

A small tinge of fear fluttered through me, but I pushed it aside. I'd already said it once; I could say it again. "I love you. I love you, Marco."

His expression shifted from shock, to awe, to wonder, then to overwhelming joy. And he rammed back inside me even harder than before.

I cried out. He was so rough and deranged.

I dug my nails into his back, dragging them down while he pounded into me over and over.

"Say it again," he growled.

"I love you."

He thrust harder.

"Again."

"I love you."

Harder still.

"Again."

"I love you. I love you. Yes! I love you!"

He claimed my lips, kissed the ever-loving hell out of me while he fucked me with wild abandon. He pinned me to the wall harder, pressing himself against me until I could barely take a full breath, and I loved it, loved the weight of his body.

His hand roamed over my back as he drew me closer, as if he wanted to be buried in my skin, and if he could, I would let him.

"I love you, Catalina," he moaned into my ear.

A feeling came over me—something sudden and strong that I'd never felt before. It shot from my head down my spine to my legs, filling the entirety of my body—bliss. Pure, unfiltered bliss.

It shook me to my core. Tears of pleasure and joy fell from my eyes, and Marco kissed each one, while he rammed the entire length of his cock into my cunt.

Then my body trembled. My toes curled and my pussy throbbed.

"That's it, mi pequeña reina viciosa. Come for your king. Come knowing that I love you—that I would live for you, die for you, kill for you."

I did. I came screaming as every cell in my body exploded. I felt like a rocket launching straight into the stratosphere—and all I could do was hold on to him so I didn't end up lost in space.

But he kept thrusting, once, twice, three times, then he roared, and I kissed him. I kissed my king, my devil, the other half of my soul as he filled me with his come. And then, I felt complete.

"Ready?"

I peered up at Marco. He was dressed in a black shirt, black pants, and black combat boots.

Normally, I thought he looked like his nickname, The Devil, because of how sinfully handsome he was. But now? He looked like death, and it made my blood pump a little harder in my veins.

Down, girl. You can celebrate by riding him later.

"Yes." I stood, and he grasped my chin, tilted my head up, and kissed me with such gentleness and tenderness I almost melted.

"I know you're my vicious little queen and that you can withstand anything, but take care of yourself for me. I'd lose my mind if anything ever happened to you."

I squeezed his back. "I promise, but you have to do the same. If you die, I'll drag you back from hell just to kill you myself."

He laughed, and I smiled along with him. "Yes, my queen."

We stepped into the elevator hand in hand. Marco's driver was waiting for us outside. Our men were set at their stations, knew their orders, and were ready to carry them out to the fullest.

My body hummed in delight, and when I looked over at Marco, I knew he felt the same. After waiting so long, our day of reckoning had finally arrived.

We made our way out to the lobby, where added security—Marco's own men—made sure we left safe and sound.

Approaching the entrance, Marco slid behind me as he opened the door.

"Lina!" Marco pulled me to him, spinning around, blocking my front.

Glass shattered in the distance, the pieces spilling over the marble floors. But I didn't understand why.

Time slowed.

"Marco?"

His eyes were so warm, filled with so much love and affection. He had the most beautiful smile on his face, yet his chest was wet, and whatever it was began to seep into my clothing.

I recognized the smell first, the metallic tang.

When I touched his chest, it came away red, full of blood. I stared up at Marco, wide-eyed. Then he went down with me. His expression turned serene, then he closed his eyes.

I didn't hear the additional shots, nor the screams, or the people running for their lives on the street.

All I saw was Marco, unconscious, laying in a pool of his own blood.

No.

"Marco." I shook him.

No!

"Marco." I lifted the entirety of his torso up and down as if his muscles, bones, and sinews weighed nothing more than a feather. But he didn't move.

No!

I balled my fist, hit his chest. I hit him one, two, three, four, five times, but he never *once* opened his eyes. He never twitched, never smiled, never laughed. Nothing.

"MARCO!"

Twenty-One

Catalina

We rushed Marco to his hospital, where they had his blood work and entire medical history on file.

The staff here was ready for him, so when they got the call from Marco's men, they took him back immediately.

I watched as the love of my life, the man who brought sunshine and color into my world, who matched me in every way and was the only sanctuary I'd ever known, was brought back into surgery on a stretcher.

I was numb. Empty.

I hadn't cried, had barely spoken to anyone besides giving simple instructions. All of my energy was with him.

Even if we were rooms, worlds, dimensions apart as the doctors fought to keep him with us, he had my everything. And every piece of me was begging for this all to be a dream—some sort of horrible nightmare where when I awoke, I'd roll over into his arms and find him safe and sound.

One of his men led me to a chair, and I followed without complaint.

I sat down and waited. A flurry of bodies passed me to and fro, but I saw none of them, couldn't remember a single one of their faces. Not until a single pair of white shoes filled my vision.

The man was dressed in scrubs, with a sad look on his face.

"Ms. Salazar? Can you hear me? Are you all right?"

Had he been calling for me?

It was like a light switch turned on and I finally recognized the man. It was Marco's surgeon.

"Marco? How is Marco?"

The surgeon took a deep breath.

"We had to do intensive surgery."

My world crumbled.

"The bullet didn't pierce his heart, but it collapsed one of his lungs and caused several other injuries. The surgery itself was a success, but..."

"But what?" I bit out.

"We've had to place Marco in a medically induced coma to give his body time to heal. We've done all we can on our side, but it's up to him now to pull through."

I wanted to yell, scream, throw something at him, or *kill* him.

He hadn't done enough. If he had, Marco would be here. He'd be the one standing in front of me, with his beautiful, radiant smile, and calling me his queen.

"Ms. Salazar..." The surgeon paused, his eyes becoming hard, his jaw firm. "No, Catalina. Without Marco, many of us wouldn't be here today. I know how much he means to you and how much you mean to him. I promise you we will do everything in our power to take care of him." Then he took a deep breath. "They say coma patients can hear their surroundings. Tell him to fight for us, to come back to us, to you, and he will."

Tears nearly fell from my eyes when I saw Marco.

His skin was ashen and pale, its normal golden hue somehow dull and muted against the bright white sheets. He had tubes sticking out of his arms. And while he was breathing, he was so unbelievably still, as if he were half dead.

No!

I went to him, sat on the edge of his bed, carefully picked up his hand and held it in my own. His arm trembled, and for a moment I thought he'd come back to me, but it wasn't him shaking, it was *me*.

I steeled my nerves.

"Marco," I whispered, squeezing his hand, stroking his cheek. "You promised me. Don't you remember? Just a few short hours ago, I told you if you died, I'd go to hell and bring you back. So, you can't. Okay? You can't leave me."

My voice wavered, but I forced myself to push on. "There are so many things I have yet to experience in this world, and I want to experience them with you. I want to spend every day, every night, for the rest of time with you. I want to grow old with you. I want to learn about life with you." I nuzzled his hand. "So please, please, I'm begging you, I'll get down on my hands and knees if you need me to, but please, don't give up. I need you, Marco. I can't survive without you."

I kissed each of his knuckles and held his hand to my cheek as a single tear slid down my face.

"Ma'am?"

I wiped it away and looked up, finally recognizing the man

who had stuck beside me while Marco was in surgery. It was Carlos, someone Marco told me he trusted.

"Your men are here to see you, as are several of the capos of the Torrino Famiglia. Would you like to meet with them?"

I looked at Marco once more, traced his cheek with my fingertips, then smoothed his hair back from his head. I took in each cord and tube, tucked the blanket around him, then hardened my heart.

Felipe did this to him. I didn't know how, but he was the only one who had a reason to kill Marco. And now, I would destroy him.

I leaned into my fury and rage, let it simmer under my skin and fuel my strength, then I turned to Carlos. "Let them in."

The capos of our families filled the hospital room, each strapped with a mixture of weapons while they waited for news from the shooting.

I straightened my back, and when I spoke, my voice was hard, commanding. "Marco is recovering right now, and when he opens his eyes again, I want to make sure he knows we got the bastards that did this."

Some men grunted in agreement.

My eyes touched each of Marco's capos. "I know I'm not Marco, and that I have no reason to ask this of you, but help me get revenge for him, for daring to touch a single hair on his head."

Carlos stepped forward, drawing my gaze. "Ma'am, Marco has instructed us that should anything happen to him, we are to follow your every command. You are our boss, our Doña. Whatever you need us to do, we will."

I fought through the emotion welling up inside me. Marco had given me control of his familia? Had he suspected what was going to happen?

"When did he make that change?"

"He asked us to watch and assist you if needed before he went to Italy. He changed the hierarchy the day he returned."

How could he... why did he? I didn't even know who he was when he left for Italy, and yet he'd left his entire familia in my hands? *How could he be so foolish?*

Then I stilled.

Hadn't he told me all along? That he'd give me anything, give *up* anything if it meant having me?

Marco had stalked me, long before we'd ever met at my birthday party. And he always called me his queen. He wasn't being irresponsible. He simply believed in me that much. *He'd always believed in me.*

My vision blurred as tears filled my eyes, but I clenched them hard. *No. I can't. If I start crying now, I won't stop. I'm barely holding it together, but I have to until he's back to me.*

I squeezed Marco's hand, cleared my throat, and surveyed Marco's—no, our men.

Not a shred of doubt clouded their faces. They were almost militant in their stance. It was a direct reflection of their respect for Marco, and whatever he had done had ensured they would never question me.

Their loyalty and confidence in me was almost overwhelming, but instead of fighting against it, I accepted it.

"We move on as planned. Stake out Felipe's mansion and give me a final head count on how many guards he has."

Our men nodded.

"Have Felipe's men arrived at his warehouses?"

"Yes," Joseph said.

When I spoke again, my voice was low, cold, full of fury. "When you're torturing them for information, make it hurt. I want them to writhe in pain, beg for death. Cut out their eyes, pull off their fingernails. Break them in *every* way possible. They went after Marco, and they are going to pay the price for their actions."

I squeezed Marco's hand again. "And when you're done, I will join you at Felipe's mansion. But do not touch him—Felipe Alvarez is mine."

Twenty-Two

Catalina

"It's starting," I breathed, running my fingers through Marco's hair.

Our men were out there, getting the justice Marco deserved.

He hadn't moved, not once, and the doctors said it was too soon to know anything. That I had to wait.

I'd always thought I was a patient person. I'd waited for years to be free from my father, spent months working on investigating the trafficking, but for the first time in my life, I couldn't stand it.

Now, when I needed it most, time seemed to move at a snail's pace. I kept checking my watch, thinking hours had passed, only to find it had just been a few minutes.

"If I could, I'd take your place," I whispered. "I'd take all the pain, the hurt, anything, *everything*. I'd take it for you."

I kissed his forehead, tucked the blanket around him again, then smoothed out the wrinkles.

I couldn't stop myself from moving. If I didn't touch him, then I'd pace. If I didn't pace, then I might scream, sob. Wail the entirety of my heartbreak so loudly that every person in this hospital would hear it. And that was the one thing I *refused* to do.

When this was all over, when my Marco was back to me, then I would. I'd release the bundle of emotions fighting inside of me, ripping apart. But until then, he needed me to be strong, to believe that he'd come back to me, and he would; I just had to wait, no matter how agonizing it was or how long it took.

I'd do anything to bring him back. I'd crawl across hot coals if it meant having one more second with him. If it meant hearing his voice, his laugh, feeling the strength in his body as he wrapped his arms around me, calling me his vicious little queen.

Something changed in the air, like an electric charge surged through the room. And when I looked up, shock flooded through me.

"Jo?"

She rushed toward me, and I barely had time to stand before she threw her arms around me. "I'm so sorry. I came as soon as I heard."

"Heard? But how did you get in?"

Did the door open? Could I have been so distracted that I missed it?

But two men were outside guarding the room, and another two were guarding the main entrance to the wing. She shouldn't have been able to get past them, and if she did, my men would have called.

"Yes, it was on the news. Are you okay? Did you get hurt?"

"I'm okay. I didn't get hurt, but Jo, how are you here?"

A small, sad smile appeared on her face. "I have my ways. One day, I'll explain them to you, but for now, let's take care of Marco."

"I... what? Take care of him? How?"

She simply shook her head, took my hand, and stood beside him.

"Johanna, what is going on—"

"You would do anything to save him, wouldn't you?"

My world, which had stilled the moment Marco had been shot, suddenly came roaring back to life. "Yes," I said, without a second of hesitation.

"Then give me a moment."

She never moved, but there was something different about her. The air around her seemed denser, humid, as if there was an unseen pressure that shouldn't exist. I wanted to ask her more, to know how she got here, why she was here, and what she was doing, but I didn't.

There was nothing I wouldn't do to bring Marco back to me —no matter the price.

The pressure suddenly dissipated, and Jo turned to me. She took my hand and placed a single small pill inside my palm. "Give this to him and he'll be fine in a couple of hours."

I stared at her.

Was she serious?

But there wasn't a single breath of doubt in her, and the way she stood before me, so confidently relaxed, made me feel like this wasn't the first time she'd done something like this.

"What is this, Jo? Why are you doing this?"

"I know what you've gone through and how hard you had to fight. I don't want that for you anymore. You've finally found someone who loves you, who treats you the way you deserve to be treated. And I will do anything in my power to defend that for you. It's time for you to be happy." Her eyes shifted to my palm, then back to my face. "I know it might be hard to trust me right now, but please, think about the last couple of weeks of our friendship. If you could trust me then, please trust me now."

Then she turned and walked away.

"Jo!" I called out to her, but she was already at the door, and by the time I reached it, she was gone.

I threw the door open, startling my two guards.

"Where did she go?" I yelled.

"Who, Doña?" one of my guards said.

"The blond woman that just left."

"Doña, no one has come in or out of this room for the last hour."

"But—"

They looked at me like I was crazy. Maybe I was.

I stepped back into the room, my legs shaking, as I closed the door slowly.

She was here. Wasn't she?

She had to be. I had the pill.

I tightened my fist around it. Maybe a doctor had given it to me, and for some reason, I'd imagined it to be Jo. Or maybe she had been here, and this pill was some sort of new, experimental drug.

I didn't care what it was as long as it brought Marco back to me.

I crushed the pill, mixed it with water, and stroked his throat to make him swallow. Then, I waited and hoped with every piece of my heart this would work.

Thirty minutes went by.

Then an hour.

Then two.

Did I make a mistake?

I shook my head.

Regardless of whatever Jo had given me, I still trusted her.

Maybe I'd become too soft. Maybe falling in love with Marco had changed me. But ever since Marco walked into my life, he'd made it better, which meant I had to believe in myself and my decisions.

Marco would regain consciousness, and I hoped it would be before I'd need to leave. Our men were almost done with the raid, and I needed to be there to end Felipe at his mansion. But I didn't want the first thing Marco saw when he opened his eyes to be an empty room.

I rested my head on his hand, stroking his wrist. Closing my eyes, I focused on the pounding of his pulse. Sometimes I thought it grew stronger, and I'd sit up, thinking this was finally it. He'd open his eyes, be fully recovered, and everything in my world would be right again. But he never did, and each time that happened, my heart sank a little more.

"If anyone would have told me a few months ago that you would come to mean so much to me, that I'd fall so hopelessly in love with you, I would have laughed in their face. Now look at me." I turned my head up to him, watching his eyes, hoping for a flutter, a movement, *something*, but he was perfectly still.

"Didn't you tell me I have a responsibility to you, Marco? Well, you have one to me too. You need to take responsibility for turning my entire world around, changing all my plans. Making me *feel*, making me open my heart up to you. And the only way you can do that is by staying with me until we're old and gray."

I palmed his cheek, stroking it softly. "I really want to see you like that, with silver hair and wrinkles around your eyes and hands. I want to make memories with you, Marco."

I opened my mouth to say more, to confess all the secret hopes and dreams I had for our lives, but then my phone beeped.

Joseph: We're done here and we'll be at Felipe's mansion in an hour.

I held the phone to my forehead, squeezing my eyes closed.

I'm almost out of time.

Then I felt something, a small twitch in my hand. At first, I thought it was me. But then I felt it again—a quick, hard jerk—and when I looked at Marco, I saw the impossible. His eyelids were twitching, as if he were about to open them.

I yelled for the guards to get someone—a nurse, doctor—anyone. Nurses ran into the room; they were pulling at his wires and tubing, shouting something, but I didn't hear them. All I could focus on was Marco. And when his eyes slowly opened and found mine, I collapsed.

He reached out and grabbed me; he was so fast, so strong as he wrapped his arms around me, dragging me towards him, like he'd never been shot at all.

I clung to him, tears pouring from my eyes, and he held me just as tightly.

"Lina," he whispered. "Lina." He kissed each cheek, my nose, my forehead, my jaw—anywhere he could reach—saying my name over and over. Tears filled his eyes, and he kissed me again.

I cupped his head, clinging to him, refusing to let go while he fisted my hair and kissed me repeatedly.

Marco, my world, my entire universe, the light of my life, was back to me.

"We need to check your wounds," a nurse said from somewhere behind me.

"Later. I need my woman," Marco growled, his eyes never leaving mine.

"But, sir—"

I glared at her, and she froze.

Of course, she was right. This was a medical miracle. But I

could have lost *him*. Now my Marco was back, and I needed to know this was real, that he was truly here, coherent, moving. *Alive.*

"Don't make him say it again," I hissed.

Slowly, Marco's lips tipped up, first into a grin, then a full smile with the dimples I loved so much. And he kissed me once more.

Distantly, I heard the door close, but I didn't even care. I would have let him take me right there, even with everyone watching. It didn't matter. Nothing mattered outside of him.

He stripped my shirt and my bra, and I pushed my pants down, while he shifted, dragging the hospital gown off of him.

He opened his arms for me, and I straddled his waist, pressing my lips against his.

I kissed him with reckless abandon. The world could've been falling around me and I wouldn't care as long as I had him in my arms. And when he pulled my panties to the side, and I sunk down onto his cock, we moaned.

He filled me, stretched me to the brink, a sense of completion tearing through my body. Then he thrusted inside of me.

I held him as close as I could as he kissed me over and over, bit and sucked my lips. I parted them for his tongue and he rubbed and wrapped his own around mine.

I rocked my hips in time with his and when he pulled back, he took my bouncing nipple into his mouth. He lavished it, sucked it hard, fucked me even harder. It was wild. Desperate. Everything we *both* needed.

I held onto him for dear life. And he never let go of me, not once. He smacked my ass, gripped it, my hips, my back, fisted my hair, always making sure I was tied to him.

I dragged his mouth back to mine, needing his taste on my lips once more, needing to feel his every breath, and he fucked me even harder.

"Marco," I cried out. "My Marco."

"Catalina," he moaned.

I stared into his beautiful dark brown eyes—filled with such desire, desperation, and love for me.

"I love you. I love you. I love you!"

He bit my neck, trailed kisses over it and up my ear before biting it too. "I love you too. I love you so much. I'd crawl through hell to come back to you. I'll always come back to you, mi pequeña reina viciosa. *Always*."

"You better. You fucking better." I moaned, burying my mouth into his hair to smother my cries.

But he kept pumping faster, harder, ramming into me wildly, and I couldn't take it anymore.

I came crying out into his shoulder, as he turned his head into my neck, shouting, spilling into me.

I don't know how long we stayed like that. Truthfully, I didn't care. But eventually my legs ached from straddling his thighs.

He somehow knew and shifted, laying back on the bed, pulling me with him, holding me to his chest while I slid my legs between his.

I ran my fingers over his back, his sides, listened to the strong beating of his heart.

"I was so scared, Marco," I whispered.

He slid his fingers through my hair, tucking the strands behind my ear. "I know, mi pequeña reina viciosa. I heard you, every single word you said to me. I'm sorry I made you so afraid."

"Did you know, before? That someone was going to shoot at us?"

He shook his head. "I was just lucky enough to see the sun reflect off of the muzzle."

"I'm going to fucking hang Felipe from his balls."

Marco's expression grew stern. "I don't think it was Felipe this time."

"What? Why?"

"Because the gunman wasn't pointing at me. He was pointing at *you*."

My eyes went wide.

"If I didn't reach for you right then, you wouldn't be here, Lina. He was aiming for your head."

Someone tried to kill me.

Someone tried to kill me and Marco pulled me out of harm's way.

He took the bullet for me.

Marco almost sacrificed his life for me.

I punched him in the chest, hard.

"Ow! I am an injured man, you know."

For half a second, my anger quieted.

But then he smiled, and I hit him again.

"Don't you ever fucking do that again, Marco. You don't take bullets for me!"

He grabbed my fist, brought it to his lips, and kissed it as though my anger was nothing.

"If the choice is between your life and mine, I'll choose you every single time."

Twenty-Three

Catalina

"Do you want to postpone?"

I buttoned my pants. "No. This has to happen tonight."

I knew that, and so did he.

Marco had been discharged, much to the utter bewilderment of the hospital staff. But even though he was fine, my nerves were a wreck.

I tried to tell myself nothing bad was going to happen. It was the most logical conclusion. We had more people, were better prepared. We'd sealed off the exits to Felipe's house by car, and while he had a helicopter, we'd taken his pilot hostage at one of the warehouses.

We would win, we *should* win, but based on what Marco had said, we might also have another enemy that we hadn't accounted for.

I didn't think it was my father. He may have wanted to kill me before, but from the last messages I'd seen, he hadn't changed the terms of his deal with Felipe. So who wanted me dead?

293

Did it have something to do with the trafficking? Were we closer to finding the victims than we realized, or was it something else?

I never really thought about my death. I wasn't afraid of dying, but I wanted to live out of spite for those who wished I was gone.

My freedom and finding my sense of power were more important to me than anything else had been. They were my reason for survival.

But that was no longer the case.

My gaze drifted over to Marco as he pulled on a clean black shirt.

He was my purpose now. I wasn't sure exactly when it had happened, if it was the first time we'd kissed, the day I'd called him after a panic attack. When he barged into my house after my father's men had tried to kidnap me, the gun range, or even before then. Maybe it was that night at my birthday party. But somewhere along the line, he'd become such a big part of me that nothing else mattered.

And I'd just gotten a tremendous, horrific example of what life would be like without him.

The last few hours had been horrendous. I didn't want to go through that again, and knowing Marco would throw himself in front of anything to save me, even die for me without hesitation, put me on edge.

If I missed something, if I wasn't alert. If I made a mistake...

Marco closed the distance between us, tilted my head, and kissed me.

"Stop thinking so loudly," he whispered against my lips.

"Stop being in my head then," I whispered back.

He chuckled, then caressed my cheek. "We knew the risks going into this. This lifestyle isn't a safe one."

I rubbed his chest. "I know. But my worst fear was seeing you in a pool of blood." I trembled at the image. It would never leave me for as long as I lived.

"I'm sorry, mi pequeña reina viciosa." He brushed my hair back, tucking it behind my ear. "While I was unconscious, it felt like I was floating in a black pool. I couldn't see the bottom and I wasn't tied down, but I also couldn't move. All I could do was lay there in the void." He rubbed my chin. "But I heard you. I heard every single thing you said, and then at some point a little crack opened and a sliver of light came in, then another, and another. And do you know what I thought?"

"What?" I murmured.

"That there was so much in my life I hadn't seen. So many things I wanted to do with you, plans I had for us, for our future. And I knew I'd be fine." He kissed my forehead. "That's the same feeling I have now."

"I'm not like that, though. I don't know how to be." I tucked my head under his and held him, gripping the back of his shirt.

His fingers trailed up and down my spine in a gentle caress. "But you do, my vicious little queen. When we left the penthouse, you had no doubts about our strategy. Yes, you knew something could go wrong or could blindside us and force us to change our plans, but you were confident, weren't you?"

"Yes."

"Then lean into that."

"But—"

"I know, believe me, I know." He shuddered. "Remember, I saw someone point a gun at you. It terrifies me you could get hurt one day, or that I might never see you again." He sighed and held me tighter. "But the same feeling I had when I first saw you, that told me you were my person, the woman who would be my queen, my equal, perfectly capable of handling my familia and walking alongside me in life, is the same feeling I have that we have to do this and *will* be fine. Can you trust me in that?"

I didn't want to. But I did. Everything Marco had said was right. All I was feeling was the fear and anxiety of almost losing him. If it wasn't for that, Felipe would be dead by now.

I was confident I could and *would* take his life, and I needed to grab a hold of that feeling with both hands, not just for me, but for Marco and our families.

"Yes," I whispered.

He kissed me again, and I fisted his shirt in my hands. When he broke the kiss, he gently bumped his forehead against mine. "Good girl, now let's go raise hell."

Pop. Pop. Pop.

The war had already started by the time we arrived.

Marco and I pulled in behind the barricade of bulletproof SUVs our men used to block the exits, while Felipe's men fought to open a path.

We'd never let that happen.

Dashing to the back of our own SUV, I grabbed the bazooka while Marco adjusted it on my shoulder. Together, we set the targeting system, and he covered me while I fired.

Boom!

I shot through two SUVs, killing six men. One exploded, sending another group running for their lives.

Felipe shouted at his men, and their SUVs reversed, fleeing back to his mansion.

"Follow them!" Marco shouted.

Marco and I scrambled back into our car and drove after them.

I tried to shoot out their tires, but they were returning fire too quickly for me to get a clean shot.

Six groups of our men trailed behind us, shooting at anyone they could.

Spotting an opening, I rolled down the window, keeping myself close to the car, cocked my shotgun, and fired.

The bullet hit perfectly, breaking the axle of the car directly in front of us. It wiggled, the driver over-corrected, and it flipped.

Marco immediately swerved around it, then gave my thigh a squeeze—a silent nod of praise—and I loaded the shotgun again. But it was too late.

Felipe and his men made it to the mansion and closed the electric gate in our faces.

Ramming it would be a death sentence. We'd make it through the barrier, but the barrage of bullets would be too much, even for the bulletproof SUV.

Marco immediately threw the car in reverse. Two of our men used their SUVs to cut in front of ours, forming a triangle of protection, and that's where we made our stance.

Bullets rained around us as we dashed behind our vehicles.

I set the bazooka on my shoulder again, but Felipe's men had one too, and they were *faster*.

"Move!" Marco grabbed me and we raced behind another set of cars.

The rocket hit where we'd been standing, exploding three of our SUVs. I fired the bazooka, aiming for the fuel tank of one of Felipe's vehicles.

His men weren't able to escape the blast. They flew. Some hit the electric fence, and it fried them alive. Others hit the wall, another car, and some were only thrown to the ground.

Now was our chance.

"Advance!" Marco shouted, taking the first group of men with him.

I followed behind him with the second. "Check your vantage points!"

Marco was likely right that the sniper who shot him wasn't part of Felipe's team, but I still wanted all our bases covered.

We shot anyone that moved, but some of Felipe's men had avoided the blast and fired back. It didn't matter; they were on the losing side.

But that didn't bring me any sense of relief. Instead, it made me more alert.

The moment Felipe realized his death was imminent was the moment he'd get desperate—and that's exactly when he'd become dangerous.

We needed to limit whatever he could use against us and fast, or else things could shift into his favor.

I took out another two men, while Marco barreled through another five and we continued forward at a steady pace.

Then I saw Felipe.

His eyes were wild, panicked, and the moment our eyes met, he ran.

Shit!

I cocked my gun, following him with the muzzle, but the son of a bitch ran in a straight line behind his men! Using them as a shield to save his own skin, and no matter how many times I fired, I wouldn't be able to get him.

I needed to change tactics, *fast*.

Diving to the ground, I set my gun up for the shot, waited until his scrambling legs nearly came into view, then pulled the trigger.

He went down, *hard*.

I fired again, but Felipe sat up, stabbing the man closest to him in the leg, forcing him to take my bullet in his place.

Fuck!

Felipe dragged himself to the front door, and I shot once more, but he swung it closed.

Then his house turned into a steel fortress. Large metal storm panels rolled down in front of every door and window. I shot at the gate, but it did nothing.

We finished off the last of Felipe's men, then Marco pulled me to my feet.

"Do you think the bazooka can blow a hole through it?" I asked.

"It should, but I don't like that he's in there while we're out in the open."

I nodded, quickly checking for any spaces I thought Felipe could defend from. There had to be a reason he'd barricaded himself in his house, and it wasn't just to protect his family. He either had reinforcements to call, or another way to deal with us.

Marco whistled, capturing our men's attention, and I made a circle in the air, then pointed to the few remaining cars, commanding them to fall back and regroup.

"Keep your eyes open," Marco warned. "He's planning something."

Our men nodded. But just as we went to reload the bazooka, the metal creaked, slowly rolling back up.

What the fuck?

I exchanged glances with Marco, who was just as confused and concerned as I was. Slowly, we approached the gates, guns drawn. The hairs on every inch of my body stood at attention as my eyes darted to each window and door.

I couldn't see any movement or anyone as we made our way to

the front steps. Slowly, the door opened, and there stood Felipe's daughter, Julianna.

Her eyes widened as she took in our army, then shifted to me, and then Marco. "Are you Catalina Salazar and Marco Torrino?"

"Yes." I lowered my gun slightly. Not that I wouldn't shoot her if I had to, but I truly hoped it wouldn't come to that.

She met my eyes and squared her shoulders, then held out her hand, revealing a small gray USB. "This has everything I have on my father. Every deal, bank account, transaction that he's made, every business venture, associate he's met with, and alliance he's formed."

I drew back. My gaze shifted to Marco's, and he nodded, confirming he'd cover me if anything happened.

I tucked my gun into the holster at my waist and took the USB cautiously from her. "Why are you giving us this?"

"My father has been trafficking women and children. He's a disgusting bastard, and he needs to be stopped."

Felipe was involved in trafficking?

Could this be what we'd been searching for?

We hadn't been able to make a link between Felipe, Fernando, and Simon, but maybe this was why. If what Julianna was saying was true, it's possible Fernando and Felipe were secretly in business together, or Felipe followed in Fernando's footsteps once he passed, and that's why he was now working with Simon.

Either way, this should help us find my missing people.

"What do you want in return?" Marco stepped closer to me. But the moment he did, Julianna flinched.

It was quick, but we both saw it. Felipe had been hurting her, *abusing* her.

Marco immediately shifted back, not wanting to make her more uncomfortable.

She gulped, her gaze focusing back on me, and when she

spoke, her voice was unsteady. "I... I can't stop him. I can't fix what he's done, not by myself." She licked her lips, then a hardness set into her. One that shouldn't have had to be there. One I recognized all too well. "Kill him. I don't care how, but kill him. And my mother."

I tilted my head. "Both of them?"

"Yes." Julianna clenched her hands. "She knew, and she supported him. She's a selfish person who only cares about herself. I know we're not saints. But that... that's not something I can accept."

"Do you realize what this will mean for you? You would be the new head of a family where we've killed off many of your men. Your assets and protection would be limited, and you would need to use everything you have to rebuild."

She rolled her shoulders back and spoke in a tone that signified her finality. "Yes. I'm aware. I know it'll be difficult, but it's the right thing to do."

I gave the USB to Marco, who passed it along to one of his men and gave them orders to get it to the right people.

I turned back to Julianna. "Where is Felipe now?"

"In the panic room. I can open it for you."

"Did he call for any reinforcements?" I asked.

"He has people who work outside of the city. They're likely on their way here. Around sixty or so."

"Relay that to our men at the entrance. Take whoever you need," Marco ordered behind me.

I grabbed my gun once more. "We have no problem doing what you've asked, Julianna. But if you're leading us into a trap—"

"I know, and I'm not. I can't... I won't live like this any longer. We're both getting something out of this." Her gaze was firm, filled with determination.

I exchanged gazes with Marco, and he nodded in agreement. Julianna was telling the truth. I knew it just as well as I knew my name. I was all too familiar with that look in her eyes. She reminded me far too much of myself, and I had to push away the sudden flash of empathy filling me.

I never wanted anyone to go through what I went through. I knew it happened, that the world was filled with monsters, but it was completely different seeing the same trauma and tragedy reflected in a stranger's eyes.

If I would have been in a similar position when I was younger, gotten my hands on information of my father's dealings, and someone would have knocked on my door who could kill him, I would have done anything, *given* them anything to escape.

Her need for freedom and power and control over her own life made me feel connected to her, and I hated that even with all of that, I still had to be wary.

I didn't know Julianna, and while her pain spoke to me on incredibly deep levels, it didn't change the fact that she was the daughter of my enemy and currently guiding us through Felipe's pompous house. Even if she wasn't leading us into a trap, it didn't mean Felipe hadn't already planned one for us.

We stopped in front of an unassuming section of wooden walls, with an expensive piece of artwork in a golden frame. Julianna pushed a part of the wall, and a small piece of the paneling slid up, revealing a hand and eye scanner. She leaned forward, allowing the machine to scan her, then typed something on a keyboard, and another part of the wall opened, revealing a screen recording from inside the room.

Felipe was on the phone, a gun next to him while his hands moved furiously in the air. Paloma, Julianna's mother and Felipe's lover, tried to press a piece of cloth to his leg to stop the bleeding, but he shoved her away.

When Julianna turned to us, her face was cold, devoid of all emotion. "As you can see, they're the only two people in this room. I've disabled the defense mechanisms. I'll walk in first, so you know I'm telling the truth."

She went to press a key, but I put my hand out in front of her. "Why did your parents go to the panic room without you?"

There was a small flicker in her eyes. Her shoulders drooped, and her voice wavered. "Because I wasn't important enough to save."

My heart broke for her, for all the pain and misery she must have gone through. I wanted to pull her into my arms, and tell her it was okay. I wanted to protect her, in the same way I wished someone would have protected me.

But I couldn't. Not until this was over.

Marco's fingers stroked the back of my spine. A small, simple movement, but one to remind me he was there, that I wasn't alone, that I had his support.

I looked at the screen once more. Panic rooms, especially of this caliber, often had a button to lock and unlock the door inside. Between that, and Julianna's parents' lack of care about her, I had to ask, "If your father thinks we took you hostage and are forcing you to open the door, would he shoot through you to save himself?"

"Yes," she whispered. Tears filled her eyes, but she turned away before they fell. "See this red dot here, next to him? This is the button to lock the room again. He likely has a code word for his reinforcements. I don't know it, so yes, he will shoot first, even if it's me."

I gave her a single nod, then turned to Marco. "I have an idea."

He narrowed his eyes. "And I'm not going to like it."

I gave him a small smile and squeezed his hand. "It'll be fine. We'll have Julianna call out to Felipe when she opens the door, let him get his gun ready, and aimed upward. Then, I will shoot him from the ground."

"You'll have a split second to get off that shot, Lina."

"I know, and I can do it." I squeezed his hand again.

He sighed, then leaned in close and whispered, "If you get hurt, I will punish you."

"Don't tease me with a good time."

He glared at me and I gave him a soft smile, then turned to Julianna. "Can you do that?"

She nodded, then pressed a key and the door to the panic room popped open.

"Dad?" Julianna called out.

On the screen, Felipe shifted and grabbed his gun. Paloma clung to him, but he shook her off and pointed to the button on the door. She moved next to it, ready to lock the door.

"Dad? It's me."

Felipe slowly stood, and I crouched on the floor.

"I'm coming in now."

Felipe aimed his gun at the door, ready to fire. Julianna made the sound of a step, but didn't move forward. Then once more. Then again and I threw myself into the room, sliding across the floor, shooting Felipe in his other leg.

He went down, losing his grip on the gun, firing into the ceiling before it fell away from him.

He reached out for it, but I shot around it, making him jerk back.

Felipe scrambled back. Marco dashed in, kicking the gun behind us, while aiming his own weapon at Felipe's head.

Beads of sweat slid down his face. He trembled in pain, but he still had the audacity to sneer. "You can't kill me. You'll never be able to get away with it. My people will hunt you—"

Marco shot him in his shoulder. "Do not ever attempt to tell my woman what she can and cannot do."

Felipe howled in pain, Paloma trembling beside him.

I stepped forward to Marco's side. "You see, I wanted to torture you, Felipe. I was going to hang you from your limbs, pull off every single one of your nails, slice at your skin for hours, while you begged me to spare your life. Get every piece of information I could from you and once I was finally satisfied, I planned to cut off your tongue, castrate you, and shove your own dick down your throat until you choked to death. But there's someone who deserves their vengeance more than me."

Julianna stepped behind me, and Felipe's eyes went wide.

"How could you?" Paloma screeched.

Julianna laughed, but it was dark, menacing. "How could I? How could I?" she yelled. "How could *you*? Neither of you have ever cared about me a day in my life. You're only with Felipe because of his money, while he's only with you for when he needs a woman draped across his arm and *willing* pussy."

Julianna's eyes bore into Felipe's. "Did you think I didn't know? That I don't know about the women you rape? Or that I have a half-sister you're trying to sell to the highest bidder all because you don't want another mouth to feed?"

I stared at Julianna in shock. Felipe was trying to sell his own child?

"This world will be so much better without you, *both* of you," Julianna spat.

Felipe glared at her, but his words lacked any strength. He'd lost too much blood. "They'll kill you too."

Julianna smiled brightly. "They might, but at least I took both of you down with me."

I lifted my gun at Felipe and Paloma. "Put your heads on the ground."

"Please," Paloma pleaded.

"You're going to die either way. It's up to you if you'd like it to be fast or slow. But know I'm being generous right now, because if I kill you slowly, I *will* make it hurt."

Paloma whimpered, but lowered her head to the ground in a bow.

"You next," Marco ordered.

Felipe glared at him, but when he tried to move, he couldn't. He fell over instead.

I waited, just for a second, taking pleasure in the way they trembled before me. Their terror brought a smile to my face.

Then I shot them both.

I turned to Julianna, her face firm, accepting of whatever I might do. "I'm not going to kill you... Marco?"

He placed his hand on my hip. "Yes, my queen?"

I whispered softly so that only he could hear. "Would you agree to us signing a contract of alliance with Julianna, to keep her safe until she gets on her own two feet?"

He squeezed my hip and nodded, then spoke loudly enough to make sure our men outside could hear. "Whatever you need, Julianna. We will do it for you. We will help you build, restructure—"

"And help you save your sister," I said.

Julianna's face fell, tears pouring from her eyes, and for the first time, she looked like the seventeen-year-old girl she was. "Thank you. Thank you, thank you. *Thank you so much*!"

Footsteps thundered down the corridor, then into the room. "Boss!" Carlos yelled, "The women Felipe and Fernando were going to traffic? We found them!"

Twenty-Four

Marco

I drummed my fingers on the steering wheel while Catalina reloaded her gun beside me.

Her eyes flickered to mine. "You feel it too, right?"

"Something about this is off. It was too easy."

She nodded. "I know it's not possible for that to be all the trafficked victims and that we'll need to find the ones that had already been sent overseas, but we've spent *months* searching for them. Now, with Julianna's information, we suddenly have them in less than an hour?"

I hummed in agreement. "Julianna was an unexpected variable. Since she's been searching for her half-sister for years, it makes sense that she simply had access to direct information we couldn't."

"But it was still too easy."

"Yeah." I stroked her thigh. "Let's just deal with Felipe's reinforcements, then go to the bunker and save whoever we can. That's all we can do for now."

She squeezed my hand, and I put the car into gear.

By the time we made it back to the front entrance, it looked like World War III had taken place. Cars were on fire, flipped, some with men still trapped inside. The air was tinged with smoke, car fumes, the metallic smell of blood, and fried human skin, a scent close to barbeque. Gunshots rained around us as police and ambulance sirens sounded in the distance.

I came to a stop behind the barricade of our men and grabbed a machine gun.

Catalina adjusted the strap of the gun on my shoulder, then turned to Joseph. "How are we doing?"

"We're all right, but we have a couple of people who need to go to the hospital as soon as we've cleared the way. One at least has a concussion, another got shot in the shoulder, and a third is unconscious from the backlash of an explosion."

Catalina nodded, then looked up at me. "Let's finish this quickly, then."

I nodded and stepped forward.

"Cover him!" she ordered.

I planted my feet, inhaled, and fired. Each shot was beautifully violent, ripping through cars, trees, and light poles. Every one of our enemies went down in a miraculous spray of blood.

Catalina and her men took care of anyone I missed, and by the time I'd let go of the trigger, it was over. There were no movements, no more gunshots. No moans or cries. Nothing but the fires raging around us—the sign of our victory.

Even though this had ended in the best-case scenario, and most of our men could go home tonight, safe and sound, unease gnawed at my gut.

Something about traveling to the bunker concerned me. I couldn't pin down the feeling, but my intuition screamed I needed to be careful, figure out a way to protect us, protect *her*. But why?

Sam had verified the route, the bunker, the guards there,

everything. I wasn't like this when we'd come to this battle or when Catalina had been mowing down our enemies beside me.

But now? It felt *different*. A full-blown klaxon was ringing in my skull, warning me that if I wasn't careful, I could lose Lina—my world, the entirety of my essence—tonight.

Catalina slipped her hand into mine and when she looked up at me, her dark brown eyes were filled with so much warmth it forced some of my fear away.

I needed to feel her, hold her in my arms. Maybe then I could silence enough of my worry to figure out my next steps.

I kissed her, and everything was suddenly bright and alive again. Each soft kiss invigorated me, gave me strength. Then I rested my forehead against her own.

"Lina—"

She placed her hand on my chest. "What are you scared of, Marco?"

"I know you might not believe me. You don't have any reason to. But something keeps telling me you'll be in danger if you go to the bunker. You should stay here."

"I believe you, but I'll be just fine."

I shook my head. "How can you say that?"

"Because nothing is going to happen to me if I'm with you." She caressed my back, drawing little circles on my skin. "I trust you, Marco, completely. But no matter what we do, danger is part of our lives. And if someone is out there trying to kill me, we won't ever truly be safe until they're dead." She tilted her head to the side. "Wouldn't it be better to find out who it is now and take care of it than spend every waking moment terrified?"

"I don't want you willingly walking into a trap, Lina. I won't risk you."

"You don't have to. But we don't know who it is or why. What if they come after you instead? What if they hold you or someone from our families hostage?"

I sighed, running a hand through my hair. She was right.

"Marco, we have a chance to do something really good here. A chance to save a lot of people and make so many wrongs, right. If you think I could be hurt, then let's use what you're feeling as a gift, and make sure we're as prepared as possible. That's all we can do."

"But what if it's not enough?"

Her eyes watered, but the way her lips slowly tilted into a soft smile stole my breath away. "You almost died, Marco. But you came back to me, and that experience has left me with a brand-new perspective." She wet her lips, drawing in a deep breath. "When you were laying there, I knew you'd never leave me. I never doubted you then, and I won't doubt you now. I will always have the utmost faith in you, in us. I think something's off with this too, and if you have a concern or worry, I will always listen to it. But didn't you say you had plans for us? For our future? Believe in those, and believe in us. We will always come back to one another. That's just how things are going to be."

I brushed a small tear away from her face and kissed her again. "You're so courageous, my vicious little queen. Every moment I spend with you leaves me completely in awe."

"Then we'll spend more. As many moments as you want. Our entire lives, even."

I buried my head in the curve of her neck, inhaling her sweet scent. I loved being surrounded by it, smelling her on my skin, my clothes. She was my home, my sanctuary, and if she could have such strong strength in us, in *me*, then so could I.

I stood to my full height and called Anthony.

He answered on the third ring. "It's good to hear your voice, boss. You had me scared for a second."

The memory of the muzzle pointed at Catalina's head flashed into my mind, so real I had to turn my head and breathe her in to remember she was safe. "I got lucky. Listen, I need you to head to the bunker with your group. You're closer, so you'll get there sooner. But be careful, check your surroundings, and bring the heavy artillery."

"Will do, boss."

I hung up and called Carlos over while Catalina yelled for Joseph.

I waited for both of them to arrive, but before I could speak, Catalina turned to Joseph. "We will continue to work together with the Torrino familia from here on out. We will assist them, as they have assisted us. Pass the message along to the men here and follow any orders Marco gives you like they were coming from me."

Joseph's eyes flickered between Catalina and me. Then he nodded. "Understood, Doña."

I squeezed Catalina's hip in silent thanks. Yet again, she was putting her faith in me.

"Carlos, Joseph, I need you to stay here and make sure anyone who needs medical attention gets to the hospital."

"Yes, boss," Carlos said.

"Good. Once we leave, I want you both to wait twenty minutes, then pick a group of four men and send them after us. Make sure they keep their distance. We don't know what we're walking into, but they're our contingency plan if something goes wrong."

"We will take care of it," Joseph said.

I gave them a curt nod, and they stepped away, leaving Catalina and me alone.

She squeezed my hand, interlacing our fingers. "We should go reload."

I followed her and strapped myself with everything I could think of. Then we slid into an SUV.

I started the car, but when I went to put it in gear, Catalina stopped me, squeezing my hand. Her grip was warm, firm. I wanted to hold her, rest my head in the crook of her neck. Feel her fingers run through my scalp, until every ounce of fear left me, but I couldn't, not until this was over.

"Ready?" she asked.

I turned her hand in mine, studying the differences. Hers was so small compared to my own, her skin a tanned shade of gold that was darker, luscious, the most beautiful thing I'd ever seen. "Lina, I haven't opened myself up or shared my vulnerabilities with anyone since my parents were killed. Not until you. So I need you to stay safe. If you need to run, run. If you need to fight, fight. If you need to leave me behind—"

"I won't do that, Marco. Don't *ever* ask me to again."

I sighed.

"Marco—"

"I love you, Catalina. So if I'm lacking, take care of yourself for me. You own everything that I am, and I won't lose you."

"You won't. You *won't*," she said again, firmly. Her voice held so strong and sure that without another word, I threw the car in drive.

I didn't know how tonight would end, but my Catalina would make it home safely. No matter what, I had to sacrifice in her place.

The buzzing in the back of my mind grew louder and louder every mile we drove.

I scanned the road at every stop and turn. There were no obvious signs of danger—no one was trailing us and anyone we passed never paid us more than a second of attention before moving on with their night. It was all seemingly normal.

Still, the nagging sense of dread grew.

Catalina placed her hand over mine, and it was only then I realized how hard I had been clenching the gearshift. I turned my hand to hold her own and glanced over at her. She gave me a soft, reassuring smile, then resumed scanning our surroundings.

She was just as alert as I was, her body coiled, ready to react at the first sign of a threat, and while I wished she were somewhere else, *anywhere* else, her presence gave me strength.

I checked the time on the dashboard. Anthony should have already arrived at the bunker. Normally, he'd call once a situation had been resolved, but it was odd he hadn't confirmed he'd found the women. Were there more guards than we expected? More traps? Had something happened to him?

Catalina squeezed my hand again, and I took a deep breath. Worrying like this wasn't like me, and I didn't have enough information to anticipate what might happen. If I didn't calm myself down, I could make a mistake that would bring my worst fears to life.

As we turned down the secluded road leading to the bunker's hidden entrance, my anxiety shifted into a full-blown scream inside my skull. I gripped the steering wheel tighter, my knuckles turning white.

Then I saw it—one of our SUVs was ahead, engulfed in flames. A sudden bit of silver caught my eyes, and I slammed on the brakes, throwing my arm out in front of Catalina to keep her from hitting the dashboard. The tires squealed as we skidded to a stop just short of a spike strip laid across the road.

"Are you okay?" I cupped Catalina's face, looking her over.

She patted her chest and took a deep breath. "I'm fine."

I put the SUV into park. "Stay here in case that vehicle is going to explode."

Her eyes narrowed, but then she pressed her lips together in a tight line and gave me a single nod.

I drew my gun, slowly approaching the SUV, keeping a safe distance. The smell of charred metal, human flesh, and smoke burned my nostrils.

As I grew closer, I counted four bodies, and one of them had been driving—Anthony. Bullet holes riddled the side of the SUV and penetrated through the armored exterior.

They never stood a chance. I shouldn't have sent him.

Death was inevitable, especially in this line of work. But Anthony was my cousin, and I'd sent him and his men to die. Their blood was on my hands. They were my responsibility, and I'd failed them.

I took a step closer, then an urge to run came over me so quickly that I moved before I'd even consciously realized I was doing so.

The air filled with gunfire.

They're trying to kill me first, then her. If they shoot our SUV with the same rounds as they did Anthony's car, she'll die.

"Catalina, run!" I waved my arms frantically, sprinting toward her while the enemy fired at me.

Catalina burst through the door with a grenade in her hand. She pulled the pin, and threw it at the shooter. It exploded, buying me time to get to her. But the shooter was too fast.

We dashed toward the woods as bullets barraged our vehicle. I grabbed Catalina around the waist, pulling her against me, and threw us both into the brush just as Anthony's SUV exploded.

My ears rang, and I blinked rapidly, trying to clear my blurred vision, while Catalina laid peacefully in my arms.

She wasn't moving.

"Lina?"

Nothing.

"Catalina, wake up!"

I shook her, my heartbeat pounding in my ears.

"Catalina!"

Her eyelids fluttered, then she stirred with a soft groan.

I ran my hands over her body. "Can you hear me? Are you hurt?"

She blinked, then shook her head slowly. "I'm okay... I think." Her gaze sharpened as she focused on me. She squeezed my arms, shoulders, rubbed my chest. "Are you hurt?"

I kissed her head. "No, I'm fine, but we need to move."

I cocked my head to the right where the raging flames from the SUV would conceal us, but would also leave us blind. "Stay low," I whispered.

Catalina nodded, her body tense as we crawled through the underbrush.

As we made it around the burning vehicle, a voice cut through the air. "I hoped that explosion would take you out, but you're like a fucking cockroach. No matter how many times I try to put you down, you just won't die."

My breath caught in my throat.

No...

It couldn't be...

"Anthony," I whispered.

Catalina stilled beside me.

"Come on out, boss. Don't make this harder than it has to be." His voice was light, yet dripping with malice. It was so different from the one I knew.

Anthony was the joker, the one who acted like life was a game. Now he was trying to kill me? My own cousin?

We crouched lower to the ground. He didn't know where we were... yet.

Anthony's voice rang out, this time closer to the street. "You know, when my father told me he killed your mother and father, I told him he was crazy. I thought he was the worst person in the world. How could he turn on family when we're all each other has? But he swore that your mother had done something to his brother. That he was no longer fit to rule. He would have gone after you too, but you know who stopped him? Me. *I* killed my own father for you and look at how you repaid me!"

The words hit me like a physical blow.

He killed his father? My uncle had killed my parents? And he knew?

I tried to find their killer for years! The bastard had fucking helped me investigate! That's what got me into gathering intelligence on mafia families in the first place. And all that time, it was one of our own.

I fisted the dirt, wanting to rush to him and beat him until there was nothing left. But if I tried, he'd shoot me. I couldn't even curse at him. If I did, I'd leak our location and put myself and Catalina at risk.

Catalina's grip on my arm tightened, her body taut, lips twisted into a snarl as her rage fed my own.

"You became obsessed with Catalina. I thought it would pass. I *believed* in you. Then you went to Italy and let me lead. I loved it. Every ounce of it. Having people look up to me, listen to me, *obey* me? It was incredible! And what did you do when you came back? You gave it all away to *her*! You want me to answer to some bitch all because you wanted some fucking pussy? Are you insane?" Anthony's voice grew shriller, more unhinged with every word.

"I knew you'd lost your mind then," Anthony spat. "You didn't even realize I knew all about the trafficking, because I worked with Fernando, Simon, and Felipe while you were gone. If it wasn't for that bitch, Julianna, you would have *never* found them. I hid all the evidence because you couldn't be trusted. All you cared about was what you thought was right, instead of what opportunities and profit could be made. Without you, this famiglia will flourish under my command."

He knew...

He knew about everything.

When we were little, Anthony was my best friend, my confidant. Somewhere, after my parents died, he'd changed. It was just a little, but it was there.

I thought it was because he was grieving, too. He spent so many nights over at our house to get away from his own father that he'd become like a brother to me. But I was so deep in planning everything, their funeral, the future of the famiglia, trying to keep us afloat that I didn't pay attention. I didn't see him, and now, my men and Catalina's familia had suffered because of it.

Catalina squeezed my arm again. "It's not your fault. Don't let that motherfucker make you doubt yourself for one second. You're better than that," she whispered in a sharp voice.

I nodded. She was right. That didn't erase the guilt I felt, but now wasn't the time.

Anthony fired another round of gunshots. Then he stepped into the street. His face was twisted and deranged. Sweat coated his brow, and his grin was wide, like a cat that had caught his prey. But it was the small black object in his hand that made my breath catch in my throat.

It was a detonator.

"You have two options," Anthony yelled. "Since I missed at the penthouse, either you and your bitch come out here and kneel in front of me, so I can make sure I get you both this time, or I press the detonator in my hand and blow up the bunker. It's your choice."

Shit!

Catalina had to stay hidden while I got the detonator away from him. But the bunker was over five-hundred feet away, and there was no way either of us could rush Anthony before he pressed the button.

It was also possible Anthony wasn't alone. If he was working with Felipe, he may have kept the guards at the bunker alive, giving him reinforcements, while ours, at best, were fifteen minutes out.

Catalina's voice cut through my thoughts. "I have an idea."

I turned to her, and the determination on her face chilled me to my core.

"No," I said firmly.

"You don't even know what it is," she hissed back.

"I know it involves you sacrificing yourself. No, Lina."

Catalina's eyes bore into mine. "Marco, do you trust me?"

"Of course I do, but—"

"He wants me. He wants you to suffer by watching me die. That's why he aimed for me at the penthouse and not you. That's why he keeps mentioning me. If he thought you were on his side, he might let you live."

My jaw clenched. "No, he won't!" I snarled in a whisper. "He's too far gone for that."

Catalina pressed on. "Marco, he still wants you to suffer. He thinks I've replaced him, so he wants the competition out, and he wants to make you beg for my life. Like he said, you're too hard to kill. He's not going to kill me until he knows you'll see him do it. He wants that power over you. That's why he wants us on our knees in front of him."

"Lina—"

I reached for her, but when she took my hand, she slipped a zip tie around it and tightened the cord. Every muscle in my body tightened.

No.

Shock flooded my system. I pulled, trying to free myself, but she'd tied the other end around a bush. I could break the branches, I *would* break them, but not before she'd put her plan into motion.

"Lina, please. Please, don't do this."

"When you get free, give me a distraction. That's all I need."

"Lina, please. *Please*!" I yanked on the bush. It bent, but didn't break. I pulled harder and harder, trembling as I strained every muscle trying to move, to stop her, but I couldn't.

Catalina stood, circling around the opposite end of the burning SUV, going back the way we came. The flames casted her in a glow of red, yellow, and orange streaks, like a dragon ready to mow down anyone who stood before her.

But when she turned to me, she wore a soft, sad smile. "I love you, Marco Torrino," she whispered. Then she stepped out into the night.

I opened my mouth to call out for her, to scream, roar, do *anything* to bring her back to me, but then she held up her hands. "Anthony! I'm coming out!"

Anthony smirked, his voice dripping with sarcasm. "Well, well, well. Now this is unexpected. I must say I'm shocked. I honestly thought you'd put up more of a fight. Where's Marco?"

"Dead."

I stilled.

Was that her plan?

"You expect me to believe that?"

"I don't really care what you believe, Anthony. I'm here; isn't that what you wanted? Let my people go."

I took a deep breath. I needed to calm down and focus. Catalina didn't have long. She needed me to give her a distraction. If I didn't do it at the right time, her plan would fail.

I patted my pockets for anything that could help me break the tie, then my fingers brushed against something near where Catalina had been lying—A switchblade.

She left it there for me.

I freed myself and circled around a tree, shrouding myself in darkness while I watched them.

I couldn't sneak up on them. Anthony was facing my direction and would spot me before I even got the chance to approach.

So how could I...

Then it hit me.

I'd have to leave her, dash toward the bunker and make enough noise that Anthony would turn toward the sound, giving Catalina the opening she needed. She was small, but her movements were quicker than mine, and damn sure faster than Anthony's.

It could work. But then why didn't she let me go out there and deal with him? Then it donned on me.

She'd told him to let her *people go.* If this didn't work, she'd take complete responsibility for their lives instead of me. Even now, even when we were so deep in shit that it had taken me a second to get my bearings, she was there, protecting me, watching out for *me.*

We're going to survive this, and when we do, I swear on every fiber of my being I'm going to spank her ass raw.

But for now, I had to wait. She'd give me a signal somehow, and I would not miss it.

"Remove your weapons," Anthony said.

Slowly, she dropped her guns, knives, even the grenades.

There's one missing.

I counted them one more time to make sure, but I was right. She hadn't removed the tactical blade in her left boot. Her pants were too bulky to see it easily, but I'd watched her slip it there earlier.

Anthony didn't notice. That motherfucker was too busy checking out Catalina's ass as she bent over.

I'll rip out his eyeballs for even thinking about it.

"You know, you're a terrible actress. You claim Marco's dead, but you haven't even shed a tear," Anthony said.

"Clearly I was a great actress, if you thought I gave a shit about him." Her voice was steady, emotionless.

Anthony sneered. "That's fucking bullshit!"

"I didn't ask for his help, he offered. I didn't ask for your family or whatever it is you think he gave me. I didn't ask him for anything." She shrugged. "Matter of fact, I told him multiple times to leave me alone, but he couldn't. He pursued *me*. He stalked *me*. And I think you're just angry that the little bit of affection I gave him was enough for him to turn his back on *you*." She smirked.

The lie rolled off her tongue expertly. She'd switched back into her façade that had helped her survive all those years with her father.

But Anthony didn't know anything about Catalina, and he'd grossly underestimated *my queen*.

Rearing back, he punched her in the face. Catalina went down, and it took everything in me not to beat him until his bones caved in and I tore his limbs off with my bare hands.

But that was it—the signal.

I dashed through the forest, drawing Anthony's attention.

"MARCO!" Anthony screamed.

Bullets flew past me as I ran towards the bunker.

Then a different scream pierced the air—a screech of pain and agony.

I whirled around to Catalina kneeling on top of Anthony. Her knife to his throat. Anthony writhed beneath her, blood spewing through the air.

My vicious little queen had cut off his wrist.

I sprinted back to her, relief washing through me the closer I got. Grabbing the detonator, I switched it off, then stalked toward her.

She watched Anthony, her every muscle tense and alert as I approached. "Are you okay?"

"Yes." Even though that was far from the truth. My uncle had killed my parents out of jealousy and hatred, and my cousin had betrayed me, and tried to kill the love of my life. But she was alive, and that was all that mattered.

She held a gun out for me and stood, pinning Anthony down with her boot. "I wanted to kill him. But he's your cousin. If you want—"

I shot Anthony in the head, and when Catalina stepped back, I emptied a clip into his chest. But his death didn't help the seething rage boiling in my blood.

"Marco..." Catalina's voice was soft now, tender and caring.

I pulled her into my arms, burying my fingers into her hair as I held her head to my chest.

She clung to me, and like a calm to my storm, the fear, anger, and fury slid away until there was nothing but her, my vicious little queen.

Gently, I cradled her head in my hands, brushing away Anthony's blood from her face as I examined her cheek. Nothing was broken, but there would be a nasty bruise tomorrow.

"Do you have any idea how scared I was?"

"I know," she whispered. "I'm sorry, but it was the only way."

"It wasn't and we both know it. You did that, so if something went wrong, I'd be safe. That I wouldn't be able to blame myself.

But mi pequeña reina viciosa, I can live through anything, but I can't live without you."

"Marco, you've gone through enough tonight. I just didn't want that on you. I... I could handle it."

I glared at her. "Yes, you did. And you almost got yourself killed. If you think I'm going to just let that go, you have another thing coming."

"But isn't that what you did earlier for me?" She grinned innocently, as if she hadn't almost just given me a heart attack.

"Touché, mi pequeña reina viciosa, just remember that when all of this is done, you will be punished."

She kissed my cheek. Then her expression turned serious. "We can take a second if you need to process. Our men should be here soon."

I took a deep breath. Catalina was safe, but we still had a job to do. "No. It's better for me if I keep moving. Let me call our men to let them know what happened, then we'll go to the bunker. And any surprises we come across we'll handle, *together*."

She nodded, linking her hand with mine. "Together."

Catalina and I dashed through the woods, using the dense foliage as cover in case Felipe's men were still alive. Reaching the bunker, we found five bodies strewn across the ground.

Anthony had likely killed them before doubling back to ambush us.

Apparently, he couldn't be loyal to anyone.

Catalina and I exchanged a glance. If Anthony had killed these men, had he killed the women, too?

I fished out the keys from one of the guard's pockets and opened the door.

The stench hit me first—a mixture of piss, shit, blood, and sweat. I stepped inside and when one of the women flinched, another scent became apparent, one that made my stomach churn. She'd been raped recently. And it sickened me even more to think it might have been Anthony's doing.

Dozens of women huddled in the far corner of a large cage, their bodies pressed together in a desperate attempt to hide them from being targeted. They were filthy, their clothes tattered, stained with blood and grime.

But it was their vacant eyes that broke my heart. There was no fear or hope there. But when their gaze slowly moved to Catalina, a flicker of emotion finally crossed their faces. Pity.

They think she's going to be locked in here with them.

How could anyone do this? What these women had gone through...

"Lina," I whispered, my voice barely audible, "I'll unlock the cages, but I think I should stay outside." The last thing these women needed was another man in their space, even one here to help.

Catalina gulped beside me, then nodded stiffly. Together, we opened the cages, but the women didn't move.

My heart ached as I looked at them. We had saved their bodies, but it would take a long time before they found their souls again.

I stepped outside, leaving Catalina alone with them, and called Carlos.

"Carlos, things here are... they're bad. I need you to get any women who can stomach cases of sexual assault and trauma here to help. Tell them I'll pay them double, triple whatever they earn, anything they need, as long as they'll come. These women... they can't have men around right now."

"Okay." Carlos's voice was tinged with the same agony I felt. He took a deep breath. "Okay," he said again, more firmly this time, "I'll make the calls and have them bring food and water."

"Towels, blankets, and clothing, too."

"Yes, boss. What about the men? They're coming down the road right now."

"Have them get whatever they need to set up a temporary shower, then establish a perimeter. Also, get someone to bring two buses. We'll let them stay in the condos until they're ready to go home."

"Will do, boss."

I hung up with Carlos, listening to Catalina's voice, so soft and soothing as she spoke to the women.

Eventually, someone moved, another woman sobbed, and it felt like the air had gotten easier to breathe.

Whatever Catalina had said had gotten through to them. They finally understood we were here to *save* them, not hurt them.

Catalina peeked outside of the door.

"Can I stay, or do you need me to leave?"

She shook her head. "No, they're okay with you for now, but the rest of our men might trigger them."

"I know. I told them to stay away, and Carlos is reaching out to anyone we can for women who are willing to come help."

The corners of her lips tipped up, just briefly in thanks, but her eyes were filled with sorrow. "Could you call Joseph too? His mother Ruth told me about everything, and I'm sure we have people who will help."

"I will." I kissed her head gently.

"Marco." She gripped onto the door handle like it was the only way she could stay standing. "This is all... it's terrible. I-I can't even imagine what these women have gone through." She bit her lip, then stared up at me, her eyes pleading. "Do you... do you think one day they'll..."

"Yes, Lina. They will." I didn't need her to finish. I brushed my hand against her cheek. "Whatever help or support they need, we'll get it for them. It will be hard, but one day, they'll be able to smile again. We'll make sure of it, won't we?"

Her eyes filled with tears, but she refused to let them fall, nodding. "We will."

As I kissed her softly, I made a vow to her, these women, and our families. We would dismantle the trafficking ring. We would hunt down every person involved and make them pay for what they'd done. And we would do everything in our power to help these women heal and rebuild their lives. No matter how long it took, we would get them justice.

Twenty-Five

Catalina

Six months later

"Is that the last box, ma'am?" the art handler asked.

"Yeah." I wiped my hands together, cleaning off the dust. "I think it is."

The man left, and I surveyed the empty mansion around me. It had taken a long time, but with Marco's help, I'd finally gone through every piece of Fernando's mansion.

We'd dug up files, USBs, old contacts, kill lists, accounts I didn't even know he had, the works.

Between the information we'd gained from Julianna, and the things we'd found here, it was enough to go after my father.

Simon had been forced to step down as a senator and was now under criminal investigation. His property had been seized, his bank accounts frozen, and the press had gone after him like a pack of wild hyenas.

His worst fear had come to life.

Losing his reputation, watching him fall from grace had been the best thing I could ever ask for. And once he went to prison, I'd make sure he died there.

The media hounded me to give an interview, and at first, I'd said no. I thought keeping my past to myself was better than sticking it out for millions to see. But Marco and Estelle reminded me that my voice deserved to be heard. So when I finally sat down with the interviewer, I didn't hold back.

I'd told them how Simon had threatened and abused me every day of my life. I made sure the world knew how terrible a father he'd been, how I'd been lucky to survive and escape him. Even insinuated I wouldn't be surprised if some of his associates were in on his illegal activities.

By speaking about my trauma, other organizations offered their services to me, and I'd been able to pass that assistance to those that needed it in my familia.

While the trafficked victims had gone home to their loved ones, it would take a long time before they were whole again. We'd been able to find several women sent overseas and brought them home—even Julianna's younger sister, Lilia, who was pregnant from one of her attackers—but there were plenty that were still missing.

Some women no longer had families or any way to support themselves, so after Marco and I had finished searching Fernando's mansion, I sold off his extensive collection of artwork and used that money for them.

They now had houses, clean clothes, whatever food they desired, and received a monthly check to make sure they could support themselves fully.

Naya had been a blessing with filling in the gaps on how to help the women and what to offer them. And Jo had given us information on how we could provide access for education and job assistance.

I hadn't asked her about the pill she'd given me or about any of the other oddities that day. She'd been there for me and supported me blindly. The least I could do was return the favor.

After all, without her, none of this would have been possible. If Marco hadn't been able to face Felipe with me that night, I would have died by Anthony's hands.

But even with all the good, there were times I worried about Marco, especially lately. He'd found out so much in such a short time.

After we made sure the women were safe that night, and went home, he'd held me as if some shadowed being would steal me away from him.

After I moved in, he seemed better most days. But sometimes his smile was tighter, not as bright as it used to be, as though Anthony's betrayal had darkened the way he saw the world.

There were a lot of reasons I wished I could bring that man back from the dead only to kill him myself, but with what he'd done to Marco? The way he'd dampened some of his joy? If there was an afterlife and I saw him in it, I'd rip him to shreds.

Marco kept himself busy, staving away the grief plaguing him, and over the last week, he'd been working especially hard, coming to bed late at night. But when I asked him if I could help somehow, he'd always tell me no and hold me tightly until we fell asleep.

Strong, tattooed arms wrapped around my middle, and I smiled. *Speak of my devil.*

He dropped a kiss on my neck. "Are we done?"

"Mhmm. The piece the art gallery picked up today is worth $1.9 million. There's a lot we can do with that money. And the closing is scheduled for the 24th."

"Have I told you how amazing you are?"

I shifted, turning back to meet his eyes. "How amazing *we* are. I couldn't have done any of this without you."

He smiled, and today it was brilliant, his dimples on full display. Then he kissed me. "Let's go get cleaned up, then. I have a surprise for you."

I sighed, melting back into my seat across from Marco in Le Jardin de Nuit. "That was amazing. The food is always incredible here."

Marco's eyes warmed as he brought my hand to his lips. "Good. I'm glad you enjoyed your meal, because this place is now yours."

"*What?*" I shouted, my heartbeat thundering in my chest.

"Do you remember the first time we came here?"

"Of course I do... but Marco. This is too much. This place must have cost a fortune."

He chuckled. "You insulted my wealth then, too."

"Because you're always spending it on the wrong things!" I slapped his chest, but he grabbed my hand and kissed it once more.

"No, I spend it on things that will make you happy, and not only do you always enjoy the food here, this was the first time I ever heard you laugh. Did you know I thought you would stand me up that night?"

I smiled at the memory. "No, but I had a feeling when I saw you waiting outside for me."

"When you got out of your car, it felt like a dream come true. You, my vicious little queen, are all I've ever wanted. And all of this—" he waved around us "—is only a speck of what you deserve."

I couldn't fight him when he spoke like that, my heart just floated away, leaving me nothing more than a mess at his feet. I reached across the table with my other hand and held his. "Is this why you've been so busy?"

He hummed. "Only some of it."

"Some? Marco, what did you do?" I glared at him.

"You'll see."

When we left, Marco opened the passenger car door, then pulled out a slip of cloth.

I raised an eyebrow. "What is this for?"

He stepped closer, crowding me against the car. Then he bent down and whispered in my ear. "For a bad girl that won't stop asking questions. Now, are you going to behave, or do I need to punish you before giving you your surprise?"

A shiver raced down my spine, and if he hadn't piqued my curiosity, I would have kept being a brat to get my punishment. "Yes, Daddy," I whispered.

He growled, the warmth of his breath dancing over my skin. "Good girl." Then he tied the sash behind my head, picked me up bridal style, and gently placed me in the car.

I squealed at the sudden movement. But before I could say anything, he kissed me. A long, slow kiss, and with one of my senses taken away, it was even more intense.

Each caress of his lips on my own sent tingles through my body. His hands were warm and firm as he cupped my head.

I reached for him, my hands landing awkwardly on his back as I slid them around to his chest, but then he pulled away.

I pouted, and he laughed, then he buckled me in, gave me a quick kiss, and closed the door.

It was odd not being able to see.

Before I met Marco, being alone in the dark was the only time I felt like I could be myself. It was my safety net, but also where I relived the nightmare that was my life. It was helpful and hurtful, solace and terror.

I used to listen to footsteps to judge when my father would beat me. Now I listened for Marco's footsteps with excitement and anticipation, because being in his arms felt like exactly where I was supposed to be.

Marco had changed me for the better, and I didn't think I'd ever be able to find the words or actions to express the full depths of just how much he meant to me. But I'd try, for as long as I could—my whole life if I was lucky.

Marco slid in beside me, put the car in gear, then placed his hand on my thigh. Turning his hand palm side up, I scratched the center softly while he drove.

We never spoke, simply basked in each other's presence and the low music on the radio. While I didn't know where we were going, I knew we'd left the city. Lights blared brightly even with my eyes closed and the blindfold on, but they'd grown less frequent, until all that was left were the streetlights and occasional cars.

I wanted to ask him where he was taking me, but I didn't. Whatever he'd done and put so much thought into was for *me*. Still, my heartbeat sped up a little when we parked.

"We're here," he said breathlessly.

Is he nervous?

He squeezed my hand, and I felt for my seatbelt, taking it off while he opened my door. Then he scooped me up into his arms again, and I giggled, clinging to him.

"You know, if you took off this blindfold, I could walk and you wouldn't have to carry me."

He chuckled. "And who says I don't enjoy carrying you?"

"I'm just saying it would be more practical, plus your arms will get tired after a while."

"Lina, I bench press three times your weight to make sure I'll always be able to carry you, anything you want, and our future children, without a problem. Now respectfully, my vicious little queen, love of my life, master of my heart and soul, shut up."

I laughed, even as my cheeks heated, burying my head in the crook of his neck.

Finally, he set me down and guided me to turn before taking off my blindfold.

I blinked at the buildings in front of me. To the left was a guard station and parking. In the center was a row of houses and what looked like an eight or nine-floor building of... apartments? To the right was a large, four-floor beige building with flowers at the entrance and a sign that read "Welcome To The Studio."

"Marco? What is all of this?"

"I wanted to do something for the trafficked victims and their families. We've brought some of them home and set up housing for those that don't have anywhere to return to, but we had to rush everything. Some have parents that are older and need their own assistance, not to take care of someone else. Others need medical and psychological help. Several have missed years of school and will need support to get their GED. This—" he motioned around us "—is a place just for them."

He pointed to the rows of houses. "These houses are set up for the families. We have three nurses on call who can help with any type of care they require." He pointed to the tall building beside them. "These are condos. There's ninety condos, all over one-thousand-two-hundred square feet, fully furnished and ready for them to move in. And the studio—" he pointed behind me "—is their learning center. If anyone needs a therapist or medical attention, they can go there. If they want to exercise, there's an indoor swimming pool, tennis, volleyball, and basketball court, and a library. There are even instructors that we've hired—all women—

to hold classes. They can be tutored here as well in any subjects they want to learn."

Tears rolled down my cheeks as I took it all in. This place... he'd built a sanctuary for our people. "How... how did you do all of this? Why...?"

His smile was radiant, dazzling, even with my blurred vision. "I had help. Naya and Jo gave me a lot to go over. This is what I've been working on, and as for why. Well..." He got down on one knee.

My hands flew to my mouth, and I took a step back, shock flooding through me.

What is he doing? He can't be. Is he...?

"I know how much your familia means to you, Catalina. I know you feel responsible for them and I respect that about you. But I don't just want it to be yours, or mine. I want it to be *ours*. I knew you were the one for me the moment I laid eyes on you two years ago. I didn't know how I'd convince you or what we'd go through, but what I did know was I wanted to go through it with you, together. That's all I want. You are all I need in this world. I love you, Catalina, and I'm asking, truly begging you, to give me the highest honor I could ever have. Marry me, please, my vicious little queen."

My entire body shook. But when his beautiful brown eyes filled with tears, I rushed to him. I threw my arms around him and collapsed as my knees gave way. He caught me, just like I knew he would, and I kissed him.

I kissed him over and over. I kissed his cheeks, his head, hugged him as tightly as I could.

"Please tell me that means yes," he whispered, his voice trembling.

"Yes! Yes, yes. *Yes!*" I kissed him again, and he grabbed me, tangled his hand in my hair, poured every bit of his love for me into our kiss, and I did the same.

When we finally broke apart, he took out the ring.

It was so intricate with a clear, large, black diamond sitting in the center of a white gold band, surrounded by smaller, clear white diamonds in the form of a flower. The smaller diamonds followed the band down until the middle in a beautiful pattern, while the sides had small, detailed scrolls.

"Do you like it? If not, we can—"

"It's perfect, Marco. Just like you."

He grinned, and I gently wiped away the single tear that had fallen down his face, then kissed him again. "I love you."

"I love you too, Catalina, and I always will."

EPILOGUE
CATALINA

Today was the day I'd always dreamed about.

I'd once thought that dream had died. That when my heart was broken, and it felt as though I'd fallen off a cliff and plummeted into an endless abyss, I'd never find myself again.

But I did.

Then Marco came into my life, and I started to believe that I could be more. That my dreams weren't childish fantasies, but something that could actually come to life with this incredible man who saw and wanted me for who I truly was.

And now it was finally here—the day I'd become Marco Torrino's wife.

I'd always heard weddings were supposed to be stressful, but ours wasn't. Even in the small, chaotic moments, Marco and I would lock eyes and laugh, kiss, take a deep breath, and work through the problem together.

He was my rock, my confidant, someone who understood and

loved me on such a deep level that I'd begun to learn how to love myself.

The feelings he invoked in me were ones I never thought I was capable of experiencing: joy, bliss, happiness, ease, *calm*.

With Marco, my life was peaceful and serene, regardless of what was happening around us. I was lucky just knowing he wanted to stay by my side, but when he asked me to marry him, I felt like I'd won the lottery.

And I had.

Our wedding planner had done an excellent job every step of the way. She'd listened. And the venue we'd booked was perfect.

Marco stood outside beside a lake, waiting for me under a beautiful wooden arch covered in an array of red, white, and pink flowers. Our families, even Julianna and Lilia, were seated comfortably with a beautiful, tall arrangement of the same flowers and candles at every end.

Carlos stood beside Marco as his best man, Joseph and Samuel as his groomsmen.

Jo had been the most incredible maid of honor and had fluffed my dress before walking out the door. Soon, she and my bridesmaids, Naya and Olivia, would head down the aisle.

Then, all that was left was me.

I took a deep breath. I didn't have any pre-wedding jitters. For the first time, I had friends, family, and a man that loved me just as much as I loved him. But I had to calm down and make sure I didn't lose my composure and trip over my own two feet.

I looked at myself one more time in the mirror. My nude-ivory, A-line dress flowed perfectly around my body. The ribbed corset was tied just right, enough to make sure the dress stayed in place, but not so tight that I couldn't breathe. The off-the-shoulder mikado sleeves brought a beautiful architectural simplicity to the otherwise glittery gown, and the thigh-high slit would make Marco's heart race.

My train wasn't too long, my makeup light and airy, highlighting my golden tanned skin, with just a hint of red at the lip. And my hair was perfect in its half-up, half-down style with the diamond encrusted tiara Marco had given me as a wedding gift.

I checked the time.

This music would start in under a minute.

I took another deep breath then shook out my hands, trying to get my excitement under control, before stepping out into the hall. When I reached the bottom stairs, Ruth was there to give me away.

I'd chosen her because if it hadn't been for her honesty and trust in me, I would have never allied myself with Marco. And while he'd always told me his goal was to be with me, no matter what or how long it would take, Ruth had given him a way. Without her, I likely wouldn't have the happiness I did in my life now.

Ruth's eyes shone with tears as she grasped my hands. "You look beautiful, Doña. Let's get you to your man."

I gulped and nodded, not trusting myself to speak, then took her arm as we slowly made our way down the aisle.

As I passed our family, seeing their cheerful smiles and the way they clapped for us, more tears came to my eyes, but not a single one fell until I saw Marco.

He was stunningly handsome. His suit was perfectly tailored, with a matching ranunculus from my bouquet and the watch I'd given him as a wedding present.

But it was his gaze that struck me. The love and affection there and the brilliant smile that lit up my entire world.

He thanked Ruth, and we helped her sit down in her chair, then he grasped my shaking hands with his own.

I barely heard the officiant, and if it weren't for Carlos handing us the rings, I would have missed my cue entirely.

"Do you, Catalina Salazar, take Marco Torrino to be your lawfully wedded husband?"

I didn't hesitate for a moment. "I do."

Marco slipped my wedding band and ring onto my finger, a gorgeous mixture of white and black, light and dark, just like us.

"And do you, Marco Torrino—"

"I do."

The crowd laughed, and more tears gathered in my eyes at his eagerness. I slipped his wedding band on, which matched the same blend of white and black as mine, and had the night of our first date inscribed inside.

"With the power vested in me, you may now kiss—"

Marco pulled me into his arms and kissed me. Kissed me as if he was starving, like he'd waited his whole life for me, and I kissed him back just as deeply.

"May I now present, Mr. and Mrs. Torrino!"

The crowd roared around us, and it was the only reason we broke apart. Sparklers, rice, and flower petals went in every direction. It was complete and utter chaos, and the most beautiful celebration I could have ever asked for.

As we walked down the aisle, I thought about how good my name sounded with his—Catalina Torrino—as though our union was predestined, something infinite and unbreakable.

And when Marco scooped me into his arms and kissed me once more, I knew it had to be. He was my king, my soulmate, my equal in every way, and I would always be his queen, regardless of anything that came our way, even death or the end of time.

I would always be *his*, and he would always be *mine*.

The End of Crowned In Blood

Want to read about a woman scorned and the beast that helps her believe in love again? Scan the QR code below!

Don't forget to visit my website or join my newsletter to get a special bonus scene with Catalina and Marco, all the latest updates, ARC opportunities, and more!

About the Author

Melissa had a difficult time speaking as a child, and thus writing became her best friend. There she learned the power of emotion, how to communicate heartbreak, sadness, tragedy, and still hope for something better: the happy ever after.

She loves to write imperfect, possessive heroes, that will risk their lives for those they love, strong heroines that can hold their own, and steamy scenes that grab you by the throat and bring you to your knees.

Melissa lives in a small town off the coast of Egypt, and is a huge mythology buff, with a love of all things magical, supernatural, paranormal, and steeped in lore and fantasy. When she is not writing Melissa can be found singing and dancing her heart out, or up, late at night, contemplating space and the universe with a large cup of tea.

facebook.com/MelissaCumminsAuthor

instagram.com/melissacumminsauthor

bookbub.com/profile/melissa-cummins

pinterest.com/MelissaCumminsAuthor

patreon.com/melissacummins

Acknowledgments

Morgan, you're a gem. Thank you for your amazing edits, hilarious comments, and threats. They nourish my soul.

Evelyn, thank you for working so hard and coming in clutch!

Marie, Claire, Kiersten, and Samantha thank you so much for beta reading this book and sharing your thoughts, feelings, and stories with me. You all truly touched me and I appreciate you!

To you. Yes! You! Thank you so much for reading my novel. Knowing that you took the the time to read it is beyond amazing to me. You help every author to move forward and publish their next book. So thank you again, take care, and I can't wait for you to read my next book!